BLACK STAR
CONSTELLATIONS

TIM MEYER

EVIL EPOCH
PRESS

BLACK STAR CONSTELLATIONS

"How to Kill a Bear with a Bow and Arrow", "Aperture", and "Siren's End" were previously published in *The Switch House,* 2018 by Evil Epoch Press.

"Lost Import" was previously published in *Sharkasaurus!,* 2017 by Fossil Lake.

"Grume" was previously published in *The Book of Blasphemous Words,* 2017 by A Murder of Storytellers.

Cover Images

Copyright ©Shutterstock/Sergey Nivens

Copyright ©Shutterstock/Miloje

International Standard Book Number (ISBN): 978-1-7323993-1-0

Printed in the United States of America

ALSO BY TIM MEYER

Novels:

DEMON BLOOD SERIES:
Enlightenment
Gatewayys
Defiance

The *SUNFALL* series (co-written with Chad Scanlon and Pete Draper):
Sunfall: Season One
Sunfall: Season Two
Sunfall: Series Three

In the House of Mirrors
The Thin Veil (A Novella)
Worlds Between My Teeth
Less Than Human
Sharkwater Beach
The Switch House
Kill Hill Carnage
Lords of the Deep (co-written with Patrick Lacey)

eBooks:

The Organ Harvest: An October John Novella
Demon SQUASH!: A One Hour Special (CAR NEX series, Book 6)

BLACK STAR
CONSTELLATIONS

BLACK STAR CONSTELLATIONS

Constellations are just stars until someone shows you what they are...

THE STARGAZER

(THE BLACK HILL #1)

1959

*T*HE SABLE SKY held many stars, some of them bright and obvious and some of them invisible to the naked eye. Novice stargazer, Blake Weber, peeked through his telescope and peered up at the cloudless night, reveling in his new view of the endless black canvas, the stars that twinkled in and out of celestial existence. As an amateur, Blake was grateful for any clear glimpse into the cosmos. Residing not too far from the city, he wasn't always blessed with visible skies. Pollution from neighboring cities and industrial factories had eaten up the majority of his nights; he could count on both hands the number of haze-free nights he had seen since he'd gotten into astronomy about six years ago, after retiring from teaching English Lit at the local university. On most evenings, Blake squinted through his scope and saw nothing but a wall of man-made clouds, a barrier between him and the hidden treasures the galaxy had to offer. On nights as clear as this, Blake considered himself the luckiest man in the universe.

Damn lucky.

"Coming to bed?" Miriam asked from the doorway that led into the attic, where Blake had set up shop. "It's almost midnight."

He still had to remind her that he was retired now, and the position of the clock's hands no longer mattered. He could stay up until two or three if he chose, as long as the morning wasn't filled with doctor's appointments or household chores he couldn't escape from. "No, my love. If it's okay with you, I'd like to take advantage of the clear night."

Miriam rolled her eyes, smiled, and told her husband she was heading to bed without him, but that she loved him and hoped he got in some quality stargazing before the drowsiness settled in and stole him away. It was important that he had his hobbies after retirement, things to keep him busy. She knew that, told him so on many occasions. He nodded, shuffled across the room and kissed her on the forehead, wished her good night and the sweetest dreams.

The second she left, Blake went back to the telescope. It was a basic model, one he'd ordered from the Woolworth's catalogue for two dollars. There was a five-dollar model, but Miriam nixed that idea the second he had brought it to her attention. That was okay with him. He was an amateur. He didn't need anything extravagant; just something to make him feel a little closer to the stars, and the two-dollar model was more than enough.

Some days he wished he wasn't so old. There had been talks on the radio and in newspaper articles that speculated the human race was destined for the cosmos, that launching a person into the stratosphere would soon no longer be exclusive to science fiction novels and moving pictures. That, in a few years, the government would have the ability to send someone into space via a rocket ship. Blake figured that would happen sooner or later, and he wished he'd been young enough to be one of those lucky individuals. But at sixty-nine years old, that simply wasn't his future.

But he was happy watching. Catching a glimpse at the stars from afar, the way the night blinked, an endless sea of bright little eyes. He felt small studying the solar system. There was so much out there, most of it beyond what the two-dollar telescope could show him, and the realization that space was truly endless, an infinite vacuum of energy and mass and *science,* hit him like a punch to the kisser. Knocked him for a loop. If he dwelled on the topic for more than a minute, he needed to sit down. Thinking about the universe's amorphous qualities and what may lie beyond (or behind) it made Blake feel like nothing, a hollow version of himself. He felt smaller than a speck of dust, a non-registrant on the cosmos' census.

Space. The most interesting subject in the world. It made him wish he'd studied the sciences instead of language, but everyone has their regrets and that was Blake's. He lived with it. The college had paid him well and his retirement was cruising along swimmingly. Miriam helped keep him in check, made sure he didn't blow their savings on nonessentials, like five-dollar telescopes.

He had himself a look at the sky fifteen minutes past midnight. He knew this because he had checked his watch after he saw what he couldn't possibly have seen, because what he'd seen was... well, *impossible.* He glanced down at his watch and made sure it wasn't three in the morning—because, at three in the morning, hallucinations would be a reasonable excuse for seeing the image that had appeared before him. But it wasn't that late, and his concept of time was true—a quarter past midnight. Miriam had only wished him goodnight fifteen minutes ago, and that made sense in that somewhat weightless head of his.

Then why did he see it, that bright black circle in the sky?

He knew how that sounded when he tried to describe it to himself. *Bright and black* were antonyms and couldn't possibly be used in unison to describe a single noun. But...

That's what it was, he thought. *Bright and black.*

It looked like a star, and Blake had seen his fair share of stars to know that much. But it wasn't a star, couldn't possibly be one—the dark qualities aside, it wasn't shaped like one. It was moving when he'd locked onto it through the scope. At first he thought he'd spotted a blackhole or a supernova, but he'd actually seen the latter before in a book and the active circular object definitely wasn't that. Could have been a blackhole, but blackholes don't move. Not like that, he supposed, though he didn't know for sure.

What was it?

A black star?

He pulled his eye away from the lens and scanned the sky without the telescope's help. The stars were themselves, and he could spot the Big Dipper, the Little Dipper, Orion's Belt, and all the usual constellations. He had no trouble locating them, no problems at all.

But when he returned to the telescope, it was as if they'd up and left. He couldn't locate any of the constellations, no matter how hard he looked. The sky was different, the stars rearranged. And still, he could see the black stars—if that was what they were—floating among the black backdrop above him, above *them,* above the world.

A strong case of the shivers hardened his skin, and Blake backed away from the telescope. He needed a break. Not just from tonight, but many nights. He started to doubt if he'd ever look through the telescope again. The fear that had come over him—he never wanted to experience it again. And it was strange because he didn't know what he'd seen. How could he be *that* afraid of something when he didn't know what it was he was afraid of? The concept startled him, shook him more than the bright dark spots floating amongst the blackened sky.

One more look.

Just one more.

He couldn't help himself. He returned to the telescope, had his glimpse of the well-lit galaxy. The black stars were still there, and they were falling. He watched them descend through their opaque backdrop, crash to earth, and land on the hill that overlooked the small town of Ludlow, Ohio.

The Black Hill.

Blake let his eyes linger there, on the shadows that covered the Black Hill. Misshapen things were born in those shadows, things with long extensions, appendages that bent back and forth, things that shared no definite form. They laid claim to the Black Hill.

That was the last night Blake Weber peeked at the sky.

That was also the night Blake Weber went crazy, the night he grabbed his ax from the garage, shuffled into the bedroom, stood over his sleeping wife, and split her head in half.

LOST IMPORT

290 Million Years Ago

FROM THE MURKY *bottom, she rises.*
The surrounding water vibrates, overloading her sensory system. She senses food, something plentiful, somewhere near the coast. Her tail propels her toward the meal. As she moves, something sweet makes its way into her nostrils. Something palatable, something delicious. Something she craves.

Blood.

Lots of it.

Fully titillated, she glides through the cloudy waters, lugging power and the desire for violence toward the coast.

Today

The scissors slice through the yellow tape and the celebration is so loud, Dr. Patrick Hammond can hardly hear his own thoughts.

He's smiling, but only because he has to. If he doesn't, Dr. Curry will chew his ear off later in private. Hammond slaps his hands together over and over again listlessly, making nice-nice with Curry and the rest of the public. The watch on his wrist rattles with each applause. He checks the time, the countdown to doomsday.

This is bad, he thinks. *Very bad.*

Curry smiles for the flurry of flashes that follow. He waves at the crowd as they toss questions at the stage. There will be plenty of time for a press conference later, once the demonstration is complete. He ignores them for now and continues to flap his hand at the media like a pigeon wing. A foolish grin pulls his face taut.

Hammond knocks his knuckles against his mentor's shoulder. "We need to reconsider this."

Curry shakes him off, continuing to address the crowd as they shower him with deafening praise.

"I'm not messing around, Kristoph."

Curry, refusing to let go of his happy charade, leans back and whispers to his protégé, "Not now."

"Yes. Now." Hammond's lips practically kiss his ear as he speaks. "You know I haven't finished testing the circuits. The transistor was acting funny just yesterday."

"No time!" Curry shouts, but pleasantly so. He keeps his face trained on the reporters, accepting their congratulatory noise for an uncompleted job.

"But, Kristoph, the engineers haven't finished signing off on—"

Curry twists around once more, giving the crowd his back. His face contorts, the bone white of his teeth filling up his open mouth. His lips zig and zag as his rough voice trembles. "Do what I say. Now!" His words are barely heard over the applause and the barrage of questions. "Prep the room. Power on the Omega Transit and for Christ's sakes, get your shit together, man. We have history to make."

The big boss rotates back to facing the crowd, wearing his smile like it never left. The cameras roll on, blinding flashes of light flicker, and the public's display of affection carries on.

Hammond retreats, ducking behind the Omega Transit, wishing he could disappear, run away, get as far away from the lab as he possibly can. He knows the dangers a throw of the switch might bring. During the long and punishing process, failures haunted them every step of the way. How Curry can sign off on something so elementary in progress, so apt to flounder, he'll never know. This isn't a demonstration of a finished product—it's advanced trial and error.

And the margin for error is infinite.

She shimmies through the brown, billowing cloud of lake dust. Light flits on the surface, bouncing in and out of her eyes. The smell of blood is bold here. She's getting close; she can taste the coppery flavor on her tongue. The phantom tang almost nourishes her. Her belly grows warm with bloody prospect.

She wonders what's ahead. What's hurt? What's bleeding? Why is there so much of it? Perhaps it's coming from one of her own. She contemplates whether she'll eat her brethren. Figures she might. Flesh is flesh, blood is blood. It's all the same once devoured.

She whips her tail rapidly, the idea of muscle, flesh, and blood too influential to slow her down. She sails forth, craving the slaughter.

Hammond pulls down on the lever. The Omega Transit erupts with life. Bright, eye-stabbing light casts the room in a heavenly glow. Hammond looks away. He finds Dr. Curry, who's staring straight into the LEDs, that stupid grin continuing to occupy real estate on his face. His eyes balloon with joy, mad with power.

I have to stop him, Hammond thinks. *He can't possibly predict what will happen.*

Curry spins, faces the crowd. They're over clapping now, finished chatting over each other. They stand in silence and witness the Omega Transit buzz with life. A few cameras flash off, but otherwise, Curry has their undivided attention.

"Ladies and gentlemen," he says like a circus entertainer. Hammond thinks that's what he's become. "I give you the Omega Transit. The very first portal into another world. Into another time."

Oohs and aahs circulate the crowd.

An animated Curry paces the stage. "Today will go down in history as science's greatest accomplishment. Today, we will attempt to draw a beast that once lived almost 300 million years ago into our world."

Incredulous gasps. Nervous laughter.

"No joke, ladies and gentlemen. No parlor trickery. This is the real deal. One-hundred percent scientific breakthrough."

Hammond eyes the machine. It's about six feet tall, constructed of solid steel. Ten feet wide. Its frame is circular, moon-shaped, but hollow in the center where the wall between worlds stands. The bright lights are embedded in the frame. In the center of the portal, where things come through, a hazy veil exists, the only barrier between a different place and time. The barrier looks like a liquid curtain. It sparkles with shades of purple and blue, always moving like the waves of a busy bay. Hammond focuses on the control panel where a million switches and dials sit, unprotected. He wonders how many he can smash with his fist before Curry's handpicked security squad rushes over and stops him. Not many, he thinks. He can feel the brutes' eyes settling on him, reading his thoughts.

"How does it work?" a member of the press shouts from the crowd.

Curry laughs and most of the crowd joins him. "A magician never reveals his secrets. If I divulge such secret information, what's to stop other corporations from replicating our design and profiting off our discovery?"

That answer satisfies only a small portion of the curious gathering.

"How *does* your company plan on profiting from reintroducing extinct creatures?" a woman asks, raising her pencil in the air. "I mean, do you plan on opening an amusement park or something?"

This tease gets the majority to chuckle.

"No, no," Curry says, slowing his giggles. "Nothing like that. We plan on selling off our discoveries to labs around the world who can research these beasts. Maybe by learning about the past we can better serve our future."

It sounds like bullshit, but no one questions him.

Another reporter raises his hand in the air. Curry calls on him. "What do you plan on bringing back for us today?"

Curry smiles. The crowd grows completely silent. "Today," he says, "we're going to bring back one of the first sharks to ever stalk the prehistoric waters. Xenacanthus."

"Xena-what?" someone asks.

"Xenacanthus." He directs the crowd's attention to a projection screen. There's an audible click and an illustration appears, depicting something that resembles a combination of modern day shark and an eel. "Relatively small in size. Not dangerous. At least not to us air-breathers." No one laughs at that joke. They're too entranced by the possibilities. "Right. Well, there you have it. They don't grow longer than six feet. They feed on smaller fish. If things go according to plan, the Xenacanthus will be our first successful import."

There's a dragging silence, and it feels like forever until someone speaks again.

"You mean..." the woman reporter says curiously, keeping her pencil raised, "you've never actually done this before?"

Curry loses a piece of his smile. He narrows his eyes. "Well, no. Not exactly."

"But what if... something goes wrong?"

He acts like the idea never occurred to him. "Nothing can go wrong, my dear. You will witness the most wondrous scientific advancement history has ever seen. I assure you."

The crowd shrinks back, feeling less confident, less jovial. Curry's overconfidence has sucked every drop of excited energy from the room.

Hammond knows his chance to stop this is now. He plots.

She enters the sector of violence. Burgundy clouds explode around her like fireworks. Ragged chunks of muscle and meat float by. She snatches what she can in her jaws as she passes. The small gobbets are not enough. She needs her fill.

She pushes through the bloody curtain and bursts into a clearing. Ahead, she spots her own kind, five of them, thrashing within another rolling fog of crimson. There's another creature there, a larger creature. In its mouth, wriggles one of her sisters. The creature bites down, tearing through cartilage with ease. Her sister's head detaches from her body and floats toward the surface, a trail of rusty nebula following in its wake.

She dives forward, joining the fray. The creature snaps at another shark, missing by the length of its tooth. The shark goes for the neck and sinks its mouthy daggers in. It comes away with a chunk of flesh, but it's nothing. The dinosaur reacts by clamping its jaws around the shark's tail, severing it in one bite. In its last moments of distress, the shark dives to the sandy bottom of the lake, seeking safety. It can't out swim death and in minutes, the poor fish floats belly-up, towards the sky.

The vision of watching the slaughter of her own kind unexpectedly infuriates her. She lunges forth, burying her teeth in the dinosaur's back, just below where a giant, fan-like fin rests along its spine. She makes sure her teeth are good and sunk before tearing away a mass of meat. The finned dinosaur screams in agony as a ruddy smaze blankets the visibility factor. She lets the meat float away as she readies herself for seconds; this isn't about food or nourishment anymore—it's a territorial war.

As she and the rest of her army strike again, their campaign of death is cut short by a blinding flash of light. It blinds her. She can see again. But there's more flashing. More blindness. Next, there's black. Then, something else.

A burning sensation in her eye sockets. A different kind

of light infiltrates her.
   She can't breathe.

"Shut it down!" Hammond pleads. "Shut it down now!"

Curry jockeys for control of the switchboard. Hammond shoves him aside. Behind the mad scientist, he spots the security squad rushing toward them.

"Stop! You fool! You'll mess this all up!" Curry throws an elbow and connects with Hammond's jaw. The force of the blow knocks the young doctor backwards, sends him falling on his ass. The security squad reaches him and it takes the three of them to corral the eager fool. "Do you have any idea how much damage you've possibly done!"

The audience looks on in shock. Some of them, non-media attendees, search for the exit, wishing themselves far away from this public relations nightmare. Curry notices this and confronts them.

"Please! Don't be alarmed. Everything is under control." He turns to the machine, twirls a few dials and pokes a few buttons. A loud sound that reminds him of an air conditioner condenser kicking on fills the silence. The lights on Omega Transit dim and dance with operational readiness. "Ah! Yes! Just as we predicted. See these heat patterns!" He points to the control panel. The five dots on the monitor pulse and glow red. "It's a heat map. We've set the directional navigation coordinates 290 million years in the past, focusing on a portion of the earth indigenous to Xenacanthus. Those must be them!"

"What's that larger dot?" the pesky female reporter asks. Curry wants to snap her pencil in half. "Is that a Xena-camu-thesis, too?"

Not wanting to admit a certain degree of incompetence, he simply replies, "Yes." No one asks for him to elaborate, but he feels the need to add, "Must be the mother of the group, the leader of the pack."

Hammond yells from the floor, "Shut it down, Curry! You

don't know what you're doing!"

Curry grimaces. "Guards—remove this man. Kick him out of the building and have his level ten access revoked."

"Are you firing me?"

"Goddamn right."

Curry spins back to the machine. "Ladies and gentlemen," he tells the gathered, "let's explore the past in the future."

He throws the switch and the portal begins to crackle and sizzle, and the room smells like fire.

More light.

It hurts. It burns.

She feels herself change. Her body feels like a wet rag being wrung out. She has no concept of this and starts to panic. Her lateral line twists and wrinkles, feels like someone is bending her body in half. She hates this feeling. Survival mode kicks in and she starts to thrash. Unable to breathe, she bites the fleeting shadows, attacks the bright pulses of light.

There's one final flash before she wakes up in an alien world, no longer herself. Now she's part of something bigger.

Something unnatural.

In the center of the room sits what the Omega Transit brought forth through time. Curry can't believe the images his eyes convey to his brain, thinks it must be some mistake. He checks the screen and sees all five heat patterns are gone.

"Oh, dear God," he says, realizing what has happened.

"I told you," Hammond says. He marches forward, away from the guards, all of whom had let go of their prisoner when the portal brought through the giant monstrosity. "I goddamn told you."

"We can send it back," Curry says. As he speaks, the

Omega Transit barks and hisses. Dusty-brown smoke unfurls from the top of the control panel. Electric glitter fires off, explodes like handheld sparklers on the Fourth-of-July.

"I warned you about the transistor!" Hammond grabs his boss by his white collar. He shoves him against the control panel. Sparks continue to flare around them, dancing in the air like festive pixies. "You overconfident fuck, I warned you!"

Curry shakes his head. "We spent years perfecting it. I don't understand."

Hammond opens his mouth to hammer home another *I-told-you-so*, but his words mean nothing and he knows it. Together, they turn and face what Curry's carelessness has brought upon them.

In the center of the room, a dinosaur-like creature with an enormous sail on its back, at least twenty feet long, thrashes around, snapping its powerful jaws at the crowd of frightened onlookers. Eel-like creatures with dome-shaped snouts protrude from its midsection as if they belong to the creature's body, like its arms and legs. They snap at the air, wildly whipping around like speared snakes. They wheeze as they struggle to breathe, their bodies not built for land. The shark-like eels bite its carrier body, removing chunks of flesh with each strike. This instigates the dinosaur-like creature, enraging it, causing it to charge the collected crowd.

The audience shrieks in unison as they realize the thing is coming for them, and they've backed themselves into a corner. They start to panic and run, bowling into one another, knocking each other to the ground. They trample the fallen, colleagues and strangers alike, frantically searching for an exit.

"What is it?" Hammond asks, from his zone of safety, near the edge of the stage.

"It's a Dimetrodon. A land predator of that time period."

"And its friends?" He points to the shark-like eels. "Are those our Xenacanthus?"

Curry nods and looks back at the map, where the heat patterns glowed only moments ago. "They must have been too close together. We drew them through at the same time. They must have amalgamated."

"How do we fix it?"

The switchboard fizzles and pukes smoke.

Curry swallows a rush of sadness. "We don't." He grips Hammond's shoulder. *"We run."*

She can't breathe, but she can snap her jaws. She bites her host, rips away flesh and blood, but it gives her no satisfaction. The alien world will kill her, this she knows. Her objective: eviscerate her host, whatever the cost. It's the least she can do.

As she lashes out to accomplish this, other creatures scurry past her. She has no sense of what they are and doesn't care. She snaps at them as if they threaten her very existence. Her sisters nip at them too. The sister on her left catches an alien in her mouth, bites down, watches hot streams of blood spurt like a volcanic explosion of lava. The thing cries out and scarlet erupts from the open hole in its face. She enjoys watching this and lunges at the next alien she sees. She grabs a female (she can smell its sex) by her leg and chomps down. She feels its bones break under the force, and tastes coppery liquid in her mouth.

Blood is blood, she thinks. Flesh is flesh.

The carnage continues.

The crowd tries to rush past the creature, but the monster is deceptively fast, not as cumbersome as its body suggests. The head matching the rest of its lizard-like body does most of the damage; it's able to bite and shred through flesh, targeting anyone who enters its attack zone, its range of motion. It backs a small group of survivors into the corner of the lab and selects its prey, not wasting time on being too choosy. If it has its way, everyone will meet the teeth. One man dodges its jaws and ducks under its arm, but finds himself in the maw of one of the shark-like eels. His death is quick, but not without pain. The bite tears out most of his stomach, and before the man enters an unconscious afterlife, he sees his tangled mess of innards slop on the floor before him. The female reporter discards her pad and pen and attempts to escape, but the Dimetrodon fills his mouth with her head, bites down across her shoulders. It swallows her neck and cranium whole, and a crimson geyser erupts, showering the rest of the throng in scarlet.

Screams ripple across the room. Some are silenced as the creatures continue their onslaught. A red lake takes shape on the floor, spilling toward the stage.

Hammond grabs his mentor's collar. "You're not going anywhere. You're fixing this."

"Try to stop me," Curry barks.

Hammond reaches back with his fist before flinging it forwards, knuckles connecting with the center of Curry's face. The floodgates in his nasal passages open, releasing a crimson waterfall down his lips and chin. The impact knocks Curry on his back.

"Fix this," Hammond says, reaching back with another fist.

"All right!" Curry struggles to his feet. "The Omega Transit is technically still open. If we can lure it close enough, maybe we can draw it into the portal and send it back."

"Got it." Hammond turns, faces the creature.

Each one of the shark-like eels has their faces stuffed with human parts. The Dimetrodon whips its head back and forth, slinging a prominent member of the Channel 7 News team into the air. Ribbons of blood follow the sailing body. The man lands twenty feet away, hits the ground like a stuffed doll, and never moves again.

Hammond cups his hands over his mouth and yells. "Hey!"

It takes several minutes before the Dimetrodon grows bored with killing media folk and sets its sights on the stage. It sneers, puffs of wet air exploding from its nostrils. It licks its bloody maw, savoring every drop of human flavor.

Then, it charges the stage.

"Do it now."

Nothing happens. Hammond locks eyes with the creature's.

"Curry, do it now!"

The Dimetrodon leaps into the air, crashes on stage. It shakes its body, launching droplets of sweat and blood into the air, a fine, almost magical mist. Its spiny sail moves with a certain fluidity.

Hammond knows it's ready to attack.

"Curry, what are you waiting for!" Hammond turns, faces the control panel.

No Curry.

Out of the corner of his eye, he watches the emergency exit door close behind his mentor.

"I don't believe it." But in truth, he can.

Without thinking, he runs over to the mouth of the Omega Transit and faces it. Behind him, the Dimetrodon's claws scratch the stage. It's on the move. Scurrying toward him.

"Here goes nothing."

Hammond jumps into the sparkling portal, and he feels the teeth of space and time chew him apart and the belly of the universe digest whatever remains.

TEN YEARS LATER

"And that's how string theory works. Mostly." Professor Campo gives the class of two hundred the thumbs up, the way he ends every lecture. The students scrape themselves up from their seats. Over the hustle, he tells them, "We'll continue this discussion on Thursday."

The auditorium empties, except for one lone student. The student hops down the stairs, toward Campo's desk with a budding confidence that unsettles his professor.

"How's it hanging, Professor Campo?" the student asks as he reaches the area around the professor's desk.

Campo looks up from his papers. He sees the young man's eyes, knows exactly where the conversation is going before it gets there. "Can I help you?"

"Oh, I believe you can, Campo. Or is it... *Curry?*"

Hearing his previous surname cuts him deep. He tries to play it cool, acting confused, but his silence betrays him. "I don't understand."

"Don't give me that shit." The student folds his arms across his chest. A pain-strained expression overtakes his features. His cocky attitude has been erased, replaced by a trembling fury. "I know who you are."

Curry swallows the cottony feeling in his mouth. He figures it was only a matter of time before he faced this moment. Ten years is a long time to get away with such a thing. In a way, he's almost glad the time has come. He thinks this moment will unburden him, release the guilt. "What is it you want?"

The student's eyes water. "I want you to bring him back."

"Who?"

"My father."

Curry shakes his head. He doesn't understand.

"My father. Doctor Patrick Hammond."

The name brings back the worst memories. "Son, your father..."

"He's alive."

Curry shakes his head. "No. There's no way."

The student disagrees. "They never found his body."

"Even if he made it through the portal, he wouldn't have survived. The atmosphere 290 million years ago—it was different. The air was different. His lungs wouldn't have acclimated. His skin wouldn't have handled the severe temperature change."

"Maybe he adapted."

Curry bores into him with a hard gaze. "No," he says. "No, that's not possible."

"Bring him back," the student says. Droplets leak from the corners of his eyes. "Bring him back, goddammit, or I'll out you. I'll tell the authorities. I'll tell the entire world who you really are."

Curry sighs. His options are few. Killing the kid might be easier than trying to resurrect a dead man. "I'm sorry for what happened to your father."

"No, you're not. You left him there. Whatever happened that day, you left him there to die. With all those people." He pounds the desk with his fists, rattling the coffee mug and scattered notebooks. "What was it? What killed all those people. A fucking dinosaur? I've read the reports. They said those people were eaten by sharks."

"I don't know what happened."

"Liar!"

"Shhh," he says in a whisper. *"Keep your voice down."*

"Help me go back and find him. I know he's alive. I... I know it."

"You don't know a damned thing."

"I see him."

Curry tilts his head to the side. The kid is clearly disturbed. Another result of what happened ten years ago, a byproduct of his impetuous mistake. "You see him?"

"In my dreams. He's still alive. Living in the past. He comes to me. Talks to me. Tells me to come find him."

"Uh-huh."

"He has a big, bushy beard. He's always naked. But alive. He eats... dinosaur meat. Prehistoric fish. Whatever it takes. Some days, he doesn't eat at all."

"Dreams."

"I see him."

"Right."

Another fist shakes the table. The coffee mug shimmies near the edge. It teeters, then falls. Smashes into several pieces.

"That was my favorite mug," Curry says.

"Help me. Or I tell everyone."

Curry closes his eyes. "Fine. Two weeks. That's all I'll

give you. After that, if we don't find him, we part ways and we never see each other again. Deal?"

"Two weeks? It'll take us years to build another Omega Transit!"

Curry smiles. "No. It won't."

The student squints. He doesn't understand.

Curry rolls his eyes. "Because I already have a replica." The smile never leaves his face. "And she's fully operational."

290 MILLION YEARS AGO

The water pours over him. He scrubs his beard, washes it out with cleansing oils he extracted from indigenous plants. Once clean, he uses the oil to coat his body. It's been weeks since his last bath. He doesn't know when he'll get another. He's been hunting a pack of herbivores. One of their corpses will provide him with a week's worth of meat, an opportunity not to be missed.

Once showered, he removes himself from the small lake with the crystal clear waterfall. He dries himself off in the heat and grabs his watch, the only remnant from his home world. It no longer tells time, but the compass still works, and that sometimes comes in handy, especially at night. During the day he doesn't need it. He knows where north is according to the position of the sun. He glances down at the watch, sees the compass is off. It's no longer pointing north. Now, it directs him east.

Strange, he thinks. Why would it suddenly stop working?

As he tracks the vagrant herbivores, the idea eats at him. East? Why east? It doesn't add up. Soon the idea overtakes his brain. He even becomes less hungry until his appetite fully dissolves and there's nothing but the want— no, the need—to explore the east. He needs to know why the compass is directing him there. He doesn't believe in a higher power, but the event appears divine.

As he treks east, leaving the herbivores behind, he realizes what it could mean. He thinks back to his old world. He thinks back to his experiments. He thinks of how compasses

31

operate.

It's following an electromagnetic pull.

He runs as an idea hits him. A theory. A sound hypothesis. What makes such a pull that would draw his compass east?

A portal, he thinks. A big one.

He storms hills, crosses rivers, dodges carnivores, and climbs over mountainous terrain. Finally, in the middle of a grassy field, he sees it. It stands alone, tall and shiny, just like he remembers. He drifts ahead as if trapped in some hypnotic trance, tears in his eyes, hoping it's no dream, hoping everything he sees is real.

He reaches the portal and puts his fingers through the glassy barrier, purple and blue sparkles shimmering on his flesh. He smiles as the cold sensation flows over him, freezing his blood. It feels like an angel wrapping its arms around him, bringing him home.

Home. It's where he goes.

NO MAKEUP

*S*HE EXAMINED THE violent yellow stain around her eye. The purple evidence had all but disappeared. Good. The less purple, the better. Purple was hard to cover. Especially that deep, eggplant shade. So deep and dark and almost black. At least the mustardy tint could be hidden with the proper concealer.

She glanced down at the open disk on the edge of the sink. It stared up at her like a cyclopean eye, all-knowing and full of righteous judgement. Grabbing the flesh-toned stick, she heard footsteps behind her.

"No makeup," a strained, husky voice said.

She cringed at the sound. While she held the wondrous, yet not overly expensive product, an entire army of imaginary ants scurried down her vertebrae. She kept her trembling hand still. This act of defiance would cost her.

"Please," she said. "I beg you."

"No makeup," he repeated.

It wasn't easy to avoid eye contact with him. Without glancing back, she knew he was loitering in the doorway, blocking the exit. No way around, no way through. He was bigger than her. Much bigger.

She was skin and bones. He was muscle and mass and

much more now. Hard to look at, what he'd become. She stared at herself instead. The bruise. That faint reminder.

Reminder of what you did.

Some bruises never fade.

She bit her lip. "I have to work."

The door jamb creaked behind her and she closed her eyes, imagining his broad shoulder pressing against it. His shadow formed on the bathroom walls, darkening the already-dull floral wallpaper, the one she had always wanted to paint over, but never found the time.

"No makeup."

She could smell his breath. If Hell had a smell, this was it. Sweet woodsmoke. Burnt bones and buckets of blood. Huffed air rolling off the devil's tongue.

She closed her eyes. "I have to go in today. I can't... can't be late again."

A grin. "I know. You have work to do. Feed me."

The bone around her eye throbbed, pulsed with knuckle-knocking pain.

"Philip, please..."

"No makeup," he said with a belly full of laughter.

Some bruises never fade.

2

The pot was hot and Gavin was too busy chit-chatting away to notice. He reached for the handle, but found glass and yelped like a puppy whose paw got stepped on.

"You okay?" Alana from bookkeeping asked. She stood across from him, arms folded under her breasts. Her lips barely moved when she spoke. "Should I... call someone?"

Gavin flapped his hand in the air like the yellow towels at Steelers games. After the burn faded some, he stuck his fingers in his mouth and sucked on them, some childish instinct rendered ineffective. The burn reached his bones and dug into the marrow, setting his whole hand ablaze. "Mm-Uh-key."

"Huh?"

He rolled his eyes and spit out his fingers. "I'm okay."

"Oh. You sure?" she asked, squinting at the sight of his hand. It had already started to blister.

"Yes. Totes. For shizzle." Gavin smiled and folded his arms across his chest as if nothing had happened. "Sooooo... how's about that movie on Saturday?"

"Uhhhh, I'm going to pass. But thanks for the offer."

She started to walk out of the room, but Gavin stepped in front of her. "Come on," he said. "Wait. Is it the fingers? I told you I'm fine."

"Not the fingers, creep-o."

Creep-o burned him deeper than the coffee pot had. Heat bubbled beneath his skin. She must have seen him turn red, because she stepped back, her face slack with immediate fear.

Her eyes fell away from him. "I'm sorry. I didn't mean to—"

"It's fine," he said through pursed lips.

Alana bolted from the break room and scurried toward her cubicle. Gavin watched her the whole way, imagining what they could do together between the sheets, if only she gave him a chance. The thoughts were totally NSFW, so he kept them to himself, as he so often did.

He snapped out of his perverted reverie when he heard footfalls on the carpet behind him. He turned and saw Anne Zolof handling the coffee pot properly, managing to pour herself a cup without incident. Out of her curious peripherals she caught him staring.

"Hey, Anne," he said, noticing she had noticed his gaze.

She replied with a weak smile, one that said either I'm not interested in talking, or I'm not interested in *you*. He figured he was dealing with the latter, because that was (mostly) always the case. To say he was sick of it was an understatement. He wasn't a bad guy. Far from it. He had a decent paying job, worked the regular nine-to-five, leased a brand-new car every few years, lived in a luxury apartment in downtown Pittsburgh. There was no reason he couldn't score himself a date. He wasn't Leonardo DiCaprio, nor did he resemble any other popular celebrity, but he wasn't Frankenstein's monster either. He was somewhere in between, your average American male in his mid-thirties.

Keyword: *average.*

He stepped closer. "How's it going, Anne?"

A cursory look in his direction before continuing her efforts in making the perfect cup of coffee—enough cream and sugar to kill that bold flavor most of the men in the office preferred. She took her sweet time and although Gavin knew she was doing this on purpose, hoping—God, *praying*—he'd leave, he stuck around, lingering like the stench of a dead house mouse wedged between the walls.

Once close enough, she backed away, abandoning her coffee.

"What's the matter?" he asked. It was like he had leprosy. The last time he checked, his skin was pure, free from stains of any kind. Except for the fresh, open blisters on his hand, but Anne hadn't seen them yet. He made sure by tucking the accident in his pocket. "Jesus, Anne. I'm not going to hurt you. What the hell is wrong with—"

"I'm sorry," she said.

For the moment those two words tamed his rising rage. He breathed slowly, in through his nose, out through his mouth, just like mother had taught him. "It's okay. Just having a rough time lately. I didn't mean to get so mad."

She nodded as if she understood rough times.

"What..." he asked, catching a glimpse of the side of her face. "...is that?" He inched closer, holding his unmarred hand out, the burn continuing to cool off in his pocket. Close enough to examine the discoloration around her eye, Gavin treaded carefully. He wanted to move the dangling golden strand obscuring a clear visual path to the violent evidence, but he didn't want to overstep his boundaries. Although, whereas ninety-nine percent of the office didn't notice or pretended not to notice Anne's swollen feature, Gavin vocalized his discovery. Most boundaries Gavin didn't mind crossing, but in this particular instance an invitation was necessary.

"It's nothing."

Of course it isn't, he thought. As expected, she wasn't going to cooperate. "Can I see?"

She glanced up from the floor, her eyes settling on him briefly. Slowly, she tucked the rogue strand of hair behind her ear and craned her head to the left, granting Gavin's request.

He stepped closer once again, this time going all the way, within a finger's stretch. He hovered around her, tilting his head back and forth, observing the faded blemish from all angles.

"Philip?" Gavin asked.

Her eyes found the floor again.

"That bastard."

"It wasn't his fault." She sniffled. Her nose gargled the soup within as her eyes birthed tears from their corners.

Gavin put a hand on her shoulder. Although they weren't friends and never once spoke outside of break room run-ins and business-related phone calls, they felt close in that moment. Janice Lesley strolled into the room casually and glanced up from her morning itinerary. She spotted them and opened her mouth to speak. Gavin waved her off before her concerned words hit the air. She disappeared back the way she came and Gavin turned back to Anne, placed his injured hand around her back, draped his arm over her shoulder, and pulled her close. She rested her head on his chest and cried. He immediately felt the wetness on his shirt and tie, but he didn't care—in that moment he felt mighty and important and more than *average*.

"It's okay," he told her. "It's going to be okay."

But it wouldn't and she knew it.

3

The drive over there was mostly silent, but Gavin bled some information from her, thankful she hadn't clammed up completely. For the better part of the work day she sat in her cubicle like a stone statue, staring at her computer mindlessly. Gavin wondered how her job was impacted, or if Jerry and the rest of the bosses noticed her behavior. Anne wasn't a particularly cheery person, but she was never the speechless solitaire she had been today. He figured they hadn't noticed, or if they *had* noticed, decided to cut her some slack. In their shoes, Gavin would have done the same, though he wouldn't have ignored her behavior and the faded shiner taking up real estate on her face.

Someone has to help, he thought. It was his time to shine. His time to rise above mediocrity and leave ordinary behind.

He shifted uncomfortably in the driver's seat as he pulled off the highway, guiding his leased Camry down the exit ramp. "How long has this been going on?" He didn't expect her to answer, but she surprised him.

"Some time," she said with a frog in her throat and a shrug on her shoulders.

"I can't believe it. *Philip.*" Gavin knew Philip as well as he knew the corporate slave-masters of the company he worked for; he'd seen him in Facebook photos and once a year at the Christmas party. In those photos and at that annual soiree, Anne had seemed happy at her husband's side. If ever questioned, Gavin would surmise they had a healthy, happy relationship with no glaring evidence of domestic abuse. "That son of a bitch. What kind a man lays a hand on a woman?"

That was a question Anne couldn't answer, but one Gavin could with great detail.

Gavin's father was never in the picture; the drunk left when he was six and never came back, much to the delight of Gavin's mother and his two older sisters. He never bothered reconnecting with the old man because his mother constantly told him stories about who he was—a low-life, scum-sucking rodent—and how he was—in all likelihood—dead. "Buried six feet under by now," she had claimed many times. Gavin never saw the sense in searching for a dead man.

Later in life, his mother had many boyfriends. Some good. Some bad. Some in between. Some he noticed. Some he didn't. Only one was ever abusive. His name was Hank Peamont or Peabody, Gavin never could remember which. But his first name was Hank, that much had fused with his memory; he had read the name tag on his Costbusters uniform every day the bastard came home from work. Sometimes he was sober, but often he was not.

One day he got much too grabby for Mama's liking and she swatted him a bit too hard across his cheek. Hank's rage flipped like a coin, and instead of remaining playful and horny, he turned bitter and violent. Not usually choleric, his veins bulged on his neck and forehead. The first punch hit Mama in the kidneys and she dropped to the bedroom floor like one of Hank's empty beer cans. The second was an open-palm strike across her face, hard enough to jar loose one of her molars. Gavin came running when he heard the impact and the breathless yelp that followed. At sixteen years old, he confronted Hank Peabody or Peamont and told him to get the fuck out and never set foot in their household again. Hank laughed and demanded the scrawny whelp learn to mind his manners when addressing adults, while Mama begged him to leave and shouted to the world that everything was fine, that Gavin hadn't heard what he thought he'd heard. Gavin disagreed with both of them and approached Hank, chest puffed and fists clenched. The next thing Gavin knew he was lying on the floor, blood spilling from his nostrils in rushed rivulets. Pain hammered him from all angles, and he opened his eyes to see Hank on him in full mount, a blur of fists striking down on him. He covered up best he could, but Hank—the more experienced fighter—landed almost every punch. It took a week to recover from the beating, but the emotional impact still affected him. Every now and again he thought back to that day. He never discussed it with Mama, and he never saw Hank again after that.

A few years ago he researched the name on the Internet, but there were way too many Hank Peabodys and Peamonts and not enough desire on Gavin's part to take the search further. Mama had said Hank was nomadic anyway, drifting from place to place every few months or so, and probably settled down in Alabama or Mississippi, living out of rat-infested motels, existing on fast food and energy drinks, working dead-end job after dead-end job, drinking his way to a slow, lonely death.

Hope so, Gavin thought as Anne pointed at the next street sign.

"This one," she said.

Gavin pulled himself out of the past and turned onto McCollum Lane. She directed him three houses down. He guided his Camry in front of house 236 and parked next to the curb. He spied a shadow in the window curtain, second-story bedroom. It was stationary and he couldn't tell if that was Philip awaiting his wife's arrival or a piece of furniture strategically blockading the view of curious neighborhood onlookers. He remembered from Facebook how large Philip was and thought how easily the swine's body could take up a whole window.

Large means slow, Gavin thought, thinking back to Hank Pea-something. Hank was lean, but muscular. The opposite of Philip Zolof. If things got physical, Gavin figured he'd fare much better against Philip than he had Hank all those years ago. Plus, Gavin had matured. He knew how to fight now, or at least thought so. He hadn't been in a physical altercation since that tangle with Hank, but UFC highlights had taught him so much over the past twenty years.

Though it probably wouldn't come to that. Gavin played the scene out in his mind: he'd knock on the door and Phil would answer. He'd calmly explain the situation and outline how the next few minutes would go. Gavin would request Anne's essentials: toothbrush, toothpaste, a few day's worth of clothes, a few hundred bucks for food. Then he'd tell the prick to think long and hard about writing a satisfactory apology, something on paper (for legal reasons that may come in handy down the road). Gavin would tell Philip if he played his cards right, maybe Anne would consider giving their marriage another shot. Until then...

Get your shit together, Philip, Gavin practiced silently.

He opened the door, setting one foot on the pavement. "Okay. Here goes nothing. You're staying here." It sounded like a question, but they had already agreed on this part of the plan.

She sat still, staring past the window, into worlds of her own.

He slammed the door behind him, bounced up the driveway and skipped up the stairs. With a knock on the door, his heart pranced in his chest.

Fuck, I can't believe I'm doing this.

Whatever it took to elevate his averageness.

The door creaked open when his knuckles touched the painted fiberglass, allowing a three-inch view inside. "Hello? Philip?"

No answer. The bastard's car was in the driveway, so he knew he was home. Unless... *he was at a neighbor's house.* Gavin hadn't considered that possibility.

He tapped the door twice more and called for Philip once. Then he entered the living room cautiously, expecting a swinging baseball bat to greet him. No baseball bat came and neither had Philip.

The living room was dim and unkempt. Magazines had been haphazardly piled on the coffee table. Some had fallen on the floor and were left there, days, weeks, or months ago. Clothes—shirts and pants and underwear—were strewn in wrinkly mounds on the couch. The faint amalgamated smell of Chinese takeout and bourbon ruled the air. Gavin bumbled across the wooded floor, hoping to alert the homeowner of his arrival. In the event Philip was armed, he didn't want to startle him or worse—provoke an itchy trigger finger.

There wasn't a sound in the house save for the occasional drip of a leaky kitchen faucet. No noise interference whatsoever. If Philip was home, he had to have heard Gavin's intrusive presence.

Gavin cupped his hands around his mouth and yelled, "Phil!"

No response.

He listened closely.

Upstairs, something shifted. The rustle of a bed sheet.

Phil, you lazy bastard. "Phil, it's Gavin. I work with Anne, your wife. We... we need to talk."

More movement above, animated this time. Something fell on the floor and broke. A TV remote or a cell phone, something electronic. He heard several plastic pieces scatter across the wooden floorboards. "Phil, I'm coming up. For Christ's sakes, you better at least put pants on!"

Gavin grabbed the banister and ascended the stairs, drawing out each step, making as much noise as possible. He wanted Phil to know he was coming. If he was waking out of a drunken slumber, it might take more than a few loud words and heavy footfalls. It might take a splash of water, or a few slaps to the face, but Gavin wouldn't go that far. If the bastard didn't want to wake up and face the music, so be it; he'd grab what Anne needed and bounce the hell out of there. Confrontation avoided. A job well done.

He skipped the last stair and entered the small hallway. The bedroom door stood before him, left ajar. Behind it, the sound of cool silk rubbing against moving flesh.

"Goddammit, Phil, I've had enough."

He rushed forward and pushed open the door.

The room was empty.

He opened his mouth, the speech to Philip on the tip of his tongue. The words were never born and died inside him. The smell knocked him back, that awful, alien stench. It seeped into his nose, curled around his brain and constricted, suffocating his thoughts. His lungs burned as if he had inhaled flames, a mouthful of bright, glowing embers. He immediately felt sick and wanted to purge the contents in his stomach, the egg salad sandwich he ate for lunch. His eyes scanned the room, his heart thudding faster and faster.

"No makeup," a voice said.

Gavin's eyes followed the voice. In the corner of the room he had previously inspected and viewed unoccupied, Philip crouched. His head rose, along with his portly figure. His eyes burned orange, pupils ablaze. Webs of purple veins traveled across his colorless flesh. He was naked, his flaccid member jiggling like an impaled worm. With a wonky gait, he started toward Gavin.

"Good girl," Philip said with a running grin.

Sensing shadows behind him, Gavin spun.

"I'm sorry," Anne said, continuing on with her miserable charade.

Folds appeared on Gavin's forehead. "What the hell is this?"

Anne tilted her head down, searching the floor for answers, but there were no answers, only the high-gloss urethane floorboards, the sheen so shiny she could see herself clearly in its reflection. She could see Gavin too, see every wrinkle and fold on his confused face. As expected, Philip cast no reflection.

"I'm sorry," she said again, the only two words she seemed to know.

Gavin whipped around and faced the naked man, sensing imminent threat. Something wrong was taking place in the Zolof household, something so elementally wrong. He felt the otherworldly shift as soon as he crossed the front door's threshold, but at the time there was no way to identify the magnitude of this strange mood. It had only been a feeling, like the world had fallen off its axis, a pepperoni sliding off a carelessly-constructed pizza. The foul odor in the bedroom had sent his senses askew, bringing his fear and paranoia to life. The ghastly sight of Philip scrambled his sanity, and he had now entered an uncharted epoch of rationale, blurring the distinction between right and wrong, real and imaginary.

The blubber on Philip's arms rippled as his arms shot out. Plump fingers reached for him. Too overwhelmed by the moment to move, Gavin stood there, dumb, watching the smile stretch across Philip's face, the corners of his grin grasping for his earlobes. "No makeup," Philip said, and in that moment Gavin noticed a knife sticking out of his shoulder. Rusty crust surrounded the blade's point of entry. As Philip closed the gap between them (reaching and reaching), the other stab wounds became clearer. Little slits small as buttonholes riddled his pale body, and there simply wasn't enough time to count each mark.

"Sixty-seven," Anne said, reading his thoughts. "I stabbed him sixty-seven times."

"What—"

Philip gripped Gavin's neck with both hands. He pushed him back against the wall. Gavin's head slammed into the sheetrock. The drywall gave and cracked and coughed white dust.

Anne dropped her head into her hands and sobbed. "Sixty-seven times and he *still* won't leave me alone."

Gavin tried to speak, but Philip squeezed and with one loud crunch he severed his ability to communicate verbally. The hot coffee pot had nothing on the pain associated with a crushed larynx. He could feel the plumbing in his throat break into morsels, flecks of bone and cartilage.

"I'm sorry, Gavin. You understand, don't you? He won't let me go. *He won't leave me alone!"*

Gavin didn't understand, but was starting to. He glanced ahead, peering into Philip's eyes, those auburn circles. They glowed and glowed and brightened until it hurt to look. Gavin closed his own eyes and prayed, begging for this to end, to cap his suffering. He struggled to breathe, his broken voice starting to feel like a softball lodged in the pit of his throat.

Philip granted his wish soon enough.

"No makeup," he said, then took his fat fingers accompanied by sharp, overgrown nails and started clawing away at the flesh in front of him. Ribbons of skin were shredded from Gavin's face, dribbles of blood flowing closely behind.

Gavin wanted to scream; he opened his mouth, but choked instead.

Choked and died.

4

The buzzer went off at 8:32 AM and Anne reached for the SNOOZE button. At 8:37 she realized she was running late. She rolled off the empty bed and landed her feet on the floor. She sprinted to the bathroom. Popping the toothbrush in her mouth, she looked at herself in the mirror. Madly scrubbing her teeth, she squinted, straining to see the yellow circle around her eye. Barely there, a ghost of what it once was.

Pleased, she smiled. A second later there were footfalls behind her, coming from the bedroom, and her mood died, along with the curve of her lips.

She spun and faced an empty doorway. No one there.

No Philip.

Her smile returned.

Maybe it's over. Maybe it's done. I gave him what he wanted and he's leaving me alone!

She returned to the mirror. Spitting into the sink, she placed her toothbrush back in the holder and then reached for the cabinet. Once opened, the first thing she noticed was the makeup disk. It sat there, still, yet begging for attention. She turned to the doorway one more time, making sure she was alone.

Alone.

At last.

Quickly, she opened the disk, swiped a generous amount with her finger, and started dabbing the skin around her eye.

"No makeup."

She froze.

No.

"No makeup."

"Oh, God. Please."

Put it down.

The makeup disk fell from the sink, crashing on the porcelain below. The plastic broke and scattered.

"No makeup."

"Leave me alone."

You will never be alone.

But she was alone. Really, she was.

"Do it," Philip said.

She looked at her eye in the mirror.

"Do it," he said again. "Feed me."

Her lower lip trembled. Tears came. Next, the violence.

She balled her hand into a fist and drove her knuckles into her eye until it swelled and swelled, and eventually purpled.

Bruises that would never fade.

THE CHORUS BOY

THE BOY IN the back row sang like an angel.

After Highland Elementary's winter chorus concert, I approached the boy and asked him how he'd gotten so good in such a short amount of time.

Austin Rivera came to us from three states away on a transfer, and, after I'd listened to his tryout, I didn't think the kid had much in the way of his voice. My assistants, Mr. Becker and Ms. Charlotte, disagreed with my analysis and suggested we add him to the chorus, even suggested he perform in the winter show. I told them how impossible that would be; getting him up to speed on what took us months to prepare. But they persisted. Eventually Principal Evans stepped in and made the decision for us; he claimed the boy's parents were adamant he join, as chorus was his favorite activity at his previous school, and the parents—like always—got what they desired.

I didn't put up a fight.

In truth, I hardly cared. He was a good kid, a smart kid, and honestly his voice wasn't all that bad. Sometimes it's not the strength of an individual, but how well they fit in with the rest of the group. I didn't think Austin Rivera fit in well with our chorus—he was too baritone and we already had at least six other boys who fit that role. We didn't need another. But still... the parents insisted. Wouldn't take no for answer.

Like I said, fine with me. We made it work. It took a lot of practice, a few extra hours a week I'd never see in my paycheck, but we got it done. Austin had caught up to speed. It was a borderline miracle.

But when it came time to perform...

He crushed it.

I mean, the kid hit every note with absolute perfection. When I say he sang like an angel, it's not hyperbole. The angelic sounds his vocal cords produced earned him—and the rest of our chorus—a standing ovation that rattled the gymnasium's windows. The bleachers shook as if an apocalyptic earthquake had struck the center of the Garden State. It was unlike any applause I'd ever received in my ten years as the school's chorus instructor.

So, like I said, after the show, I asked Austin plainly: "Where in the world did that lovely singing come from?"

He smiled knowingly, shrugged his shoulders, and said, "Papi, Mrs. Horner. *Papi.*"

And then he ran away, into the crowd of parents searching for their superstar children, attempting to find his own and celebrate the performance of a lifetime.

I didn't think much of the kid's response at first—I'd chalked "Papi" up to some extra help at home, maybe from the boy's father. I even brought up the occurrence to my husband, Tom, a few days after the concert. We were eating dinner and I set down my fork near the edge of my plate. I told him the story. I told him about the kid's strange answer and how it didn't sit well with me.

"What's so strange about it?" Tom asked. "Maybe he got some extra help."

"Maybe," I said, and then thought Tom was onto something. Maybe it wasn't all that weird. Maybe I was thinking too much into it. Maybe I was burnt out from all the extra hours I had put into the show. Maybe this was one of those things I'd obsess about over the course of a week, and then a month from now it wouldn't matter. Maybe a few years from now, I would forget all about Austin and his peculiar reply.

I wish that had been the case.

"I know how this sounds," I said, dropping my hands on the table. "But it was almost as if the singing hadn't come from him. But when I asked him about it, he knew exactly what I was talking about."

"I don't understand."

"Austin. It was like someone else was singing through his mouth."

Now Tom put down his fork. He stopped chewing. "That sounds—"

"I told you I know how it sounds," I said with a faint smile. But I wasn't smiling on the inside. On the inside I was going a little crazy. My heart pumped a little harder and my nerves tingled.

It was that voice, I think. It had infected me in some way, the angelic way it had hit my ears.

"You were there," I told him. "You didn't hear anything... different?"

Tom shook his head. "No. It was a hell of a show, though. I'm very proud of you."

Even his kind words weren't much comfort. I kept replaying the concert over in my head, that voice. I kept hearing those heavenly sounds coming from Austin Rivera's mouth, a fifth-grader who had had approximately two months less prep time than his classmates.

And then, I heard the name *Papi,* over and over again. In my head. Even while I slept.

☆☆☆

I didn't revisit Austin Rivera's response until after winter break. After music class on the first day back, between the bells, I pulled the boy aside.

"Austin."

"Yes, Mrs. Horner," he said, grinning, almost as if he knew what I was going to ask.

"I wanted to ask you about Papi."

I thought he was already smiling as wide as he could but he proved me wrong.

"I wanted to know how he helped you prepare for the chorus concert. You sang so lovely, Austin, and I'd love to share any wisdom he might have given you with the other students."

He kept smiling and shrugged.

"Nothing?"

No answer. His lips were sealed, unmoving, holding down that knowing smile.

"Who is Papi, Austin?" My mouth was completely dry. I don't know why, but just saying *Papi* made my tongue itch. "Is he your dad?"

Austin giggled like he'd been tickled. What I'd said wasn't meant to be a joke, but who knows, maybe it was. One I wasn't in on, that was for sure.

"No? Not your dad?"

Time was ticking. The bell would ring any second.

Austin shook his head slowly. For a second, I thought he was urging me to take another guess, but he surprised me and opened his mouth. Still grinning, he said, "Papi's right behind you."

A chill swept through me.

I turned and saw nothing. A hallway half-full of students hustling to their classrooms. Certainly no one who went by the name of *Papi* stood present.

I rotated back to Austin but he was already halfway down the hall, heading to his next stop—Mrs. Berman's science class. He waved at me over his shoulder, and, in a jubilant voice, yelled, "Bye, Mrs. Horner! See you in chorus!"

I was certain that I'd lose it. After hearing the voice during the winter concert, the sounds that couldn't have possibly been Austin Rivera's vocalizations, and, after our brief exchange in the hallway, Austin introducing me to a person who wasn't there, I'd concluded the kid was either messing with me or he had an imaginary friend who'd stuck with him past the age of when imaginary friends were deemed acceptable. I prayed for the former, but every time I convinced myself it was all a great big joke on the veteran chorus teacher, I heard echoes of that angelic harmony, those beautiful, unique and inspiring vocalizations.

Or better known as *Papi*.

Manuel and Sabrina Rivera were in my office during my fourth-period lunch the next day. Twenty minutes into our talk, I asked about Papi.

"Has he ever mentioned anything like that to you?" I felt my face bunch up, wrinkle like dirty laundry.

The couple paused, hesitated, and then stole a look at each other. In that moment, I knew Austin had told them about his imaginary friend.

I waited for one of them to say something, *anything*. I allowed the silence to breathe as long as it needed.

Manuel spoke first. "Did he say something about..." He gulped. "...Papi?"

My palms grew sweaty. My heart spasmed in my chest. Still, I put on a warm smile, hoping to ease the mood. "Yes. He did. I asked him about the concert and commented on how well he had performed. He said Papi helped him." I didn't want to tell them about the hallway, not yet.

"I see," his father said, sounding almost hurt by the news.

His mother shifted uncomfortably in her seat.

"Is that... I'm sorry," I said. "Is it a sore subject? Would you rather speak about something else? How about Texas? Quite far from New Jersey. Do you miss it there? Family? Friends?"

None of those topics tipped the mood. An awkward silence lingered.

"I'm sorry," I said again. I didn't know how much apologizing I'd end up doing before our meeting would adjourn, but I suspected a lot. "I didn't mean to bring it up. It's just... I dunno. I have some uneasiness toward your son's.... whatever it is. The other day in the hallway—"

I told them about Austin and how he'd informed me that Papi was with us, spying on our conversation. *Watching us.*

"I just think Austin is a little old for imaginary friends; that's all. I'm just playing the role of concerned educator."

Manuel cleared his throat. "Did you bring us here to talk about Austin's future or something else, Mrs. Horner?"

"Manny!" his wife scolded.

He waved her off. She kept quiet, but she looked like she had much more to say.

"I can explain," I said, though I didn't need to. The truth had been written all over my face. "It's that voice. It's hard to forget..."

"Well, forget it." Manuel stood up and headed for the exit. "Let's go, Sabrina."

Austin's mom didn't move, not at first. She stared at me, pleading with her eyes. After a long beat, she stood up and trailed her husband to the door. Before leaving, she glanced back over her shoulder and said, "Don't talk to it.

"Whatever you do, don't talk to it."

In the three weeks after I had spoken with Austin's parents, the kids began to get sick. Not all of them. Just those involved with the after-school chorus program. The nurse's office sent home a bulletin citing bronchitis and laryngitis, two sicknesses not usually considered contagious, but, for some reason, they were passed around the classroom like a bowl of Tootsie Pops. When the kids went out, they stayed out. They never came back.

I knew the absentees and Austin's *Papi* were somehow

related. I had no evidence other than what I'd felt, what I'd heard, and had witnessed of the Riveras' reaction to their son's imaginary friend. I knew I had to do something before the whole school fell under the spell of *Papi*.

Luckily, Mrs. Rivera came to me before I decided to do something impulsive.

I opened my car door and sensed someone behind me. I turned and saw Sabrina Rivera, her head hanging low and her hands folded in front of her as if she were a sinner and I was her confessional.

"Mrs. Rivera," I said softly, my voice hitching.

"Mrs. Horner." She glanced up at me. "I need to talk to you."

I led her back into the school, to my office. She sat down as she had the other day and I closed the door, but not without peeking down the hall, making sure no one had seen us. Then I made my way over to my chair, plopped down, and folded my hands on the desk.

"This has happened before," she said, her voice trembling.

"What has?"

"The kids. The sickness." Her eyes were wet, threatening to push tears over the brim. "Papi." She said the name as if it were a dirty word. "In Texas. It's why we moved here, Mrs. Horner. This thing, it's following us. My son."

"What is it?" My skin hardened with gooseflesh. I wasn't sure if I wanted her to tell me, but I had to know. For the children's sake, I needed to know what we were dealing with.

Sabrina Rivera's lower lip quivered. *"El Cuco."* Another dirty-sounding word that came off her tongue like a wad of spit.

"El Cuco," I repeated.

"Si. They're demons or evil spirits. They attack children."

"I see. And Papi is this... El Cuco?"

She nodded slowly. "It happened several months ago. One day, it just started happening. We heard singing coming from Austin's bedroom. Lovely singing. The voice of an angel." She sniffled. "But when we'd go in to check it out, it was just Austin. Or sometimes..."

I waited as she collected her thoughts.

"Or sometimes there was no one there at all. His room was empty. It'd happen when he was at school. It freaked us out."

"What'd you do?"

"Did what any Christian family would do in a time like this." She breathed deeply. "We called a priest."

"Did that work?"

"No." Shifting in her seat, Sabrina tried to get comfortable. I had a feeling she wouldn't. This story wasn't coming from a place of comfort. "It did for a little while. Then it came back. The singing. Then Austin started talking about his Papi. How he'd seen an old man in his closet. Staring at him. Frightened him at first. He spent a few weeks in our bed. But then he..."

"He what, Sabrina?"

"Then Papi became his friend. Started singing with him. I'd hear two voices singing at night, in his bedroom. When I'd go in there, it'd just be him. I'd ask him, 'Austin? Austin, honey? Who is singing those beautiful songs with you?' And he'd say, 'Papi.' Always Papi." She grabbed her head as if a migraine had suddenly barreled into her. Tears came next. The woman shuddered while sobbing, and I handed her a box of tissues. She went through half of them in under a minute.

After a few minutes, Sabrina got hold of herself and continued.

"It didn't stop. The church refused to help us. Got the police involved. Even had an officer stay the night. Of course, Papi didn't come around then. It knew. The son-of-a-bitch knew when to haunt us and when to stay in the closet. It knew how not to be found.

"Next thing I know, I'm getting a call from Austin's music teacher. Says how wonderful his voice has become. Asked if he was getting any extra help at home." This part of the story sounded familiar. "We said no. Eventually, Austin started talking about Papi, his imaginary friend, the old man who lives in his closet. People were concerned about Austin's story, but by then it was too late. The children, they'd already begun to get sick."

My heart thumped. "What did you do?"

She shrugged in a what-choice-did-we-have sorta way. "We sold the house. Went in about a week. Decided to move to New Jersey. Somewhere far enough away from Melbourne, Texas. Away from Papi."

"But Papi didn't stay, did he?"

"No, he sure didn't." She sniffled and brought a tissue to her nose. "No, it followed us here. It's attached itself to Austin."

I nodded. "You said not to talk to it."

"That's right."

"Why not? I mean, maybe there is some way to reason with it."

She shook her head adamantly. "There is no reasoning with the beast. Manny and I tried. Whenever you address it, it gets angry. It does things."

"What things?"

In the chair, she sat frozen. Staring at me. I thought I'd lost her to some horrific memory. Thought she had checked out on me. But then she stood up. She lifted her shirt. Across her stomach were several scars. The wounds they covered looked to have run deep. Fresh bandages sporting pinkish stains hid more recent wounds. The injuries were only a few days old.

"All sorts of things. Whatever it wants. It has no rules. In our culture, El Cuco is a boogeyman who feeds on children. I think..."

"Yes?" I asked, wanting her to continue.

"I think it feeds on their minds. Their creativity. It leeches onto them and bleeds them dry."

"How do you know that?"

She shrugged. "I've done some research, Mrs. Horner. Throughout the years, towns who have reported similar activity—the children suffer."

"How so?"

"It's different in each case. Some towns have said that seventy percent of their kids get sick. Cancer and brain tumors. Some of them lose the will to eat. Failure to thrive in younger children. Babies. Some of them pass in their sleep."

"Jesus."

"Dios mio."

"That's what's happening here. In Highland Elementary."

"It'll start here, Mrs. Horner. But it won't end here. Next it will be the middle school. Then the high school. Who knows? Maybe it will spread to a neighboring town. The entire county. Sooner or later, the whole state. The country. These things are an infectious disease. *El Cuco* is not just a boogeyman, it's a plague."

"We have to stop it."

At this, Sabrina began to cry. She'd clearly given up any hope of dispatching the demon.

"Mrs. Rivera," I said, reaching out and grabbing her hand. "We can fight this thing. We can stand up to it."

She nodded as she sobbed, but I don't think she agreed. Of all the things the monster in the closet had stolen, hope had been the most important.

After all, it's hope that sees us through.

"Is Papi here now?" I asked Austin. "Is he in the room with us?"

After giving the room a good once over and deeming it free from the old man who lived in his closet, Austin shook his head.

"Good," I said. "Now, I want to teach you something. A very important lesson."

"What is it?"

"I want to teach you a song."

"What song?"

"A very special song. And I want you to sing it every night before bed. I want you to sing it in your dreams."

"Sing it in my dreams?" His brow crinkled along with his forehead.

"That's right. I want you to remember the song, everything about it. The measure, the notes, the lyrics. And when Papi comes to you, I want you to sing it to him."

He seemed hesitant to agree. "Okay..."

"Promise me you'll sing Papi the song."

"But why?"

"Because."

"But why?"

"Because I said so."

"Will he like it?"

"No, I don't think he will."

"I don't want to make Papi angry, Mrs. Horner. Papi is my friend."

I knelt down. "You know, Austin, sometimes we think people are our friends, but they're really not. Sometimes people will use a friendship to get things from others. It's called taking advantage of someone."

"And you think Papi wants something from me?"

I nodded. "Yes, I do. I know he sounds like a great... *person.*" I almost choked on the word. "But, I don't think he is. I think he's trying to fool you. He wants something from you and he'll do anything to get it."

Austin hung his head. "I think so, too."

"You do?"

"He started out okay. He teached me songs."

"Taught you songs," I corrected.

"Taught me songs. He made me laugh. He even took me on adventures when I was asleep."

"I know, I know. It's hard. But that's all part of his plan. Don't you see?"

Biting his lower lip, Austin nodded.

"What do you think Papi wants from you, Austin?"

The kid drew a deep breath. "He wants friends. A lot of friends. He wants to be friends with everyone, he says. He wants to teach them songs. Songs from the mundo de sueños."

Mundo de sueños.
World of dreams.
"Well, I want to teach *you* a song. A song that will make Papi go away."
Austin smiled. "Will my real friends stop getting sick?"
Tears stung my eyes. "Yes, I believe they will."
So I taught him the song. And he sang it beautifully.
Like an angel.

Three days passed.
The kids were still sick, but no more had gone out on leave. I wasn't sure if the song was working, but Austin promised me he'd sing it every night before bed. Chorus had been canceled for the last week because we were missing so many students, but I decided to stay late that afternoon. I called Tom to tell him I needed to grade some homework and I'd pick up dinner on the way home. He was okay with it and told me to take my time; he wasn't hungry yet.
After I hung up the phone, a knock sounded on my classroom door.
"Come in," I called.
The door swung open and in walked Don Hayward, head of the school maintenance department. The befuddled expression on his face threw me. He looked visibly upset about something. Holding his baseball cap in front of him, squeezing it with both hands, he looked up at me with watery eyes. There was fear in his approach, fear and childish worry.
"Mrs. Horner, I don't know exactly how to explain this..." he said, and the tone of his voice froze my blood.
"What is it, Don?"
"Well, I was downstairs in the boiler room, and I heard this... singing."
"Singing?"
"Yeah..."
"Okay?"

He sniffled and laughed simultaneously. "I... I think I saw something too. A man. At least I think it was. Anyway, he was just singing down there."

"What did the man look like?"

"He was wearing a cowl."

"You couldn't see his face?"

He swayed his head from side-to-side as if to say *maybe I did, maybe I didn't.* "Couldn't get a great look. It was dark down there. But... I don't know. He looked..."

"Old?"

Don nodded. "You know who he is?"

I didn't answer that.

Don smiled. "Had a pleasant voice. Sang almost like an angel from God's golden army."

I didn't realize how tightly I was clenching my teeth until my jaw began to ache. "So why are you telling me?"

"Well... two reasons. First, I thought since you were the chorus instructor and all."

"And the second?"

"Well... he asked for you."

"He asked for me?"

"Oh, yeah. When I told him I thought you had left for the day, he got real angry."

"What happened when he got angry?"

"I... I don't know if I should say really."

"I won't tell anyone—"

He waved my concern aside. "Not that, Mrs. Horner. It's just... Well, shoot. I don't know if I believe what my eyes were telling me."

"What was it?"

The janitor was shaking now. "Well... you see... his flesh... it began to... melt."

"Melt?"

"Mm-hm. And I think I saw horns growing out of his head. Curled ones. Like on a ram."

"Horns."

Don swallowed. "Yes, ma'am. But also, it could've been the dark playing tricks."

"It was probably the dark," I said, agreeing with him.

"Well, I suppose I should go tell Principal Evans. Maybe even call the cops—"

"Let me talk to him first? Please?"

"Oh, yeah. Sure thing." Don nodded dreamily and stepped backward, toward the door. It was as if he was sleeping on his feet. Dreaming. I knew this was an extension of El Cuco's power. "I'd hurry if I were you, though. Man seems real eager to meet you, Mrs. Horner."

Don directed me downstairs but didn't accompany me. Something told me he'd never step foot in the boiler room again. He escorted me to the mouth of the stairs and then turned around, walking away as if in a trance. He'd probably forget his run-in with the spirit by the next day; remember it only as a fleeting dream.

I descended the stairs, taking my time, mindful of the dark and potential hazards.

The air in the basement was tainted, and I couldn't tell exactly what it smelled like. Maybe cheese that had burned in the microwave. Maybe something else. Maybe it was what mundo de sueños smelled like.

Maybe Hell.

I continued along the walkway. The sound of the heating system grew louder, more distinct. The smell grew worse, giving me the sort of headache that made you want to lie down and not get up for the next four hours. I fought through it, made my way to the end of the alley. There were a few work lights stationed throughout the basement, but mostly the entire area was flooded with shadows and perpetual darkness.

I came to a dead end.

Then I heard it. Started off as a whistle, then grew louder, blossoming into a harmony. A saintly hum. Angelic in nature. Sweet. Something you'd sing a baby to sleep with. The carol rose several octaves. As the gentle, inviting singsong matured, the silhouette of a body appeared in the darkness, crossing over into one of the patches of light cast by the work lights. Like Don had warned, the figure's identity was hidden behind a cowl. The song grew louder, suddenly playing as if there were speakers in my head, blasting the solo effort directly into my ear canals. I backed away.

Then the song stopped.

"You must be Mrs. Horner," El Cuco barked.

"I know what you are."

"Do you?"

"You're a vampire."

"I have many names, in many regions, in many cultures."

"You feed on children."

"They taste best. Their thoughts mostly. Go down smooth. Vitalizes the mind. Helps me grow big and strong."

"I know how to stop you."

"Ah, yes," Papi said. "The song."

"I'll sing it for you."

In that moment, the creature grew several feet taller. El Cuco stretched as if made of clay, the shadow it cast crawling up the wall, across the ceiling. It hissed like a cat near a bath.

I backed away.

"YOU WILL SING NO SUCH SONG."

"Why not?" I asked. "Does it hurt you?"

It didn't reply. Instead, it continued to elongate, the sprawling shadow blanketing most of the basement. I didn't want the shadow to fall over me—who knew what danger its darkness contained. For a split second I could almost see through the shadows and into the realm it called home. Mundo de sueños. The realm of dreams. Of nightmares. In the darkness, I saw children. At least twenty of them, maybe more. They were holding hands. I thought I recognized their faces. Maybe they were from my chorus, maybe they were not. The shadows did their job and hid them well.

In that moment, I sang the song.

The shadows retreated.

Papi shrieked. A hideous noise filled the basement, so I opened my airways and pushed myself. It'd been years since I had explored my voice in that way. I felt good. Righteous. And... pitch perfect.

The shadows continued to dwindle in size.

I couldn't see the children anymore, but I heard them. They were singing with me, their united voices matching the quality of my own. Together, we drowned out the cries of the demonic presence, the vampiric creature that fed off the young creative spirits of the world. I didn't know how long the beast had been on its rampage. Centuries. Millennia. Longer. It didn't matter. What mattered was that it ended. Here. Now.

The chorus rose and before long the shadows were gone. They'd been reduced to nothing. In the corner of the basement, all that remained of the foul entity that had stolen my students was an old shriveled man, cowering with his head between his knees, hands pressing against his temples. He was crying.

The children could no longer be heard, but I kept with the song, singing the chorus over and over again, as loud as my pipes would allow. I still had air. Plenty of it. I could go the distance. I could sing as long as needed to see the demon out.

I stopped and glanced down at El Cuco's reduced state. "Papi," I said.

The unclothed, albino-looking thing eyed me. Its wrinkled skin moved like a caterpillar, almost all at once. Its crimson eyes found mine. Two red streams dribbled down its face.

"You can't..." it said.

"I can and I will."

In the distance, I could still hear them. The children. They were singing my song. I once said that sometimes it's not the strength of the individual, but how they fit in with the rest of the group. Our ensemble fit well. Perfectly. Together we sang the last verse and the final chorus three times, and, after that, the albino-looking creature began to melt into a puddle, which then turned into a river and ran to the closest floor drain. Where it went after that was anybody's guess, but no one at Highland Elementary ever heard from Papi, El Cuco, ever again.

A week later the children returned to school and my chorus, reportedly feeling better than they ever had in all their lives.

Austin Rivera thanked me and gave me a great big hug. So did his parents come the next parent-teacher conference.

Everything returned to normal.

And, at next year's winter concert, the entire chorus sang like a choir of inspired angels.

LOVERS' HILL

(THE BLACK HILL #2)

1972

SHADY O'QUINN PULLED two cans of beer out of the cooler, one for him and one for the lovely Margaret Eastern. He cracked the top and foam rushed to the opening, bubbling on the surface of the can. Margaret opened hers with ease, care, and a bit of kindness. No foam frothed and she took on that first sip like a gentle kiss.

"Cheers," Shady said, raising his can.

"Cheers," she replied, knocking her can against his. The clink of their meeting sounded a lot louder than one would expect.

"Can you believe it?" he asked, gazing across Lover's Hill, up at the cloudless night. The stars had come out and put on quite a show. Normally, the Hill would be populated with teenagers making out in their cars, but tonight was different. Almost everyone from town was over at the high school, celebrating. "Graduated. College next year. Seems like a dream."

Margaret nodded, trying to swallow the terrible, lingering taste of the cheap beer. No matter how many times she swallowed, the flavor remained. "Yeah, it's crazy. When you start high school, it seems like graduation is a lifetime away. Now, looking back at it, it all feels like a blink."

"Yeah, time is funny like that."

"Next thing you know, we'll be thirty and have like four kids."

Shady chortled. Kids weren't really his thing, but he was fond of the work that went into making them. "You know, Margaret, we've been going together for how long now?"

"Since the end of sophomore year." *This conversation again.* How it bored her. But a romantic evening—even one filled with stale, stolen beer and a beautiful starlit sky—wouldn't be complete without Shady *trying*.

"Yeah, so two years. Two great years, I might add."

"Hm." Tuning him out, she studied the surface of the hill. The terrain was lumpy, as if there were eggs hidden underneath the grassy surface. A lone tree stood atop the hill, the only natural formation that kept the promiscuous teens that came here company. It was the best place in town to lock lips, and everyone knew it. She'd only been here once with Shady, and had never visited the prime necking spot with anyone else. Heck, Shady had been her only boyfriend, and except for Tommy Wilkens, her old next-door neighbor, she'd kissed no one else in her entire life.

"Are you listening to me?" Shady asked. He'd gripped the can so hard it had dented.

"Hm? No, I'm sorry. What were you saying?"

Shady faced the window, looked out into the night. His lips parted just slightly, enough so she could see the whites of his teeth in the dark reflection of the driver's side window. "It's been two years, Margaret. You're going to Akron next year, and I'll be stuck here in Ludlow. We won't see each other much. I really like you." He turned to her again, and his jaw no longer clenched. "I love you, actually. And I want to be your first."

She nodded. "I know you do."

"What about tonight? It's graduation. The stars are out. Prime time for a little love-making, wouldn't you say?"

She suddenly felt sick, and it wasn't from the watered-down beer. "You know, Shady, I'm just not ready yet. I want my first time to be special."

His features fell, darkened. She felt a little threatened by his reaction. In her mind's eye, she pictured him punching her head through the window. And she didn't know why that thought occurred to her—Shady had never been violent. Just the opposite. He'd practiced and preached peace, attended rallies and concerts that hailed messages of love-not-war. There wasn't a violent bone in that young man's body, yet, in that sudden moment, everything had changed. The air felt different. Heavy. Like it was hard to breathe. And the look on his face—well, it hardly looked like a face Shady would make. Angrier than angry. A rage that equaled that of some psycho's.

His lips parted again. He spoke through his teeth, "I've been patient."

"And you'll be rewarded one day, just not—"

"When? After college? When we're married? When, Margaret?"

"When I'm ready." *Asshole,* was how she wanted to punctate that sentence, but she refrained from name-calling. It was the look she'd been given that steered her in a gentler direction. Plus, it was graduation. She didn't want to look back on this night in thirty years and remember it as the night they had argued, or worse—the night they had broken up. Shady always got upset when she turned him down. More dejected than angry, though, and this was clearly the most vexed he'd ever been.

"I've tried, Margaret. I've really tried to be patient with you."

"Stop, Shady. You're—"

"I'm what? Not good enough for you? Is that it? You want your first time to be special, but just not with me?"

"No, not at all. I was going to say you're scaring me."

"I'm scaring you?" A laugh tucked behind a breath. "I'm scaring you? Well, you're scaring me, Margaret. I'm starting to get the sense you don't really like me."

"I like you just fine. I... I love you, in fact."

Did she? She didn't know, but she hoped it would talk her boyfriend down from whatever ledge he was climbing.

"You love me?"

She nodded.

"Then show me."

She shook her head. "I'm just not ready. And I'm certainly not interested in doing it up here. This place freaks me out, if I'm being incredibly honest. You've heard the stories of what's happened here over the years. Heck, Blake Weber's place is just—"

Her head catapulted forward, and her nose cracked against the dashboard, nearly flattened against her face on impact. A moment passed where everything was fuzzy, like looking through a partially-veiled curtain. The world blurred in and out of focus, and distant telephones rang in her ears. It took half a minute for reality to slide back into view.

"I'm sorry, baby. Honestly. But I feel like that was the right course of action."

Her nose leaked steadily, blood droplets blossoming on her dress. She brought her hand to her face but was too terrified to touch the damage. It was too dark to see her reflection in the rearview, even though she'd seen his only a moment ago. But the world had grown darker in those minutes, and she couldn't see much of it. If the blood and the fireball of pain in the center of her face were any indication, the destruction was extensive. She hoped it was just a broken nose, but she feared *shattered* was more likely the case. She pictured her fractured bone jutting through her soft skin when she closed her eyes. There was no more comfort in the darkness behind her eyes than there was outside her boyfriend's Impala.

"You hit me," she said, and her voice sounded very unlike herself. Nasally and congested. Her nose *had* been crushed though, so what did she expect?

"I'll do more than that if you don't make love to me," he replied in a voice she didn't recognize. It was his, she could tell. But it also wasn't. His tone held a sinister quality. *Possessed* may not have been accurate, but it was accurate enough. "Suck my dick or *something*."

Even though her eyes were closed and she couldn't see him, she saw his face. It was there, in the darkness behind her eyes. Tentacles were poking through his skin. He was smiling an angry smile, the edges of his lips curling, reaching for his eyes. His teeth were gone, replaced by short, ivory spikes. Somewhere behind him, more tentacles whipped in the darkness, multiplying with each passing moment.

Her eyes shot open and she stared out the window, up the Black Hill; Lover's Hill some called it, but that nickname couldn't be any less accurate. There was no love here. There were shadows collecting at the hill's apex, near the tree, and she glossed over the fact that her head was slightly damaged, concussed, and that she may be seeing things. Her mind had already accepted the moving shapes and swaying dim figures as reality.

She screamed.

Turning to her boyfriend (ex if she could make it through this alive), she screamed again. His face was gone, now just a sheet of glistening carmine. Every strip of flesh had been peeled like a potato skin. The bloody mask that used to be his face rested on the dashboard as if it were some ordinary thing, a hat perhaps, something to throw back on later. His longish hair was matted with fresh blood. Deep trenches had been raked into his raw muscle. His fingertips were soiled with his own demise, dripping droplets of bright and shiny crimson. Despite his grim appearance, that smile remained; he flashed her his pearly whites, clean as if he'd just given them a thorough brush.

"Come on, baby. Give me a kiss!"

She shrieked and pushed open the door. Putting a foot on the wet grass, she slipped and collapsed on the ground. In the near distance, where visibility and shadows converged, things moved about. Long things, whipping things, things that whispered and sang nearly-silent songs. The lone tree stood still, watching the night unfold, a sentient creature residing over this dark land. Above her, the sky twisted like a tornado, the stars blinking from their palaces of eternal rest. And behind her, something crooned, and she wasn't surprised to discover the noise had come from none other than her lover.

Ex-lover.

"Just a kiss, baby," Shady said, climbing out of the car. "Just a *goddamn* kiss. Can't a guy get a kiss!"

His voice came out warbled, a scratched-record quality that caused every one of her limbs to shake uncontrollably. That wasn't him, her Shady. He'd transformed into something else in a single heartbeat. Changed. Into someone else entirely.

No, not some*one*.

Some *thing*.

But how?

It didn't make sense to her. Didn't add up. She knew there was something wrong with the hill, the Black Hill, that there had always been something wrong with it. Maybe not always. But there had been something wrong with it thirteen years ago when Blake Weber had lost his mind and cracked open his wife's head with an ax. There had been something rotten here then, and there was something rotten here now. She was sure of it.

But what?

The shadows. Twisting things. Unspeakable evils.

She looked over her shoulder and saw Shady bounding toward her, his speed much too fast for her to outrun. She had no shot. She knew it the second she saw him barreling down on her, his legs moving like an Olympic sprinter's, almost in a blur. His arms and hands had morphed into something else—two long tentacles that were dragging on the ground behind him, flopping around the grass like wet spaghetti noodles.

That got her moving faster, but not fast enough.

Within four more steps, she felt his cold embrace around her, those rubbery extensions. They curled around her, pulled her tightly against his body, which had become a slimy sheet of skin and tattered clothing.

He whispered: *"Come with me. To the dark. Across the*

rainbows, through the pearlescent realms of the other worlds. We can be one. We can be more than one. We can be infinity."

She screamed, but the second her outburst hit the air, a hand—a *human* hand—clapped over her mouth, stifling her desperate attempt to alert the nearby town. No one would have heard her anyway. They were simply too far away from civilization. Plus, she got the sense the Hill wouldn't allow her to be heard. It would hide her pleas from the world, her cries for assistance.

"I can't fight it, Margaret," she heard Shady say, *her* Shady. The boy who she'd once considered giving up her virginity for. "It's in me and I can't fight it. Much longer. Run. Run toward the town. Don't look back."

Margaret did as she was told. She got twenty steps toward the town before something behind her shrieked, a whistle that nearly split her eardrums in half. Then, the thing that had invaded Shady was on her, pouncing down on her back. She was looking at the well-lit town before the thing snapped her neck. After the force broke her vertebrae, she faced the starlit sky, wondering what those little black spots were, hovering over, floating like jellyfish among the black.

Next came eternal nothingness.

LET ME BE YOUR BUTTERFLY

1

WHEN THE METAL doors parted, opening like the jaws of some robotic shark, she found Jeremy naked in the fetal position on the pad, just like always. His entire body quivered. Thick mucus coated his flesh, one of the many side effects of his brief journey. Other side effects could include: forgetfulness; a slight, short-lasting fever; a mild case of diarrhea; irritable temperament; sore throat; blisters on the hands and feet; temporary speech impediment; and swollen ear drums, making it hard to process sound. That last one, he'd told her, felt like cotton balls in the ear canals.

She entered the small chamber, no bigger than the average walk-in closet, and offered him a hand.

At first, he didn't accept. Screwing up his feral-looking eyes, fixating on hers, he drew short breaths as if on the verge of hyperventilating or of having a full-blown panic attack. The machine's heart-rate monitor spiked near the one-sixty mark.

"It's okay, honey," she said, keeping out her hand, hoping he'd grab it. It was always like this when he returned. There was at least a thirty-second grace period where his scrambled thoughts tried coming together. He stared at her blankly, the pieces of his memory slowly joining, forming a cohesive bond.

Sixty seconds, she counted silently. *Longer than the last trip by about ten seconds.*

This was his fifteenth trip into 2120, the year everything went to absolute hell.

"Can you stand?" she asked him. "Take my hand and I'll help you."

Another moment of hesitation, but soon after he acquiesced. She pulled him to his feet, then helped him across the room, over to the small station where they kept a few medical supplies.

"You have a cut above your right eye," she said, sitting him down in the chair. "Remember how you got it?"

Jeremy's brow folded and his eyes bounced around the room, taking it all in. It was like he'd been there before but couldn't fully remember. But he had been there—he *lived* there, had for the past twenty years.

He's getting worse, she thought. *Every time he goes in, he gets worse.*

"Belle?" he said foggily. Then his face broke, the mask of confusion shattered. He looked at her lovingly, like a partner who'd gone away for two weeks and returned home should. "Belle... it's... you."

She kissed his lips, allowing their touch to linger. When the kiss became too wet, so much so she couldn't taste him anymore, she pulled back, grabbing his cheeks with both hands. She forced his eyes to hers but she didn't need to. Jeremy was back. *Her* Jeremy was back.

"I missed you," she said, pecking his forehead.

"I missed you too, baby."

She climbed off him and started attending to the gash above his right eye. He flinched when she dribbled antiseptic on it.

"Burns, I know." Belle patted the area with a gauze pad, and then applied a fresh bandage. "Good as new."

"Thank you." He stood up, stretching his limbs. "Towel?"

She fetched one for him from the closet. Helping him

wipe the viscous gel off his body, she asked, "So... how was it this time?"

He stopped wiping. Froze. Had she said something wrong? It was the same question she'd always asked, same one she'd asked the last fourteen times. "The same," he said with zero fervor. "It's always the same."

"Nothing different?"

"No."

"There must be something."

"There's nothing. I can't... I can't change what I can't see, Belle."

She nodded. "Maybe I can—"

"No," he said adamantly. "No, this is my job. My duty. I must do it."

"It's killing you," she said finally. They'd never discussed it before, the toll it was taking on Jeremy's mind. His body. She didn't want to tell him that his body was going through changes—*significant* changes—and that he'd aged exponentially each time he'd used the machine. "It's gonna kill you."

"My mistake. My price to pay."

And that was all he would speak on the subject.

2

Outside, the blood-orange skies rolled on. Lightning crashed perpetually on the horizon, the flashes blinding to anyone who stared too long. The city below lay in ruin, black and gray rubble the only remnants of the old world. A lone building stood in the middle of the derelict city, towering over the apocalyptic wasteland, the dead world that was once a vibrant and thriving metropolis. No longer. The event of 2120 had destroyed everything and everyone.

Not everyone. Not exactly. In the barren wasteland yonder, there was movement, *slow* movement, shadows that crept and crawled along that endless stretch of visible darkness. *Mutants,* he told her. *Survivors.*

Unable to stare out any longer, Jeremy backed away

from the window. Belle snuck up behind him and wrapped her arms around him, squeezing him tightly as if she never meant to let go. They both watched as more lightning sectioned the sky.

"Lightning getting worse?" he asked, more of an observation than a question. "Seems like there's always more of it."

"I haven't noticed," she lied, knowing she *had* noticed, noticed very much. Her only job nowadays was to notice things. Things about the outside world, the chaos below them, all around. She'd noticed the clouds had grown more turbulent, the streets darker, and the occasional animal that scurried through the streets in search of food had also become less frequent. Those shapeless things at the edge of where the darkness stirred had become more noticeable too, but she didn't dare tell him. The man had enough on his plate without worrying about things that couldn't reach them. That couldn't hurt them in the city's last remaining structure.

"Well, it looks like it," he said, turning his back to the window. "Can't stare too long. I'll go blind."

"Hm. It's never bothered me too much."

She led him to the other side of their laboratory where their mattress lay in the corner. She pushed him on it. "It's been almost three weeks," she said, unbuckling her belt. It was off and thrown across the room a second later. "I want you."

"Belle," he said, hardly reacting.

Next, she drew her shirt up over her head, tossed it aside. Pouncing on him, she giggled.

A faint smile wedged its way onto Jeremy's face. He held her in his arms, and, as she pressed down on him, shoving her tongue in his mouth, he looked away.

"What's the matter?" she asked.

"Not in the mood."

She climbed off him. "What do you mean?"

"I'm just not in the mood."

"Why?"

He shrugged, having no adequate answer. "I just... I'm tired. Maybe later?"

"You've been gone for almost three weeks and—"

"Maybe later?" he repeated.

"Forget it." She put her shirt back on and headed for the door, needing to take a walk around the building to clear her head.

Darkness lived there too.

3

The time machine was a confusing device to wrap one's head around. Some days, Belle didn't even understand it herself, and she'd help build the goddamn thing. Really, it was her husband's genius that was responsible for getting the job done. He'd slaved away for years—not like there was anything else to do—trying to perfect the thing. Make it not just work but make it an operational tool that could undo all of this... *madness.*

So far, no luck.

She caressed the dome-shaped head of the machine, dragging a smudge down its stainless-steel shell.

"What are you thinking about?" Jeremy asked, wrapping a towel around his naked body. He'd just gotten out of the shower, a post-time travel ritual he'd never forgotten.

She shrugged. "That this is never going to work."

"Don't say that."

She spun toward him. "Fifteen times, Jeremy. You were there when it happened, the thing that started this all. You were there when *he* released it."

"I know." He sounded depressed, and Belle knew he had every right to be. "I know, but no matter what I do, he still finds a way to trigger it. To set it off. I've tried everything, Belle. *Everything.*"

"You haven't tried sending me."

"Told you. It won't work. The machine is a direct link to *my* past. Not yours."

"What will happen then, huh?"

"I don't know, and that's the problem."

"What could be worse than this?" She pointed toward the window, the desolate scenery beyond their home, beyond the top floor of the tower.

"Obliteration, maybe? Maybe it melts our brains. Maybe reality bleeds out of view right in front of us."

"Death?"

"Almost certainly."

"And that's worse than suffering here."

"We have each other, Belle."

She stomped her foot on the hard linoleum. "Don't do that. Don't use our love as a weapon against me."

"I'm serious. It's not a perfect existence by any means, but... shit, Belle. At least we have each other. Enough food for the two of us to last the rest of our lives."

"Yeah? And who knows how long that is. Look outside. Do things seem normal to you? Do you get the impression that this world will last another year? Another five?" She didn't want to tell him about the shapeless things, the shadows they hadn't given a name to yet because they were so distant, barely a piece of their lives. But soon they would name them. They would have to.

Jeremey didn't answer.

"No? That's because it won't. Sooner or later, everything around us will fall. Including this tower."

"It's lasted twenty years. Why not another twenty? Why not another fifty? Who knows, maybe this world will outlive us."

She began to cry, tears spilling down her cheeks. "But it won't. And you know that. Plus... what about everyone else... all the people who died. Our friends. Colleagues. Don't you miss them? Don't you miss having a life outside of... outside of us?"

His eyes went soft. Tears filled them to the brim. "I only need you."

That was the last thing he said to her before they went to bed.

4

A week passed before they began to plot their next leap. Belle made sure not to volunteer again. That seemed as useless as sending Jeremy back, time and time again. *Do you know what the definition of insanity is?*

He had looked at her with that *hardy-har-har* stare, the one with the downcast eyes. She didn't require a response because she knew *he* knew the answer.

Now they were prepping the machine for another launch.

"What will you try this time?" she asked, almost afraid to. Any time she had referenced the jumps over the last week, he either hadn't answered or answered angrily. Almost like he was finished talking about it. Almost like he was giving up.

He breathed deeply. "I don't know. I might try to adjust the calculations, go back a week earlier. Try to infiltrate the laboratory and destroy the batch before... before *he* releases it worldwide."

"Aaron," she said, and the name sounded like poison on her tongue.

"Yes," he confirmed. "Yes, him."

"Why not try to kill him?" she suggested, and not for the first time. "You could go back to when he was a baby and k—"

"It doesn't work like that." He rolled his eyes. Every explanation he'd given her over these past few months hadn't gotten through. "I only have a little play. It was designed to go back to a specific moment in time. I can't just... go back to when Hitler was a baby and stop the Holocaust. Time... time doesn't bend like that, Belle."

"So make it."

At this, he laughed. "Make it? I'm not a god, Bee. I'm a man."

"A man who built a fucking time machine."

He leered at her, all of his good-natured temperament melting away. "Why do you want this to happen so badly?"

"Because... I want to save the world."

"Do you?"

Her brow crinkled. "Of course. Why else?"

He bit his lip, so hard the skin around his mouth blanched. "Nothing. Forget it."

He turned and went for the machine, undoing his collar, ready to undress.

"You used to be into this. The first several times you jumped, you were all about saving the world. Now... now, suddenly, our love is good enough?"

He stopped stripping off his clothes, craned his neck like he was going to respond, then turned back and continued to relieve his body of clothing.

Ten minutes later, he was gone, twenty years behind her.

5

She killed the days by reading. Old magazines and books left over from the old world were her companions, and she read each day until her vision went blurry. Her head was full of stories. It was an escape, a good escape, a way to cope with the reality they had made for themselves here atop the tower. Occasionally between reads, she'd stand near the window, look out, and survey the dead lands below. The earth had turned the color of ash. Skeletons of those less fortunate lay below the dirt, she knew. Friends, colleagues, people she'd never see again. She wondered if those shapeless things were them too. Leftovers from the old word. Or maybe they were new things. New things that mimicked the old world. Things she'd never see, or experience, ever again.

Unless, Jeremy figured out a way to stop it.

It didn't make sense to her. He'd been there when Aaron released the chemical that had killed off almost the entire population. The chemical that had gotten airborne, traveled overseas, and killed off mostly everyone there too.

The entire world, dead.

Except for them. That they knew of. Over the last twenty years, they had seen figures travel through the streets below. Different from the shapeless shadows on the dark horizon. People, or so they appeared like it. Who they were didn't much matter. The atmosphere outside was too harsh to survive, and the fact that they'd survived at all surprised Belle. A part of her wanted to bring them inside, interview them, find out what it was like out there, ask them how they had survived. That was the scientist side of her. The survivalist in her knew that it was too dangerous to risk. The entire world was infected with the chemical now, the nasty, lethal toxin that was invisible to the senses but would melt the skin right off your face. She'd remembered what it was like watching people die on the television. People's skin liquefying, running off their faces like bleeding mascara. That imagery still haunted her even twenty years later. Their deaths had been seared into her brain. It lived there, imprinted forever in the catacombs of her memory.

She shook the painful memories from her mind, visions of her friends and colleagues, people whose minds were much brighter than hers, dying under the poisoned skies.

"Aaron," she thought, crying now. "Why..."

He'd never gotten the chance to answer for his crimes. The fact that he'd created such a terrible weapon (*helped* create) was bad enough, but to release the thing—she couldn't wrap her mind around it. So many deaths. *All* the deaths, really. All the deaths in the world.

Couldn't grasp what would make a man do such a thing, so she dug her nose into more books, the classics written by such notables as Charles Dickens and Jane Austen, and contemporary masterpieces scribed by the likes of Kurt Vonnegat and Joyce Carol Oates. The days flew by, and almost two weeks later, her husband returned. Naked. Covered in the goo one does while traveling between two points in time. The fluid she never understood—he had explained it to her, but not being a quantum physicist, she couldn't comprehend it. Something to do with the molecular breakdown of certain genetic coding. Whatever. It was foreign to her.

"Are you okay?" she asked, getting him a towel.

He just stood there, looking around the lab, his eyes

vacant, no thought behind them. She pressed the button on her stopwatch, wondering how long it would take to normalize this time around. Last time was abnormally long, and any longer, she fretted might do permanent damage to his brain. And then where would they be? According to him, he was the only one who could travel.

According to him.

He'd told her the machine was linked to *his* past, meaning the traveler could only inhabit *his* body. The way he had explained it was like demonic possession—the traveler was the spirit and the past body was the vessel. It only linked to Jeremy Holloway's past, no one else's. Thus, only he could travel.

"Jeremy?" she asked, wrapping the towel around his shivering body. "You with me?"

Of course he wasn't. He stared toward the window, his head a hollow shell. A zombie of a human being.

Last time it took a little over a minute. Her counter said ninety seconds. When it hit the two-minute mark, she panicked.

"Jeremy?" she asked. Her heart felt like a million butterflies taking flight. "Jeremy, come back to me."

But he didn't. Wouldn't. It was like he refused to.

Was this it? Was this the journey that broke his mind?

I can't let him do this anymore. He needs a break before he *breaks.*

He was still standing there when the machine called to her. She glanced over her shoulder, back toward the small dome-shaped thing. It invited her inside. It was waiting for her. She thought how wonderful it would be to go back, and, even if she couldn't save them, save the world, she would see their faces again, the faces of all those who were lost when the skies bled and the storms came, when the toxins soured this once great slice of existence. She could see *him* again, too.

Him.

She put her hand to the zipper on her white plastic suit. Before she could move it down past her breasts, a hand reached out and grabbed her.

"Don't even think about it," Jeremy said. The life in his eyes had returned.

6

Breakfast the following morning was quiet, too quiet, so quiet that Belle wanted to scream just to disrupt the awkwardness. Last night, he had lectured her again on the cosmic calamities of sending her into the machine. The speech had been filled with threats, how much she could tear the universe asunder, destroy everything they had worked so hard to obtain.

And what is that? she had asked him. *What have we got? What have we obtained except solitude, a pitiful existence?*

Our lives, he had answered. *Our lives, our love, our souls.*

A part of her did feel guilty that their love wasn't enough. That being stuck at the top of the tower in the center of a dead city, a dead world, wasn't truly living, even if she did have her husband with her. They had no children—their work was their children, each success and failure. All they had was each other, their love, forever and always.

Belle cleared the table, placing the dishes in the sink. She began washing them at once, still chewing on last night's verbal tussle. About two minutes later, Jeremy snuck up behind her and put his arms around her waist. She let him, didn't stop him when he nuzzled the crook of her neck. Didn't stop when he began to kiss her flesh, softly at first, but once he realized it was open season, he sucked on her skin harder.

He spun her around and she immediately hopped up on the sink. In a blink, he was reaching up her skirt, pulling off her underwear. She closed her eyes and leaned back, waited for him to enter.

The sex was short but meaningful. For her, it was a release of the tension that had been building. Sex had a way of cooling things that got too hot, an act of forgiveness. For him, allowing them to become one meant that she still loved him. At least in his mind. At least she hoped that was the message their act conveyed. Afterwards, things did die down, became less awkward.

They lay on the mattress; Jeremy dozing off to sleep; her trying to calm spinning thoughts. As she closed her eyes, all she could think about was the machine, the travel, what might be waiting for her on the other side of this black rainbow.

7

Another two-week trip. She occupied herself with more books, though, the shelves were running empty on original reads, and she had begun to dip into stories for the second time. It wasn't a bad thing. She started with her favorites, some old Michael Crichton. *Timeline* seemed appropriate, so she cracked open the paperback and finished the thing in less than a day. She dipped into some other popular fiction next, settling on Peter Benchley and Stephen King. She alternated books until she fell asleep mid-page.

The next few days were filled with books. Magazines too. She skimmed through an issue of *Sports Illustrated* from 2019, the issue after the Philadelphia Eagles had won their second straight Super Bowl, much to her chagrin, being a Giants fan and all. Remembering those days was weird. They felt like a distant dream now, one that maybe had never happened to begin with. Time was strange. The brain *was* strange. Time and the brain were not good friends nowadays; they played tricks on her. It was hard to separate dreams and the past, and the magazines and books helped keep a tally on what was real and what was not. What she dreamed.

Belle needed to go back. There was no more *want*. Cosmic calamities aside, she needed to feel the past, let it fill her. The future had been dreadful, even if she had been able to live out the rest of her life with the one man she loved, above all the rest. One man didn't make her life. One person couldn't possibly have that much power over her.

She needed to go back. Fix things. Sure, Jeremy had explained the butterfly effect. Change one thing, no matter how insignificant, and you could change the course of everything. The slightest incident—like killing a butterfly—might have grave consequences in the future.

But nothing had changed here. Everything was the same, day in and day out.

No changes.

He's not doing anything, she thought.

The idea hadn't really occurred to her before tonight. All these trips, almost twenty of them now, and he hadn't rewritten a single piece of history. Was that on purpose? Surely it had to be. Unless the butterfly theory was wrong. Unless, no matter what, the future couldn't be altered. Unless everything was written in stone from the onset of time.

No, she didn't believe that. She believed in change. The world could change; all it needed was a little push.

If people can change, so can the world.

She knew she had to try, cosmic calamities aside.

8

When he came back, she knew she didn't have much time. She was already naked, ready to swap with him. Helping him out of the machine, she guided him over to the chair. Belle wrapped a towel around his body and gave him a quick rub down.

She had two minutes, maybe more. Once she was inside, she hoped there was no way for him to draw her back safely. If everything he had told her was true, she didn't think he'd risk damaging the machine just to bring her back.

But she couldn't possibly know for sure.

Dropping to her knees, she stared into his catatonic gaze. "Baby, I know you are going to kill me when I come back. I know this might do permanent damage to us, but if it works... if it works, everything will change. Our world will be better. I promise. I... I feel it in my bones."

She kissed his freezing-cold forehead and then turned away, facing the machine. The interior glowed with blinding light. When she reached the pad the machine rested on, Belle put her hand on the small control panel harboring three dials. She set them to the exact position Jeremy always had, a step he hadn't taught her (probably out of fear of this very moment) but that she had learned by paying close attention.

The machine whined. The light brightened, forcing her to shield her eyes. She stepped into the light, letting the warmth fill her. She felt right. On the correct path. This was the proper decision, she was sure of it. Jeremy, for all his genius, had been blinded by his own stubbornness. She was the answer to this equation, not him.

It felt like she had entered a car wash. Ice-cold fluids wash over her body. She closed her eyes, unable to handle the sensations rushing all around her, filling every internal nook and cranny. Sensory overload. She felt as though she might explode.

Then she opened her eyes.

And she was somewhere else.

9

She saw Aaron's face. His smooth, not-a-whisker-on-him baby face. He wasn't smiling, very un-Aaron-like. His eyebrows were arched. He held out a folder stuffed with papers in one hand, the other hand also far away from his side. He stared directly at her.

"Are you okay?" he asked.

Belle swallowed. "I... Aaron?" The warmth that filled her was almost too much for her body to handle.

He put the stack of papers down on the table. "Jesus, Jeremy, do I need to call someone? Are you having a heart attack?"

Jeremy?

She blinked. Of course. Jeremy had said the link to the past was his, no one else's, and she guessed that was what he meant by it. The traveler could only access his body. But she couldn't seem to access his thoughts. Her thoughts were her own.

"Yes," she said. "I'm fine."

"Good. You scared me for a moment."

"Sorry. Just... been under a lot of stress lately."

He slapped her arm, a playful swat. "Well, prepping a wedding will do that to you. You're a lucky guy, you know. You should count your blessings that Belle fell in love with a surly fuck like you."

He laughed haughtily, but she didn't join him.

"Oh what?" Aaron bit his lip. "I was just joking, pal."

"I know. I know." She squeezed her temples. They were on fire with pain. "I think I better go lie down."

"Okay, I'll help you."

"No," she said. "I'm fine. Really, I am."

"Okay..." His smile returned. "Then we'll chat later. I've had some breakthroughs with the neuro-toxins. Good stuff. Deadly, but good. That sounds sick, I know, but when you see what we've done, you'll cream your pants."

Belle swallowed. None of this made her happy. "Okay..."

"I mean, it was your research, Jeremy. You helped design this." He laughed. "Are you having creator's remorse?"

"No. Just... need to lie down."

"Okay, you big weirdo."

With that, Aaron left.

She sat down on the couch in the lounge. People came in and out, colleagues she used to know but vaguely remembered. This was all too weird for her. The past was squeezing her head together, crushing her cranium. She stood up, wondering how much more of this feeling she could take.

Maybe Jeremy was right.

Maybe she was never meant to come here.

If she could pinpoint when exactly she was, maybe she could find herself. Convince herself that it was her, from the future, hijacking her future husband's body.

No. That wouldn't work. That might cause one of Jeremy's

warnings to come true. She couldn't risk that approach. Though, it would have been great to see herself that young again, that full of life. Still, it wasn't worth the possibility of everything getting blown to hell.

She retrieved a knife from the kitchenette and headed back down the hallway. There was only one way to stop this. Since Aaron was the one who released the airborne toxin, it would stand to reason that killing him was the best way to end this. Bring it all back.

Kill him, she told herself. Kill him and when you go back, it will all be different. Better. The world you loved will be there.

She almost didn't convince herself.

She headed back to Aaron's office. He was there, by himself, rifling through a mound of paperwork. She didn't knock.

Keeping the knife behind her back, she entered the office.

Aaron looked up. "Hey, you feeling better already—"

She leaped across the desk, knife in hand. Grabbing Aaron by the collar, she threw him up against the wall. His glasses were knocked loose from his head, fell on the floor and broke. She stomped on them for dramatic effect.

Why hadn't Jeremy done this? This was so easy. What stopped him? The threat of going to jail? Yeah, there was that. Even if she killed Aaron here and now, she'd have to figure out a way to dispose of the evidence, make it so Jeremy wouldn't get arrested. If he were jailed, sentenced for life, then all of this would have been a waste.

She hadn't thought of those consequences.

The sharp side of the knife was near Aaron's neck. His eyes bulged with absolute terror. He started to make noises, a quiet whimpering, as his whole body trembled. She heard his teeth chattering.

"W-why?" he asked.

"You know why?" she practically growled in response. "You're gonna do it. Aren't you?"

"I-I'm sorry." He closed his eyes, tears shooting down his face. His cheeks glistened in the pale lamplight. "I-I'm sorry.

I-I l-love he-her."

She froze. The knife squirmed in her hand, as if it were alive.

"What did you say?" she asked.

"I-I didn't mean for it to happen." Aaron sucked in short breaths. His eyes were fixed on the blade, the thing that could so easily whisk him away from the world. "It only happened twice," he admitted.

Frantically, she searched her memories. Her memories, not Jeremy's.

They had been together, she and Aaron, but that had been a lifetime ago. Or felt like it. Did Jeremy know?

I didn't cheat, she thought. It was before we were together.

"It was before you two were... were... officially dating, okay? You were seeing each other, okay? We hooked up a couple times. It was nothing serious; at least, it wasn't meant to be."

She leaned in closer, smelling a ham sandwich with a squirt of mustard on his breath. "You... still like her?"

He shook his head. "No, I... I love her. She means the world to me. Did you find it? Did you find the note I was going to leave her? Is that it? My confession?" He was frazzled now, his voice climbing higher, becoming squeaky.

The knife felt weightless in her hand. "I..."

"I love her, okay?"

She stared into his eyes. Had she loved him, too? Maybe. Once upon a time. There was something there between them, something elemental, something basic. But then Jeremy had come along, and she had taken to him and the rest, as they say, was history.

"You're going to kill me because I love her?" Aaron asked her. "You're going to go to jail because of that?"

He was yelling now. Yelling wasn't good. Yelling attracted attention. Their co-workers would overhear. Help would come.

She let go of him.

"Get out of here, Jeremy. Get the fuck out of here. We will never speak of this moment again."

"Are you going to tell someone?" she asked.

He shook his head, then hung it. "No."

"If you talk to her—"

"I won't, okay?" he said, picking up his head. *"I won't say a fucking word to her."*

And he didn't.

She stormed out of the office and ditched the knife in a nearby garbage can. Her head spun like a carousel on fire. Dizzy. Disoriented. Stumbling down the hallway, she needed to hold onto the wall for support.

Something flashed before her, a vision: Aaron in the lab, yelling. Screaming. Telling him "NO!"

Another quick flash: an image of Jeremy holding the toxin, a small dose of it.

Another: Jeremy in front of a button, finger on the apocalypse, the thing that ended it all.

Another: A push.

She snapped back to reality. The past. She was still in Jeremy's head like a parasite. An illness took her over. She doubled back to the garbage can, lunged forward and expunged lunch. When she stood back up, Aaron was in front her, his arms folded across his stomach.

"Do I need to call someone?" he asked.

"No," she said. *"I'm fine."*

She spent the next two weeks living out the past like a zombie. Now knowing what she knew, she could hardly enjoy the trip. Everything felt fake. Her whole life felt like a bad dream, one that she'd awake from only to find herself in a new nightmare.

She cried a lot for those two weeks.

When she returned to the future, she cried some more.

10

The first thing she saw when she returned was her husband's face. It was shades of red and purple, his cheeks swollen with pure anger, blended with a little bit of betrayal. She sat in the chair near the medical station, a towel draped over her shoulders, the thick gel still coating her flesh.

She couldn't look him in the eyes.

"You had to do it," he said, the same way her father would after she'd broken curfew. "You had to go back there. You had to meddle."

"What did you do, Jeremy?" she asked catatonically.

He gripped the chair handles and leaned in, almost nose-to-nose with her. "What did *I* do? What did *I* do?" His lips quivered, the rage within trumping all other emotions, including his love for her. "What did *you* do?"

Now she faced him, staring him directly in his less-than-human eyes. "You erased the entire planet. Killed everything, every*one*. And you want to ask me what I did?" She blinked, unable to comprehend how his mind was rationalizing all of this. "Because of what? Jealousy?" A laugh disguised as a breath. "If I didn't see it, I wouldn't believe it."

"You cheated on me."

"I had sex with Aaron before we were dating. It was twice. And then I met you, asshole. Aaron meant nothing to me."

"Didn't he?"

That last remark hit like an arrow, hard and fast.

He licked his lips, agitated. "I've seen the way he looks at you. The way you look at him. I've seen it close to twenty times. Every time I head back there, it's clearer. It didn't stop after two times. No, it continued. On and on. For how long, Belle?"

"Listen to me, J—"

He grabbed her neck with both hands, squeezed until her eyes bulged. Her eyes felt loose from their sockets, as if they could fall out if he applied a little more pressure. "How long were you fucking him behind my back?" His voice was a snarl.

She couldn't breathe. Flailing her arms, she reached for his face, hoping she could push in his eyeballs with her thumbs. He dodged her attempts, moving out of the way before she could find purchase on his flesh.

"You bitch," he muttered, repeatedly. "You bitch, you bitch. I only wanted to love you and only wanted you to love me."

She couldn't reply. Not enough air. The fringes of reality began to blacken. Using her last remaining strength, she positioned her right leg between his feet. Then she lifted her knee with force, smashing him right in the jewels.

Instinctively, his hands dropped their hold. Before he could realize what he'd done, before he could fix the error, she hit him again, this time with a knee to his chin. He dropped to his knees. Standing up, she immediately ran to the other side of the room, near the passageway that led to his previous life.

Her heart was aflutter, a thousand butterflies pumping their wings.

"I only... wanted to love you," he said, reaching for her. His words were slurred, but that was because his jaw had been knocked off kilter. Might have been broken, but definitely dislocated.

He crawled toward her. Disgusted, she turned, and immediately began stripping down. She was completely naked by the time he reached the center of the room. Still reaching at nothing. Grasping for the past and all it meant to him.

Nothing, she thought. *The past means nothing. The future is the only thing we can hold onto.*

He pulled himself to his feet. Wobbling, he knew he couldn't get to her before she ducked into the machine. One last desperate attempt, he made eyes at her. Crying. Sobbing like a child who didn't get his way. "Remember, whatever you do," he said, moaning now. "Will have effects."

"The butterfly, I know."

She turned. He called to her, but she didn't listen.

The blinding light had already absorbed her.

11

Aaron stared at her, blinking.

"Are you okay?" he asked.

She nodded.

"Should I call someone?"

She shook her head. "No, I'm fine."

"You're freaking me out, Jeremy. Should I get Belle?"

"Aaron," she said.

"Yeah, buddy?"

"If something happens to me, I want you to take good care of Belle, okay?" She swallowed. "I sometimes think maybe you two would be great together."

He jerked his head to the side, staring at the wall. Swallowing the invisible rock in his throat, he tapped his foot on the floor. "I... I... I don't know what to say."

"Don't say anything," she told him. "Just... if something happens."

He turned back to her. "You have my word."

She nodded, then exited the lab, headed down the hall, into the kitchenette. There she found the knife.

She figured it was sharp enough to slash open her wrists, to murder the butterflies in her chest once and for all.

THE BUTCHER FROM BROOKLYN

I.

SMOKE CURLED AROUND the bar like an ancient ghost's deadly haunt.

How exactly did I end up here?

A big-name publisher contracted me to write a novel that documented the Hell's Cadets, the most savage motorcycle gang currently active in the United States, was the answer I'd give people.

But why I stayed was a different story.

Staged in the corner of *Danny's Den,* nursing a pint of Pabst Blue Ribbon, I sat by my lonesome, doodling notes that had quickly turned into childish scribblings of shadowy monsters and under-the-bed boogeymen. In the limelight, Jackie was gearing up for her routine performance, tuning her lungs while Moose, the piano player, smashed away on the keys until his fingers were warm. In the opposite corner, Daddy Pipes and the rest of the Cadets eyed their prize closely while drinking, laughing, secretly snorting lines of coke, and insulting each other's mothers. They were a boisterous, nasty bunch, as entertaining as they were frightening.

Why did I stay? Simple answer: for Jackie.

I'd come to learn she was born in Brooklyn to a

professional drunkard and an abused housewife. When she ran away at sixteen, they didn't try hard to find her. She'd spent two years bouncing between what was left of her shattered home and the open road, shacking up with whoever would have her until she'd hit the magical age of eighteen. She'd wasted the last six months on the road with the Cadets, cruising from town to town, city to city, performing at small venues, and ingesting, inhaling, absorbing every known drug-- the ultimate road trip across this great country of ours.

Jackie Byner had talent. Born to sing. At least I thought so. Performing at places with names like *O'Malley's* and *Hole in the Wall* were not her ideal destinations. Her aspirations were aimed much higher: sell-out shows at Madison Square Garden, rolling out red carpets, paparazzi-induced blindness, and platinum-dipped records. But that wasn't how reality worked, not for everyone. Especially not for Jackie Byner.

She had the voice to succeed and just enough attitude. She carried herself like an angel with a devil on each shoulder. She performed that way too, embodying that broken-spirit persona. Traces of Marilyn fused with her routine, that *Hey-Daddy* inflection. She stalked the stage like a panther. I sensed a hidden darkness within her, a monster burrowed in her soul. I was never sure what birthed that demon—her shitty upbringing or the way Daddy Pipes and the rest of the Cadets treated her; although, she garnered more respect than their other female members. I don't know what fueled that malevolence and I guess I never will.

I'm a journalist, not a talent scout. But watching her, I knew one thing. People always talk about having *it*, that label with no quantifiable attributes. I can't break it down simply, but I knew Jackie harnessed *it*. She glowed with the effulgence of a thousand suns, her shows every bit as good as the pop sensations on the radio, those temporary American Sweethearts.

Jackie Byner was a goddess, living in the belly of the Great American Whale. She could escape this place, of course, but that would require sobriety and clean-thinking, both of which seemed forbidden under the Cadets' covert code. She was stuck and the Hell's Cadets became the glue that held her.

In another life, she was the Babe of Brooklyn, the Queen of Coney Island; here, she had become a slave to a caravan of miscreants, drunk on the power of violence and drug-fueled ambition.

Coulda woulda shoulda, Sugar-Bear. Coulda woulda shoulda.

II.

"The world is our sky and we're all stars, some brighter than others, ready to explode at any moment."

I was sitting in the sand, staring across the moon-fulgent lake, gazing at the trees beyond, the soft piano play chiming from the bar at my back, when I heard the shuffling of feet, drawing near. Shallow thoughts dispersing, I turned and saw the pale angel's face, bright as the moonlit beach.

"Hey there, Mr. Big-Fancy-Writer-Guy," Jackie said with a smile and a slight sway to her gait, as if the tender breeze controlled her balance. That was her usual pet name for me. Never Deke, and only sometimes Mr. Big-Fancy-Writer-Guy. There were other things she called me, but never Deke. I didn't mind. "Whatcha doin' out here?" She blew a big bubble with her candy-pink gum.

"Enjoying the scenery," I told her. I took a drag from my cigarette, let the smoke into my lungs and exhaled.

"Got one for me?" she asked with a playful nudge, her shoulder to mine.

I smiled and offered her the pack. Plucking one out and sticking it in her mouth, she flashed that I'm-so-fucking-high-and-loving-it grin she had. I lighted the cigarette for her and clouds of smoke appeared between us, so thick we couldn't find each other's eyes.

"He got another one," she said.

Pinching my brow, I asked, "Who's that?"

"The Butcher of Brooklyn."

I nodded. "Ah. That." It was an unfolding story that had hit the papers several weeks ago. I'd never read anything about it personally, but Jackie had kept me in the loop. Brooklyn had a serial killer. A busy one. The murderer was flooding the streets with blood, eviscerating his victims, pinning their entrails up around town like lost-puppy fliers. Sick stuff. I didn't particularly like hearing about it, but she enjoyed telling me the stories, so I listened. More so to her voice than the grisly details—I couldn't get enough of her voice.

"Yup. Killed a family of four this time. Police found their hearts dangling from a telephone line on Booker Street. Sick, right?"

"Oh yeah. I hope they catch this sicko soon."

Eyeing the lake, she shrugged. "I don't know. Seems like killers always get caught. I think this one should get away."

An odd way of thinking, but Jackie was an odd girl—odd being her most attractive quality.

I finished my smoke and cast the remains into the lake. Jackie still had half of hers left, so I waited.

She turned to me, an abrupt gesture. "Why don't you party with us?"

I knew this question would surface, but I didn't think it'd have come from Jackie. Daddy Pipes maybe. Moose or Tinkle definitely. I offered a weak shrug. "I don't think the guys like me very much." A partial fib. I *knew* they didn't like me. In fact, they abhorred my presence. It was a strange situation we had all been thrust into. I'd been contracted to write a factual account of the operations of the Hell's Cadets, very much an organized crime syndicate. Meanwhile, I couldn't document *much* of their illegal doings because it could technically be used as evidence, should their questionable activities ever warrant an arrest and conviction. To ensure this, Daddy Pipes, the president of this particular chapter, had final say in what would be published and what wouldn't. Well, more like Pipes's legal team. On the flip-side, I was supposed to deliver a journalistic account of what it was like inside the organization. All the dirty details. A blockbuster bestseller. Information that likely wouldn't make it past the final edit. It all seemed like a great big waste of time. On the other hand, I was getting paid. Quite well, too. I wondered how the publisher got Pipes and the Cadet's Grand Poobah to consent to this adventure. Neither side would tell me, but someone's palms were getting extra greasy. Anyway, everyone involved now existed in this delicate ecosystem of truth and fiction, and where that line was drawn... I had no definitive vision.

"I don't think that's true," she said.

"What's that?" I asked, pulling free from my wayward thoughts.

"I think they like you just fine."

I laughed through my nose. "Yeah, okay. Keep dreaming, Odessa."

Odessa. Stage name. Not her choosing. That was Daddy Pipes's brainchild. She had started out using her real name, but, since accumulating a small fan base, he thought it would be more exotic, more attractive (more marketable, really) to have a dark, alternate identity. I always thought pseudonyms were partially bullshit—*why hide behind a fake you?* Anyway, she didn't fight the idea. As long as the drugs were good and flowing, and her hotel rooms were booked and paid for, she didn't care what they called her.

"For real, Writer-Guy. You've never given them a chance."

"They look at me like I'm the cancer that killed their mothers."

She shrugged. "Are you?"

"Not the last time I checked."

"It's not that they don't like *you*. They don't like what you represent."

"And what do I represent?"

She tilted her head like a cat getting that perfect ear scratch. "The American Dream. And not their fractured version of it."

"Hm. Never thought of it that way." I winked at her. "How

high are you right now?"

She laughed playfully and I did too; although, it was faked and forced and undeniably so. "As high as I want to be, baby. High on the dark side of the American Dream. We're in the gutter, you and me. We're collections of leaves and dirt, watery tombs washing over us. But leaves and dirt can't drown, can they?"

I hated when she was high and philosophizing. It was like listening to a small child explain the world through their unfiltered eyes. A lot of it was nonsense, but, underneath it all, she presented the truth in some crippled capacity.

"No, I don't think they can."

Another smile, less angelic than the others. "I like you, Writer-Guy."

For a second, I thought she'd lean in and kiss me. I prepared to launch myself away from her. Not that I didn't want to taste her lips, but because of the powerful fear that Daddy Pipes was spying on us from the patio. If I so much as laid a fingertip on her, the nearest Dumpster would serve as my burial.

But she didn't kiss me. Instead, (and much to my relief) she pushed herself up onto her toes. One last puff on her cigarette and she flung the butt into the air, the breeze catching it, the cherry fragmenting into several orange flurries, zipping through the air like fireflies from hell.

"Catch you later, Writer-Guy," she said, waving goodbye.

The Great American Nightmare continued.

III.

"Which makeup is best to cover a bruised heart?"

A week later, while the gang enjoyed their endless towers of buttermilk pancakes, grease-sodden bacon, and bottomless cups of coffee at a small diner on the Alabama-Mississippi border, I was in the parking lot, sitting on the trunk of my rental, yelling through the phone at my agent.

"My hands are tied, Deke," he said.

"This is fucking bonkers, Riley," I told him. I was hot. More so than I'd been in a long time. "How much longer do they expect me to live with these animals?"

"That bad huh?"

There was humor in his voice and that fueled my fire. "I'm glad you think this is fucking funny. Last night, I witnessed one of the women take a beating like a runaway slave. I don't know for sure, but I think the reasons were prostitution and money, or lack of the latter."

"Sounds like fodder for bestseller material to me."

"You think they'll let them print this?" This time I laughed. "You think they'll let them print *any* of this?" To that, he had no answer. "I should be writing about the Butcher of Brooklyn, or something that won't get vetoed before publication."

"The who of what?"

"You know. Butcher of Brooklyn. That serial killer."

"Never heard of him."

I shook my head. "It's all over the news. You being in Manhattan, I thought you might have heard of it."

"I watch the news every night at eleven with my wife. Haven't seen a thing about it."

"Okay, Riley. Whatever."

A brief silence, then a long, disappointing sigh. "Just write the book, Deke. Another month and—"

"—Another month?" My jaw fell open and hung there for quite some time. "Riley, I could spend a whole year with these savages, and it wouldn't do any good. They won't let me in. They don't want me here. They don't want me poking around. This is a waste of time, and honestly—a waste of the publisher's money."

"Deke, this is 2017. No publisher is giving out advances to relatively unknown writers. You should count yourself lucky. This is an opportunity of a lifetime. This is Pulitzer stuff, dude. Oprah Book Club and Wally-Mart endcaps. This is—"

"They don't give Pulitzers to books with no words in them."

I hung up after that.

Jackie was making her way out of the diner, leaving the dirt squadron behind. She shimmied down the stairs and into the parking lot. She sparked her cigarette while catching my gaze. Smiling, she drifted towards me, puffing away like a bad exhaust pipe. I had just finished my smoke, but the nature of my phone call had left me craving another.

"Writer-Guy," she said seductively. "Who you callin', sugar-bear?"

I still had the phone in my hand. "No one. Just business stuff."

"Ah. Business stuff," she said, like she knew what that entailed. "Sleep well last night?"

I didn't. Not after watching the Cadets swarm that helpless woman like a pack of hostile hornets. They left her broken and bleeding in some fast-food parking lot. I watched from afar on the back of Moose's bike. She wasn't moving when we absconded. The second I was alone I phoned 911 from a local convenience store, reported the incident, giving the vaguest of details.

To answer her question, I simply shrugged.

She nodded, knowing damn well I'd tossed and turned endlessly. She moved then, slightly, as if to show me something on the left side of her face. A small bruise, which she had tried to conceal with multiple applications of makeup, stained the skin next to her left eye. I opened my mouth and she turned back to her original position.

I looked up at the diner's lengthy window. The devil stared back at me, nostrils flaring. I wanted to smash in his teeth.

"Pipes hurt you?" I asked, continuing to stare at him, not caring if the fucknut could read lips.

She didn't answer.

"Jackie..."

"I..."

"You can tell me. I won't confront him."

She swallowed her hesitation. "It was my own damn fault," she said, softly choking on sobs.

The devil continued his audit.

"He's watching us. Don't turn. Don't face the window."

Understanding, she nodded.

"I want you to tell me what happened."

"You're just gonna write about it."

"No. I won't. I would never do that. Whatever you tell me is confidential."

She sucked in a great big drag. "We had a fight. Got outta hand. I said some things. Nasty things. Then he..." She jerked her head to the side.

"First time?"

Her silence blabbed.

"Why don't you get away? Leave him. Leave the Cadets." I wanted to touch her then, grab her chin and pull her close. "You'd be just fine on your own."

"No, I wouldn't. Where would I go? What would I do?" She looked to the pavement, but the parking lot was silent. "No, I can't go anywhere. I'm such a lost cause, sugar-bear." That winking smile. "Cast me in the river, watch me float away."

"Stop being so fucking dramatic," I snapped. At that point, I was angry. Furious. Not necessarily with her. I mean—I was; the way she put herself down, the way she self-deprecated, the way she degraded herself for these pigs. It was one thing to have low self-esteem—hell, anyone can relate—but to constantly punish yourself for something you never deserved, to have all the talent in the world and an open road before you, and to throw it all away for some scumbag, some sewer-dwelling rat, some glorified mobster— well, that sent me over.

"Fuck you," she said.

Those two words hurt, but that was nothing to the beating I'd receive from Daddy Pipes if she told him what I had said.

"No," I said. "Fuck *them*." I gestured at the diner, now hoping they saw me. I resisted the urge to throw up *my* gang sign—a good old-fashioned "go-fuck-yourself" middle finger, and I'd even extend my thumb out to the side; more American than the Star-Spangled Banner itself. "Fuck them, and fuck Pipes for laying his hand on you." My eyes tingled with surging tears. "You deserve more, Jackie. A shitload more."

She snarled at me. Taken aback, I folded my arms across my chest and waited for the speech, the *you-don't-understand-how-it-is* spiel. Sure enough, I was right, and she dealt me an earful.

"You don't understand what it's like on the road," she started. "You don't come from nothing. Where'd you come from, huh? Some nice fuckin' house in suburban New Jersey? Bet you tossed a baseball with your daddy every weekend and baked pies with your mommy before she tucked you in for bedtime, kissed your little forehead goodnight." I wanted to tell her we made cupcakes too, but she was in rhythm and who was I to stop her. "'Just run away.' Like it's that fuckin' easy. What am I supposed to do? Who's gonna take care of me? No, fuck that. Tired of running. I'm right where I'm supposed to be."

"You mean who's going to give you drugs? Who's gonna fuck you night-in and night-out? Who's gonna pimp you out to the next shitsplat bar desperate for cheap entertainment and reap 90% of your pay?" I know the truth was like a razor being dragged over her heart, but I didn't care. Deep down, I wanted to hurt her. She'd been living in la-la-land for far too long and I needed to pull her back into the real world; however, the haze of drugs put up a thick wall between the two. "Get real, Jackie. You should be a fucking star. You could be, but you rely on other people. Fuck everyone else and rely on yourself. You are better and stronger than you give yourself credit for." With my eyes, I traced the top of her shoulder down to the crook of her arm. "And stop sticking yourself with dope. That's half of your fucking problems right there."

She glared at me. If opportunity knocked, she'd have castrated me.

"You think you've got it all figured out, huh?" A bitter smile replaced her scowl. "Think you're perfect? Huh, Writer-Guy?"

"I don't have shit figured out, but I know you deserve

better than this—hell, you *are* better than this. Don't throw away your life."

"Newsflash: I ain't better than this. This is who I am. This is where I *want* to be."

And there it was. I knew from experience you couldn't help someone who didn't want help. No reluctant dope fiend has ever gotten clean, so I saved my breath.

She turned and stormed off, back to the diner. I knew then I was completely fucked.

Halfway there, her grinning lips faced me. "He struck again."

I opened my mouth, but before I could ask the answer hit me. "The Butcher of Brooklyn."

"You know it," she said with that sad-happy voice I'd come to adore. "Lined the streetlights on Rockaway with severed heads."

The information sounded impossible, but I didn't think anything of it at the time. I was too upset. Too broken. Too scared of the potential fallout from our conversation.

"See you around, Writer-Guy," she said, and I wished I would never see her again.

IV.

"Be my little slice of American Pie, sticky and sweet, good to the last bite."

My bags were packed, and I was ready to go. The nightmare was over. Time to leave. My decision, not the publisher's. They could keep their money. It wasn't worth it. Plus, knowing they had coerced the Cadets into this arrangement, lined their pockets with paper, funded drugs and weapons, perpetuated their war on the American Dream, I couldn't do it anymore. Couldn't stay another second.

I'd had enough. And honestly, I'd seen enough to write the novel they wanted. Not that it'd get published.

I was getting ready to bounce when a knock rattled the motel door. I pranced over to the blinds like I was walking on spikes. Peeking through, I glimpsed none other than Daddy Pipes and the Hell's Cadets. Well, most of them. I noticed Moose and Tinkle, a few other surly gents which I had the displeasure of getting to know. Brutes, the lot.

I opened the door because, if I didn't, they'd break the fucker down.

They filed in and I sat on the bed; they surrounded me, an intimidation practice I'd seen and noted a few dozen times already. I sat because that presented me as inferior— this was a self-defense mechanism, my way of waving the white flag. I didn't stand a chance against one of them, let alone the entire gang.

"Going somewhere?" Pipes asked gruffly. He jerked his thumb at my packaged belongings.

"Yeah, I'm done, Pipes. I'll be out of your hair. Come morning, you'll never see me again."

He shrugged. "Except on the press tour."

"Press tour?" I didn't understand.

"Oh yeah. Big tour. Thirty-two cities. Signing autographs. Reading from whatever shit you scribble in that little book of yours. Oh yeah. Big tour. Lots of miles." He scanned the eyes of his followers. "And lots of money."

The animals cheered and their porky bellies quaked with laughter.

"See, your publisher already promised us the moon. Mars and Jupiter, too. You're gonna make us rich, Writer-Guy."

I hated when he used her words and he knew it.

"I think you're overanalyzing—"

"Nope. Done deal. Signed in blood."

I didn't argue any further. Whatever they had promised him, didn't matter to me. I secretly hoped the book I hadn't written yet ended up bargain-bin material.

Pipes cracked his knuckles. "So, you can't leave. Not yet."

Ah. The clincher.

"Do I need to *convince* you to stay?"

The crowd closed in around me. I squeaked out a resounding, "No."

"Good. Now, matter two. Boys," he said, motioning to the

door. "I think Deke and I need to chat mano-a-mano."

The herd ambled to the door and disappeared. They hung around outside, attending to their rowdy routines of swearing, drinking, and snorting coke.

"Odessa," he said. He never used her real name. To him, Jackie Byner was a dead girl. One of the Butcher of Brooklyn's victims for all he cared. "She's *my* lady."

"She's just a girl."

"My lady all the same." He arched over, dropping his eyes to my level. "Best leave her alone. Don't go sticking your nose in that business. Sound good?"

"You beat her."

He tilted his head to the side, gave me a sad smile, Odessa's trademark. "She's mine."

"She's just a girl," I repeated. "Young."

"Young or old, women are property. That's our code. Write it down. Put it in your book."

"This isn't the sixties. I know what your kind got away with then, but that doesn't make it okay today. Then, now, or ever. It's... wrong. Just plain wrong."

Amused, he just beamed. "You're out of your element, little boy. Don't make me remind you where you are and who's in charge."

I didn't press the matter. I sensed I could coast through this exchange if I kept my mouth shut. I did and I did.

He left without saying another word.

I'd never know if he spoke another.

V.

"Write my fucked-up fairy-tale ending."

It was late and I was dead tired. I knew the Cadets had left the motel, the collective roar of their motorcycles had carried off into the distance hours ago. I lay in bed, staring up at the ceiling, getting lost in the plastered popcorn texture. Then I glanced at the clock; it read 11 o'clock.

Time for the news. I wanted to catch up with Jackie's

Butcher. According to her, they were finding victims daily; quite a spree and the fact he hadn't been captured yet astounded me. I watched a half hour of the major cable network's program and there was no mention of the brutal crimes, something I thought would be on the front page of every newspaper, the first banner on every major website. But Yahoo displayed no such information and Brooklyn wasn't trending on Facebook or Twitter. I checked. Twice. Three times. Then I ran a Google search and came up empty.

Not a goddamn thing.

I became scared for seemingly no reason. On the surface, it appeared Jackie had made up the story. Simple as that. But there was something disturbing about the way she'd gone about it, the amount of detail and creativity involved. She was a creative girl, sure, but this was beyond crafting a story of fiction for publication or poetry or music or lyrics or... whatever.

This was slightly deranged.

I had to know.

I called a precinct in Brooklyn, the first one to come up in Google search. I asked about the Butcher of Brooklyn and the desk clerk told me pranks were taken seriously there and how she planned on tracing my number. I told her to bite my bird and hung up.

So what? She made it all up?

That was my first thought. My second was much darker.

VI.

"Even on the darkest of days, behind the clouds, the sun still shines."

The next morning, after I had my coffee and post-breakfast smoke, I strolled across the motel parking lot and headed to Jackie's room. I wanted to wish her a proper farewell, but only after I had apologized. I also wanted to set her straight about the Butcher. I was curious as hell about how she'd respond to my discovery.

That walk took no more than two minutes, but it felt like an entire existence had passed. The soles of my shoes seemed to melt into the blacktop, dragging me down like quicksand. The world felt different then. Changed. And not for the better.

I know now that the odd feeling was my sixth sense kicking in, warning me not to proceed, to turn around and never look back. But we never listen to our senses, not when there are other feelings involved—feelings like love and sympathy.

Did I love Jackie Byner? Simply—yes. But not the Jackie Byner she was or the Odessa she was, but the Jackie Byner she could have been and the Odessa she *should* have been. I wanted to tell her these things—planned to—but the universe had other ideas, other arrangements.

I knocked once, twice, three times.

I heard singing.

Jackie.

She was working out a sad song and, from the sound of her voice, I pictured her swaying back and forth in front of the mirror, a smile tugging her mouth to one side, her arms wrapped around her hips. That's what I imagined anyway. When I opened the door, I was met with a different image.

Jackie was sitting on the bed, singing and grinning wider than I had envisioned. Her face was slicked with crimson, her arms and hands stained with scarlet smears. On the bed, sprawled and shaped like a star, Daddy Pipes lay. His stomach had been cut down the middle, the incision running from his throat down to his genitals. His organs were haphazardly strewn across the room. Blood stippled the walls. The bed sheets were inked in various shades of dark merlot. Incarnadine puddles soaked into the cheap carpet.

Jackie didn't even notice she wasn't alone anymore. She continued singing, laughing along to her own depressing lyrics. I couldn't tell you what she was singing because the world faded around me, her voice drowning under my thoughts, reality swallowed by the fantastical scenery before me. I remember stumbling to my knees and trying to work out the question "what did you do?" but failing miserably.

She sang. Beautiful voice. A true angel.

Finally, I managed to squeak, "What did you do?"

She noticed me. Her eyes held onto tears. The corners of her mouth curled slightly. Happy-sad. That Odessa trademark.

"Hey there, Writer-Guy..."

The black galaxy in her arm was fresh.

Tears dribbled down her cheeks.

"Jackie..."

"Oh my," she said in the same tone as if she were checking out at the supermarket and discovered she'd left her wallet home. "This?" She motioned to Daddy Pipes's eviscerated figure. "This is... well, he asked for it."

"Jackie, I could have..." *What? What could I have done?* "Helped you. I could have..."

She shushed me, putting her finger to my lips. I tasted Daddy Pipes's blood and, in that moment, I didn't care, didn't think about what diseases I may have contracted. Lost in the sick, room-spinning daze, I beheld the young girl who had metamorphosed into a woman, the Butcher she'd dreamed of.

"Sugar-bear," she said, grinning, her teeth stained strawberry. That bloody smile would haunt me forever. "Don't you worry your head about me. I'm... *free.*"

And then she cried.

So did I.

We both did for a long time.

Until the cops came and took her away.

The Butcher from Brooklyn they called her.

PURPLE CHEESE

A **CURTAIN OF** lavender overlay clouded the back of Lucas Curry's van. Cody Arnold nursed another rip on the two-foot bong shaped like a missile silo. The burn nestled deep within his chest, though it wasn't the burn he expected. The smoke crawled inside and set his lungs ablaze. Unable to bear another second, he huffed lilac fog into the air between him and his friends.

"You better take it easy, champ," Freddie Holt said, reaching for his turn.

"Or what?" Cody asked, refusing to give up the goods. After two hits, he could already feel the buzz.

"You might regret it."

Cody snorted and stuffed his lips inside the long glass tube. With one flick of his thumb, thick tendrils of berry-purple rushed toward his mouth. He drew the smoke deeper this time and held it for thirty seconds until his insides sizzled. Slowly, he relieved himself of the burning sensation sprawling throughout his chest, releasing cottony clouds of fuchsia. He smiled at his friends, letting them know—though proud of his progress—he was not nearly finished.

Lucas and Freddie exchanged glances.

"What's gotten into you?" Lucas was the first to ask. "You

rarely smoke. Now all of a sudden you're acting like Snoop Doggy Dog? I don't get it."

Cody glared at the giant bong like it had been the one to dump him. "Mandy broke it off."

"What?" Lucas and Freddie asked in unison.

"Yup. Two years. Down the drain. Just like that."

"That sucks, man," Freddie said. "But at least that explains why you're a damn chimney tonight."

"I can't get rid of this pain in the center of my chest. Thought this would help."

Freddie reached for the bong again, but Cody wasn't done. He put the glass to his lips and ignited the purple ash in the bowl. The water within bubbled as he inhaled and filled his lungs. Watching the smoke travel up the tube and disappear inside his friend's mouth, Freddie said, "Well, that shit will kill more than the pain in your chest."

"Huh?" Wisps of magenta curled out from Cody's mouth.

"What you got there is the most potent strain of weed on the market. It's called Purple Cheese."

The name made Cody giggle. The purple part he understood, but cheese? He didn't know what about it had tickled him the right way.

"Why do they call it that?" he asked with a mischievous grin.

Lucas nudged Freddie and gave him the look that said, *you better tell him.*

"Well, story goes like this—too much of this stuff will melt your face off. Makes you trip balls. Like bad stuff. *Nightmarish* stuff. You ever hear of the Faceless?"

The dumb look on Cody's face suggested he never had. "Like, the band?"

Freddie reached for his treasured piece of paraphernalia, but Cody held onto it like a baby. "Come on, Cody. Trust me. You don't want to mess around with this stuff. Especially since you're a lightweight."

"Kid in Ohio died last week on Purple Cheese," Lucas added. "Parents found him all messed up. Said he was talking crazy till he offed himself."

"You're messing with me," Cody said, unable to conquer the giggles creeping into his throat. "It's not working." He lit the flame, listened to the magical plant crackle, and sucked down another enormous rip. "You can't scare me," he told them, violet coils escaping his lips.

Again, Lucas and Freddie looked at each other.

Freddie shrugged. "Your funeral."

He awoke in a lilac haze. It was like the smog in the back of Lucas's van had followed him home and slipped into bed with him. He threw his sheets over his head, thinking it was all a dream and when he peeled off the comforter, it'd be morning and time for work. He hated his job, but he needed it now more than ever; he needed something to occupy his mind other than Mandy's last words. *You're just not that good in bed,* she had told him. *And John Hunter is. Like really good. Crazy good. God, he makes me feel so—*

Cody rolled over to the edge of the bed, located the garbage can next to his desk, and expelled the three slices of pepperoni pizza he had for dinner. Most of the undigested meal made the can. The rest found the carpet and would stay there until morning.

He rolled over and stared at the ceiling, which he barely saw through the swirling clouds of lavender. It didn't make sense. It felt like a dream, but his senses suggested otherwise.

It's the drug. Purple Cheese.

He forced himself into a sitting position. The same purple obscurity that thinly veiled the walls of his room also occupied the atmosphere outside his window. Convinced it was all a bad dream, he swung his feet on the floor.

The world tilted when Cody walked it. He stumbled to the window, lifted the bottom sash, and stuck his head out into the alien world. Nothing but purple fog. In the distance he heard the low drone of machinery but it was too far away to identify. He retracted his head and turned back to face his room. Plumes of smoke drifted from the bottom of his door, tendrils reaching up like the furious fingers of an enraged apparition.

Fire.

That was the only explanation for the smoke.

Down the hall, he heard his parents. Screaming.

Cody surged toward the room's only exit, gripped the handle and ripped open the door, slamming it against the wall. The drywall cracked from the force but he didn't care. He had a wall of purple smoke to deal with, unfurling before him like slow rolling waves.

More screaming from down the hall.

Eff it, Cody thought.

He lunged forward into the plum atmosphere. The fog was so thick he couldn't see his hands in front of him. Following the screams of his tortured parents, he wondered if it was too late. Was he better off jumping out the hallway window? Save himself? No, he couldn't do that. He couldn't leave his parents to die in the burning house; it would haunt him until the end of time.

As he moved down the hall, listening to the throat-seizing screeches from his two beloved caretakers, the haze thinned and the door to their room appeared before him. Seeing the finish line dumped adrenaline through his veins. He quickened his pace and reached the door in almost no time at all.

Gripping the handle, he discovered the door was locked. *Dammit.* "I'm coming!" He took a step back and kicked the door left of the knob. In his first attempt he cracked the jamb. The second completed the job and the door swung in, the hinges screeching with resistance.

The two bodies kneeling on the bed were not his parents.

"Mom? Dad?"

The room was covered in the same strange fog that occupied the rest of Cody's world. It hung over them like dark rolling clouds, pregnant with storm. A thick layer of violet fog blanketed the taupe carpet. Between the floor and ceiling existed the haze, the one he had left in Lucas's van and somehow followed him home.

"Mom? Dad?"

They were his parents, yet weren't. They had their bodies. Their frames. A semblance of their external features. But their faces were not the faces of Cindy and Lorenzo Arnold. They looked...

Melted.

Like pizza cheese.

Purple Cheese.

The faceless figures knelt on the bed, facing Cody, their hands joined together, fingers interlocked. Cody couldn't see eyes beneath their featureless masks, but sensed they were there, looking right at him.

"Join us, son," his mother said, speaking through the layer of rippled flesh hiding her mouth. "Join the Faceless."

"You'll love it, Cody," his father promised. "You won't feel a thing."

"You'll be numb. Isn't that what you want?" His mother tilted her head like an inquisitive pup. "To be free of all your pain?"

"It's why you smoked the stuff. Isn't it?" The faceless Lorenzo Arnold held out his hand while waiting for his son to answer.

Cody stepped away from the bed, toward the open door. "No..."

In a blink, his parents transitioned from a kneeling position to a standing one. They jumped off the bed and onto the carpet, their feet disappearing in the swirling purple fog.

"Yes," his mother said. "That's what you want. To be faceless like the rest of us."

They lurched forward and Cody spun toward the door. His feet were already carrying him into a sprint. He didn't look over his shoulder to see where his faceless pursuers were, but heard the stamping of their feet not far behind.

Within seconds, Cody was out the front door and halfway across the magenta glow of the front lawn.

☆ ☆ ☆

Cody was halfway down James Street when he turned and saw nothing but the bright purple atmosphere. He had outrun his parents, which did not surprise him. He was half-convinced this was all a dream anyway, however, nightmares usually harbored the power to slow him down while giving the villains the gift of supersonic speed.

Cody convinced himself this wasn't a dream. It was a reality. A totally messed-up, super-bad trip based in an alternate reality that would eventually fade with time.

Time. That's all he needed. A few hours, maybe less.

This was a bad trip. A *really* bad trip. As someone who never touched drugs outside the occasional social toke, Cody was not accustomed to feeling this way. He never experienced anything but uncontrollable laughter and the unquenchable desire for packaged cheese-powdered snacks. However, he had heard stories before; the kid who ate too many mushrooms and imagined a horde of pitchfork-wielding leprechauns stabbing his ankles, or the man who unknowingly snorted angel dust and met Jesus, a Jesus who told him to swan dive off a ten-story building. He had heard the stories and laughed at them, but this—this was far from funny.

Just need to lie low and wait it out.

Waiting it out was the most logical thing he could come up with. He turned off James Street and jogged down Alexander Boulevard. He needed somewhere to hide and since he was on Alexander, he could only think of one person, the only person he wanted to see.

Mandy.

He didn't care that she'd probably curse him out for showing up unexpectedly, especially since she'd given him the boot. It was a risk worth taking. If she could witness the state of mind he was in, she'd understand. Mandy was a sweet girl. She always understood. Things would be different now that they weren't together, but still—she'd understand.

She had to.

Cody jumped up the four steps leading to Mandy's front door. The walnut-stained mahogany barrier was unlocked— as Mandy's parents usually kept it—and he let himself in. The purple fog had followed him there as well, and Cody was not surprised. Wherever Cody went, so did the purple.

And the Faceless?

As he bounded the stairs two steps at a time, he couldn't rid his mind of his parents' awful appearance, their faces twisted and unevenly blank, looking like someone rubbed out their characteristics with a pencil eraser.

If I get out of this, I'm never smoking again.

He had said the same thing last year, the morning after Carly Horvath's party; he drank a whole bottle of rum and nearly landed himself in the hospital. *If I get out of this,* he had promised, *I'm never drinking again.* One of the many he never kept.

The square-paneled door to Mandy's room sat ajar, vibrant lilac light beaming from within. He shielded his eyes as he hustled down the hall, mindful of the fact his parents were lurking not far behind. With any luck, he slipped their tail, although he didn't think so. Mandy lived close enough that they'd be morons not to check there first. Mandy had an enormous closet he could hide in, and even if his parents did come snooping, he knew they wouldn't find him there.

"Mandy!" he shouted, over the loud machinery drone, the one he heard earlier. It was coming from Mandy's room. "Mandy!"

As he pushed opened the door, his heart spiraled.

"No..."

Mandy was on the bed, naked and bent in an awkward position, a way Cody had once been familiar with. A man with more mechanical accessories than human parts knelt behind her, thrusting in a way Cody also knew well. The dragon tattoo on the android's arm gave away his identity— *John Hunter.* His chest was plated with silver, his other *non*-human arm structured from the same material. Waist down, however, was all John Hunter.

The act which Cody walked in on wasn't disturbing—it was the participants' faces, or the fact they were lacking them. Like Cody's parents, Mandy and her new boy toy wore masks of the Faceless.

"Hey, stud?" Mandy spoke through no face hole. Her tone was warm and welcoming, which made him want to run.

Invisible fingers wrenched Cody's gut. "This isn't happening."

"Oh, but it is," John Hunter said. "It's all real. All of it. You're gonna die here tonight, limp dick."

Cody's legs ran numb with fear. He used the dresser to keep himself from falling. His fingers touched something metal and sharp. He glanced over and saw a pair of scissors, the same pair Mandy used to trim his unruly hair whenever he asked.

"What are you doing, stud?" Mandy asked. Grape smoke poured out her mouth as she spoke. "Don't hurt yourself now."

"Stay away from me!" Cody held the shears out like he meant to enter a sword fight. "Stay the hell away from me!"

Shadows appeared in the purple light before him. He turned and saw his parents, the flesh on their faces forever fixed in obscurity. He raised the scissors at them, but they did not back away. Slowly, they marched on, closing the gap between them.

"Put those down, sweetheart," the thing that resembled his mother pleaded. Her voice seemed genuine, but Cody knew she was not here to help.

"Come join us, son," his father begged. "Join the Faceless. You're one of us now."

"Never," Cody whispered.

Whenever trapped in a nightmare, cornered with no outs, Cody always knew what to do.

Die.

And this *was* a nightmare. He was sure of it now. Mandy wouldn't betray him. Not like this.

He opened the scissors wide enough to fit around his

nose, and jammed the points into his eyes. He felt the blades run deep, severing tissue and tendons, and other sensitive parts he had learned about in Anatomy. He didn't stop pushing until he reached his brain.

He felt at peace almost instantly. There was no more purple where Cody went next. Only black.

John Hunter jumped off the bed and knelt next to Cody's shivering body, his feet slipping in the blood pooled on the carpet. Mandy ran to her parents' side, the three of them embracing each other, looking away from this living nightmare. Hunter flipped Cody onto his back. He reached to pull the scissors out, then decided against it. The kid was already as good as dead.

"You're going to be okay," Hunter lied to him. "You're going to be okay."

Cody smiled before he let out his last breath, a cloud of dark amethyst misting in the golden light above.

THE SKY, HOW IT SHOULD BE

(THE BLACK HILL #3)

1959

*D*EAR MIRIAM,
I am writing this to you because I think you should know. What exactly it is you should know, well, that's up for some debate. I don't know that I can properly explain the events of this evening, but I'll do my best. I'll be as brief as possible. Direct. To the point. Just as you like.

You're sleeping now. Peacefully. I made sure of that. Soundly even. Like a baby. Just like you always sleep. I've tucked you in, made sure to see you off to dreamland, just in case this is the last time I get to do so. Because, Miriam, this might be *the last time I get to do so.*

My feelings toward this thing, this thing I have no name for, this thing that has me so perplexed, has me feeling like this is the end—of not just me, but of everything. A slow and steady decline toward oblivion. This thing I've witnessed—it is horrible, more terrible than anything a person could ever know. Which is odd, because I, myself, don't fully comprehend it, only that I know it makes me feel ill inside. Sick. Rotten. Like something inside me has soured, gone bad.

We kissed each other goodnight a few hours ago. It's currently two-fifty-nine in the morning. I've been up for the past two hours debating about what to do. A part of me

121

wants to phone the police, tell them what I've seen. But the things I've seen, as unexplainable as they are, would only earn me a trip to the local loony bin. I'd be fitted for a straight-jacket as soon as I could hang up the phone. So, you see, phoning the authorities would be counterproductive. No, I think I need to study this thing first. Learn about its abilities. About it in general. Find out exactly what *it* is.

I'm going too fast, aren't I? I need to backtrack. See, after we said our goodnights, I studied the stars. It was a clear night, Miriam. Gosh, you should have seen it. The visibility was like no other night. A clean glimpse into the cosmos—that's what I had to look forward to. Only it wasn't. Our sky, I mean. It was... different. *Changed.* Like I was looking up from an alien planet, looking at someone else's galaxy. I know how impossible that sounds. And it is. Impossible, I mean. It couldn't possibly be real. I saw the sky how it should be, and it was all there—the stars, arranged in their usual template. Our constellations matching exactly what I'd seen time and time again, on clear nights such as this. But whenever I peered through the telescope, it was all gone. All of it. Not a trace of the universe I knew was present.

Something had replaced it.

I thought maybe it was the telescope itself, that something was deeply wrong with it. That it had broken since I last used it. But I didn't feel like that was the truth. And... I was right. God, I wish I wasn't.

That was when the black stars began to fall, forming constellations of their own. Moving constellations. Twisting patterns that crashed to the earth, atop the Black Hill.

The Black Hill—I don't have to tell you its history. This town has had its fill of stories about the Black Hill, the terrible things that have happened there. The countless deaths, disappearances, and hauntings. I don't know why kids continue to play up there, spend their weekends playing kissy-face underneath the lone tree. It's a bad place, I believe, a place where evil lives and breathes. It's fine if you don't get too close to it, get within its range, and I know, as long as we've lived in this town, getting near it has never been on our agenda.

But tonight, in the den, the Black Hill got near *me*. It reached out like a hand and grabbed me. Shook me. Stuck its fingers in my ear, played with my head. Everything went a little fuzzy after I saw those black stars. Like something had infected me. I no longer felt safe in my own skin.

Then I saw *them*. On the Hill. Three black shapes next to the lone tree. Humanoid shadows. Standing there. Watching.

Looking at me.

Not at me.

In me. As if there was something inside my head, something they wanted. A thought or an idea, something not easily accessible. Not through traditional means anyway.

And that's when I blacked out a little. Woke up and discovered my knees were muddy, stained with grass and other earthly products. Had I left the attic? I didn't think so, but the evidence was damning. Did I go out to the Black Hill? Did I get close to it?

I feel weird. Strange inside. Not quite myself.

I'm going back to have another look. I owe it to myself. And if you get this letter when you wake up, Miriam—you'll know that I am dead. That I stared too long at the black stars, the shapes atop the Black Hill. That I, indeed, let them touch me.

Know that I love you.

Know that above anything else.

But I need one more glance. I need to know, before I sleep, that the sky is how it should be.

Your love, forever.

Blake

GRUME

INTESTINES ONCE PURPLE-PINK and slicked with slimy crimson gore now looked like an old tangled hose splashed with spaghetti sauce. The rubbery coil poked out of the cabinet lined with canned beans and tasty greens. Morris lifted his head from his bowl of cereal and glanced at them with a certain amount of pride. A smile would have broken across his face, but his muscles and mind were spent. Everything ached. Stung. Throbbed. His temples pulsed with a dull pain akin to getting tapped in the testicles by a quick wrist-flick.

After the intestines began to bore him, he whipped his head, directing his eyes across the kitchen and found a hand on the counter next to the sink. Just one lonely hand. About two inches of bone protruded from the ragged flesh where a wrist should have been. If his memory served correctly, the wrist, along with the rest of the arm, had been stashed in the trashcan outside the garage door. He couldn't remember if he was the one to put it there, or if Brianna had.

Next, he spied the old woman's scalp. They had tossed it above the cabinet over the stove. Visible from his seat were cottony tufts of silver and the streaks of blood that ran down the cabinet doors like thin crimson tears. He thought he should probably clean the mess before *they* arrived.

In the corner, wrapped in plastic, was the body. It looked much like a packaged prime choice before leaving the slaughterhouse. Morris scooped another spoonful of Cheerios into his mouth and chewed while remembering how surprisingly hard the old woman's bones were and how many saw blades it took to cut through them all. He thought, because of their age, it would be simple, easy, no big deal.

He was wrong.

Red decorated the walls in specks and splatter; some even marred the crucifix hanging above the doorway connecting the kitchen with the living room. Morris glanced at Jesus and admired the autumn-brown flecks on his face. Had he noticed the sacred object earlier, he would have intentionally made a bigger mess.

On the floor, a lake of blood had sprawled, now a rusty pool of old jelly. Dried and crusted over.

Shoveling another spoonful of sweet crunch into his mouth, he inhaled the fresh-death odor through his nose. He wondered how long it would take for *them* to discover what they'd done. It wouldn't be long before the stench traveled to the neighbors, especially on those ninety-degree days the weatherman kept promising. Morris thought he should check out the crawlspace, maybe scatter some parts down there. That would delay their search, make it a little more difficult to track down. He'd still be playing by the rules, of course; every piece would remain on the property. A chunk or two in the crawl, a leg or a foot in the attic, perhaps that would buy them a day or two. He knew they'd check loose floorboards first. Scan the walls for holes and quick patch jobs.

No, he had to get creative.

"Morning."

Morris spun in his seat. He wiped away the dribble of milk on his chin. "Hey, sis. Sleep well?"

"Not really." Brianna opened the fridge. Behind the

orange juice sat the old woman's tongue. She knew if she opened the freezer she'd find the crone's eyes in the ice tray, frozen, because she put them there. "I never could sleep in this *goddamn* house."

The crucifix on the wall flipped upside down as if invisible fingers spun it.

They focused on the religious décor, expecting it to mystically gyrate once again.

"You pissed someone off," Morris said.

"Yeah, well, add them to the list." Brianna turned her back on Jesus and faced the fridge, scanning the top shelf for something to eat. "Didn't mother ever send one of her gophers food shopping?"

Morris shrugged. "I ate the last of the Cheerios. My bad."

"I'd expect nothing less from you, old chap." Her British accent was phony. She only spoke this way when slightly irritated.

"Relax, sis. We'll hit a Micky Donuts before the highway. I'll buy you a bacon-egg McDoodle."

She flared her eyebrows. "Extra bacon?"

"As you wish."

For the first time in the last twenty-four, she smiled. "We should hurry, though."

Morris took the cereal bowl, brought the rim to his lips, cocked his head back and poured the honey-sweet milk down his throat. Once empty, he sat the bowl back down on the table next to a meaty blob of what could have been grume, muscle, skin or any combination of the three. He poked it with his finger—a squishy shell with a hardened center like lava cooling over black rock.

"You hear me?"

Morris looked up from the indiscernible fragment of Mother. Even in death she had the ability to ruin a fine day. "Yeah, I heard you."

"They'll know. They'll be coming."

"Maybe we should wait for them."

Brianna's eyebrows lifted. "You're joking."

Morris pushed himself to his feet, using the table as

leverage. His legs weren't what they used to be and sitting for more than ten minutes made it difficult to stand again. "I'm getting old for this."

"Mother was one of the last ones."

"Still, even if we get them all. What then?"

"Then... our job is done." Brianna leaned against the wall. She folded her arms across her exposed midriff. "We can retire from this... *this.*"

"I think I'd rather settle things today."

"Morris, please. Don't be dumb."

"Not being dumb."

Her face twisted into several wrinkles. "But that's suicide."

"Yeah. I'm aware."

A smirk pushed her mouth. "You're stressed. I get it. Come on. Wanna see what I did with the pantry?"

Like a lost, broken puppy, beaten down and abandoned by its first and only owner, he followed her to the far side of the kitchen.

She opened the bi-fold doors with so much force they nearly slipped off the track. "Ta-da!"

Mother's uterus dangled from fishing wire. The fallopian tubes hung at its side like dead flowers.

"Remember how she used to lock us in here for hours. Made us say a thousand 'Hail Marys'. I still have nightmares about this fucking pantry."

Morris grunted in agreement.

"Glad I'll never have to see it again," she said, turning away.

"The heart?"

"Hmm?"

Morris faced his sister. "What did you do with the heart? You said you'd take care of it."

She winked. "Maybe it's better you don't know."

"They can't piece her back together without the heart."

"Well, they'll try. They always do."

"Of course they will. But it won't work without the heart. Or her brain. But I ground it up and mixed it in the jar of peanut butter."

Her eyes grew wide with childish excitement. "There's peanut butter?"

"Bree?"

She continued to grin and wrinkled her nose.

"The heart?"

"I put it somewhere special."

"Keeping to the rules?"

The grin disappeared at once. She rolled her eyes. "Psh. Rules."

"I'm serious. You're abiding by the rules?" He glowered at her. "Aren't you?"

A devilish smile touched her lips. "What's your deal? A minute ago you wanted to confront The Ancients. Now you want to play by their rules? Make up your mind, Mo."

"Don't call me that. Mother called me that."

"Aw," she said, pouting. "My little Mo."

He lashed out, grabbing her throat. Her eyes bulged from their sockets and for a second, he thought they might explode from her skull like pulpy grapes squeezed from their skin.

Gritting his teeth, Morris asked, "What did you do with it?"

"I... at... it."

"Come again?" He loosed his grasp, just enough so air could get out, and words. "I didn't quite catch that."

She growled. *"I ate it."* She practically spat the words.

"That's what I thought you said."

"Last night, I cut the bitch's heart into little pieces and I ate the fucking thing. Swallowed every piece. Tasted terrible, by the way. Like an old rubber shoe. I don't know how cannibals do it. Anyway, if The Ancients want it, they'll have to cut me open, baby. By then it will have digested. I don't know why we didn't think of this sooner."

"You broke the rules, the most important one." He closed his eyes. "Fuck, Brianna. You know Mother can't leave the property. *That's the rule.*"

There was no more strength to Morris's grasp. Slowly,

she pushed aside his hands. Grabbing her brother's cheeks, she smiled. "Rules were meant to be broken, big bro. Mother never played by the rules. Did she?"

"Yes, she did."

Brianna grimaced as if something sour penetrated her taste buds. "The fuck she did. There were no rules back then, Morris. She abused us, starved us, practically killed us I don't know how many times. She was supposed to be a mother to us. Take care of us. Teach us *The Way* for fuck's sake. And what did we ever learn?"

Morris let his anger fade, replaced it with regret. "We learned not to anger The Ancients. And we learned how to survive in this world."

"We learned nothing but pain and suffering and... *hatred.*"

Morris bit his lower lip and shook his head. "We learned much more than that."

"Morris..." She gently touched his cheeks with her palms. Pressing her forehead against his, she closed her eyes. "This feels right. This feels—"

The same blade he used to scalp Mother slipped into her throat. Choking, she watched a stream of blood squirt from the wound. She tried to talk, tried to reconcile, but the time for words had passed—only pain and those final gasps of air were left. Then, came the end. Swift and full of mercy.

She dropped to the floor, a red pool spreading beneath her.

Morris quickly dropped to his knees and went to work. He sliced open her belly and began sifting through the mess of parts. He dug around, located and grabbed hold of her stomach sac, pulled, separating it from her internal chamber. The bloody bag slopped on the floor. He wasted no time slicing. It opened rather easily, like cutting open a water balloon. He immediately grabbed the sac from the closed end and started shaking it, letting everything inside out. Several items fell to the slicked floorboards, most of which he couldn't make out. He found eight pieces that fit the puzzle he was trying to piece back together.

Morris spent the next hour piecing his mother's

heart back together, using her old sewing kit to reattach everything. Once whole again, he placed the heart on the counter and admired his handiwork. He couldn't believe the results, how perfect it turned out.

"Damn you, Brianna. You almost got us killed."

He never once fixed his gaze on his ruined sister.

As he turned for the doorway, he heard a thump echo throughout the house. It came from the counter. He faced the heart. It beat with authority. Pulsed with fervent rage. Danced with life.

"I'll be damned."

And he would be.

Half a million light years away, The Ancients heard the call. They awoke angry. Their screams ripped holes in space and time and obliterated microscopic worlds of varying insignificance.

Morris decided it was best not to stick around after all.

DEATH LOVER

THE WOMAN IN room one-two-twelve nibbled the ends of her fingers until they started to bleed. The man across from her placed his clipboard on his lap, peering over his glasses. She stared back nervously, letting her hands fall on her thighs. The man offered her a thin smile.

She didn't smile back, her eyes darting back and forth, examining the emptiness of the room. The hustle of the workday filled the silence, the shuffling of busy feet in the hallway beyond the door.

He wanted to say something, knew he *had* to, but the words just weren't there.

She opened her mouth to speak, then closed it. Her dusty gray eyes continued to search the room, unsatisfied with their findings. He knew she wanted to cry, let it all out, but she was putting on her best *I'm-keeping-it-together* mask.

"We don't have to talk if you don't want to," the man said. "It's up to you, Casey."

She shook her head. "I love our talks."

"What do you want to talk about then?" he asked, tossing his leg over his opposite knee. "Your house? Your job? The Yankees?" He paused, thinking if he should continue. *"Them?"*

She swallowed, and he saw her eyes fill to the brim with tears.

"We don't have to—"

"No," Casey said groggily. "No, I want to."

He eyed her carefully. "Are you sure?"

She smiled wanly. "Yes, Dr. Carson. I am."

Rupert Carson nodded and took to his clipboard. He clicked his pen to life and began jotting down notes on the pad of paper. "Good. Where would you like to start?"

Casey sighed. "I don't know. Where does one start when discussing dead lovers?"

"I guess at the beginning."

She closed her eyes. Her face drew wrinkles. Shadows climbed over her, darkening the circles under her eyes. "Okay..." Her eyes popped open and her lips quivered. "Lover number one could be a real prick sometimes..."

LOVER NUMBER ONE

His name was Chester Burton and he was a southern boy through and through. He loved fried chicken, his mama, and his precious Crimson Tide. He also loved getting shit-faced and tussling with the locals down at Harry's Bar every Saturday night. He'd walk onto a job site Monday morning with a black eye or a few faded scratches and the boys knew he'd been down at Harry's the day before yesterday. It became a joke after a while, though I hardly found it funny. It was sad. And embarrassing. Good thing my parents were dead because they would never have approved of Chester Burton. Their disapproval would have only made me want him more and I probably would have stuck around a lot longer, dragged the whole thing out.

Hell, I might have saved him.

Looking back, I have no regrets. No qualms. No aspirations to go back and do it differently. I lived with Chester for three years, and most of the time we spent together was good—no, great—and we lived like lovers were meant to live—blissfully happy and spending each day like it was our last. Our union was built on mutual loves like football, cheesy 80s horror flicks, and Ben & Jerry's. We had always connected, since the first day I'd met him down at Harry's.

(Want relationship advice, Doc? Never fall for someone you met at a bar. Never do this. Promise me?)

I kept waiting for Chester to propose, but that never happened. In the year I waited, Chester found a new lover. Her name was heroin and she was a real bitch. A costly, time-sucking, bonafide bitch of a lover. He used once every day and, when that number tripled, I knew it was time to get out. I didn't see it as a problem at first. I was twenty-four and no angel myself, but when your extracurriculars begin to consume your life, get you fired from your job and warrant eviction notices on your front door, then it's time for a change.

Chester didn't want change. He liked being with heroin. No, he fuckin' loved it. Loved it more than me.

That's why on October 8th, 2005, when I came home from waitressing and found him unresponsive on our bed, noticing the bluish tint to his pigment, I did nothing but watch with morbid fascination. He wasn't dead yet and I still believe, if I had phoned the proper authorities the second I stepped foot inside the bedroom, Chester Burton would still be alive today. Experts say differently and you may say differently, but I know how I feel inside, and my gut is rarely wrong.

Is it a crime to let someone die?

I don't know if it is or isn't, but no one ever questioned me. Chester died of an overdose and that was that. But his death wasn't what landed me here, in this place. You know that. Of course, you do. But it is important for what came later.

Why?

Because I enjoyed watching the last flicker of light leave Chester's eyes. His death excited me.

And death became my favorite lover.

Casey bit into her nails as Dr. Carson rested his pen on

the clipboard. Blood dribbled steadily from the fresh wound, and Dr. Carson removed his hanky from his pocket and offered it to her. She accepted the cloth and covered her fingers. Bright red bled through almost immediately.

"Thank you," Casey said, casting her eyes down. "Bad habit."

Carson didn't comment on the habit; his interests lied elsewhere. "Is that a true story, Casey?"

She nodded. "Yeah."

"Are you sure?" Dr. Carson pinched his lower lip between his teeth. "We've heard you tell that story before. We researched this Chester Burton from Birmingham, Alabama and found no evidence of his existence. No one by that name died on October 8th, 2005."

Casey shrugged as if this were old news. "Maybe Chester Burton wasn't his birth name. I don't know."

"You lived with him for three years and didn't know his real name?"

"His name was Chester and he was real enough."

Carson wondered.

"Besides, you don't want to know about Chester."

"I guess you're right."

"You want to know what happened in the fall of 2011."

"Yes, Casey. I'd like that very much."

"Okay, then..." She drew in a deep breath. "I know you wonder why I did it. I mean, that's your job, right? To make sense of what happens up here." She tapped her forehead. "But it wasn't my fault. Before, I said death was my lover and I meant it. Death wasn't just my lover, it was my—"

Lover Number Two

—*Everything.*

The obsession with death and whatever comes after didn't start right away; the ideas took time to formulate and fester, coming on slow like a good and powerful disease. The following summer I researched death and the afterlife to a sickening extent. Many hours were lost in my town's public library. *Nights were spent at home, combing the Internet for facts and conjectures, truths and plausible theories. I learned things about death. Did you know that male corpses can get erections? I didn't. Happens when they hang themselves, but it can happen with other causes too. I wish I had checked Chester to see if he had one. Not like I could have done anything with it, but it would have been a sight to see. A corpse with a hard on.*

Anyway, in about five years I learned everything there was to know about death and what supposedly happens to us after. I can tell you what different denominations of Christianity believe about Heaven and Hell, and I can tell you what Islamics believe about their paradise. Hell, I even studied Norse mythology and became so well-versed in their ideas that I feel like I've roamed the halls of Valhalla. I was an expert on death, not because it was a hobby, but because I fell madly in love with the nothingness sometimes personified in cartoons and movies as a scythe-wielding black robe.

I worshiped death.

And like all good worshippers, I needed church.

That was when I met Thomas Tripps, a professor at the University of North Carolina. I first noticed his golden-blonde hair coasting above a sea of students one Friday afternoon in late September 2010. I was taking a few classes, dipping my toes back in the further-education pond. I wasn't sure if I wanted to commit to a full semester, so I decided on a few classes. I was living with an old high school friend in Raleigh, commuting once a week. I waitressed at Hooters the other six days.

Thomas had a dynamite personality; he really knew how to light up a room. His students loved him, especially the girls. They formed crowds around his lectern after his session was over. It was sickening. He bought into it, of course, like most men would. He was such a tease. And can you believe it—I fell into the same goddamn trap. Fell right in. Head fuckin' first.

Two months after we met, Thomas and I were a pair. He'd

just finalized a nasty divorce and I hadn't dated anyone since Chester. We were a match made in Heaven. We both liked scary movies, buffalo wings, and he liked Ben & Jerry's too, though not as much as Chester had. I couldn't hold it against him. He was better looking and fucked better. Also, he didn't love heroin.

I decided to kill him all the same.

(I see your look and I understand the befuddled thoughts forming behind your eyes. It's the same single word the detectives and lawyers uttered when I told them the truth. WHY? Why would I kill someone whom I genuinely liked, got along with, experienced leg-quivering orgasms with, held hands in the park, and dare I say—loved. Though it's one simple word, the question is loaded; it all traces back to the skull and crossbones.

Death.

My one true love.)

I didn't know how I wanted Thomas to die, only that when I killed him it had to be epic. A big deal. When I let Chester go, there was barely a mention of his passing in the local paper. I wanted Thomas's death to garner attention. I wanted it to affect people. I wanted his death to mean something. After all, I was still a student and the subject was still death. I wanted to study what happened after he died, experience the pain of others, the witnesses of his demise. That excited me more than the murder itself.

I'm twisted, I know, but I can't help it. Watching Chester expire live and in stereo warped me in ways no one could predict. Or was I already warped, and Chester's overdose was just the catalyst, the thing that perpetuated my condition?

Guess that's for you to figure out, huh, Doc?

Anyway, that was when I decided Thomas should die in public. In front of people. In front of a crowd. And considering he was around crowds daily, it wasn't going to be a problem.

But how would I do it? Guns bored me. Poison was slow and—if miscalculated—reversible. A knife in the gut was too personal (I wasn't ready for that kind of commitment).

So, I paid a visit to the chemistry lab, had myself a chat with a professor who oddly asked zero questions about my bizarre inquiries, and gave me the recipe for a dangerous, powdery chemical cocktail designed to eradicate. I told him it was for a paper, and that seemed to squash any and all curiosities. He gave me the ingredients with a broad smile.

I mixed the deadly combination of hydrochloric acid, baby powder, and a few other items I bought in the cleaning aisle of my local department store and poured the contents into a plastic-coated container gift-wrapped in purple paper. I chose purple because that was Thomas's secret favorite color. That way he'd know the gift was from me and, in his final moments, he'd know that I was the one responsible.

Sick. Twisted. I know. But I loved the craftiness of my creation.

The package was delivered to his lectern on November 5th, 2011. Before his lecture started, Thomas told his audience that he "must have a secret admirer" and laughed, scanning the room for my eyes. He found them and winked. I winked back. He proceeded to unwrap the gift. "I wonder what's inside, ladies and gentlemen," I remember him saying. Then he popped open the top. The white dust of death shot out like a cannon, blanketing his face and chest. The chemicals went to work on his flesh almost immediately, and he began to scream and flail in agony.

The audience gasped.

My nipples grew hard, rock solid. My sex was as moist as a tropical rainforest.

Thomas clawed at his face, his voice hoarse and exhausted from screaming. His flesh came off in strips like a cheap charcoal beauty mask. Raw, oozing muscle became his prominent facial feature. The dust had entered his lungs and he began to cough and wheeze. Dropping to his knees, he clutched his throat. His airway tightened. He reached for help, but no one came, not at first. A handful of students rushed him, coming to his aid. By the time they reached him, it was too late; Thomas Tripps had died of asphyxiation. A few students were close enough to breathe in the hazardous cloud that had thinned and almost disappeared. They didn't die, but I'm told they'll never breathe right again. COPD and all that.

The important thing was that I climaxed the second Thomas's body went limp on the floor.

☆☆☆

"I can't tell you how much that story disturbs me," Dr. Carson said, his hand trembling.

"I know. I can see how." Her smile was weak, barely present. But still there. "I guess if I hadn't stolen the acid from the chemistry supply room and that teacher hadn't testified against me, I might have gotten away with it."

"Doubtful."

"Guess we'll never know."

"So how do you feel now, knowing you'll never kill again? That you'll never see your 'lover', Death, as you put it?"

She shrugged and slouched in her seat. "Who's to say I won't see him again? I see him all the time. He walks the halls of this facility. Suicides and natural causes. I don't, and *won't*, see him often, but I *will* see him again. True lovers always unite."

"Casey, I promise you, as long as I'm alive, you'll never see your lover again."

"Well, I guess we'll have to change all that," she said with a wink.

Then she closed her eyes and mouth for the rest of the session.

LOVER NUMBER THREE

Back in my cell, Dr. Carson's words repeated, over and over again, in my mind. "You'll never see your lover, death, again." The words hurt, practically ripped my fuckin' heart out. Could I go through life and never see my one true love? I knew there was no getting out of this place. No one had ever escaped here successfully, and those who'd tried were batshit crazy. I wasn't crazy. Never was. Crazy in love? Guilty. But clinically insane—that's just laughable.

I mulled over my options. There weren't many. Live in misery. Or die in peace within the cold embrace of my lover's arms.

Those were my choices.

I had no weapon, not so much as the paperclip I could have nabbed off Carson's desk. I had me, myself, and I.

And I had teeth.

I bit into my wrists. Deep. Made sure I got through the tendons and—most importantly—I tore out my arteries, chomped through them like soft licorice. Even though I was happy, I yelped. Blood sprayed everywhere—a surrealistic amount of blood—spattering the walls, creating a crimson Rorschach of the messiest variety.

I closed my eyes and envisioned my lover. Holding me. Kissing me. Smothering me. Bringing me the sweet gift of eternal rest.

ON THE EARS OF DEAF GODS

HE WOODS... THE *running... the panting... the muscle cramps... a dream? No, reality... the grinding of rubber against gravel in the near distance, the sound it makes... the yelling... the cheering... the rumble of the truck's engine... the echoes in the darkness... the final pursuit...)*

He woke with sweat pouring down his forehead, lifting himself a few inches off the mattress. Breathing heavily, he felt something warm press his bare chest and heard sweet, reassuring words whispered by a kind voice. He looked down and saw a palm placed over his heart, fingers stretched. Eyes bulging with anxiety, he turned and spotted two materializing shapes. One sat bedside with her lips puckered, a finger over them, continuing to ease him down with hushed sounds. "It'll be all right," she said softly.

The other figure, a boy, leaned into the doorway, peering into the room. The wall hid the lower half of his body.

"Where am I?" the man asked, directing his question to no one in particular.

The woman faced the open doorway, the boy. "Go fetch a bottled water, Nelson."

Nelson did as his mother requested, leaving at once.

"Where am I?" he asked again, with urgency this time.

"You're safe." She tapped his chest. "Lie down."

Knowing the woman meant him no harm, he hesitated anyway. After a brief staring session, drilling into the woman's soft eyes, he slowly fell back on the stack of pillows.

"How did I get here?"

(running... the woods... the howling... echoes in darkness)

The woman cleared her throat in preparation to speak, yet she remained silent.

"What's your name?"

"One question at a time." She sharpened her gaze. "I found you outside. You passed out."

"I was running."

She nodded, lowering her eyes away from him. "I know."

"Do you know what from?"

Once again, she was late to answer. "I do."

"Then why are you helping me?"

Something moved in her throat as she swallowed hard. Her eyes moved up the wall, and the man followed her vision as if the answers to his questions were scrawled there. He discovered nothing but taupe walls, uneven and rough from poor patch jobs. The ceiling owned several brown water stains, some darker than others. The man knew it was only a matter of time before the plaster would cave in and sprinkle the floor with chunks of gypsum and fine white dust.

The woman clicked her tongue. "Because I wanted to."

"Do you know what they'll do—"

"Yes," she said, snapping her head in the stranger's direction. "Yes, and I don't care."

The man showed her his palms, a defensive display. "Okay, okay. Just wanted to... you know... make sure."

The boy returned with a bottle of water and a cool, frosted glass. "Here, Mom," he said, padding across the room. His eyes latched onto the stranger. "I brought a glass, too. In case you prefer it that way."

The fugitive smiled. "Thank you, Nelson."

The boy handed over the items, skipping his mother and going directly to the source. "What's your name, fella?"

"My friends and fam—um, people call me Howie."

"Howie!" the boy yelled with amusement. "I like that name."

His mother smiled at the boy's delight. Her son threw an arm over her shoulder, pulling her close to him so their heads gently knocked.

"Mom's name is Helen." Nelson's mouth dropped open with shock. "Helen and Howie! Two H's!" He squealed with delight.

Howie chuckled. So did Helen. The three of them filled the room with laughter, but the joy slowly tapered off.

"Why don't you get ready for bed, short stuff?"

"Ohhhh," he said, shaking his body as if doing the Twist, directing his eyes to the floor. "All right, I suppose. If I have to."

"You do," Mom replied, poking his tummy. He giggled. "Get to bed and I'll come read you a story in a few minutes."

"Awesome!" he said, waving at Howie. "Goodnight, mister! See you tomorrow!"

Howie nodded at the boy and watched him dart across the room, disappear around the doorway.

"Sweet kid," he said.

"The sweetest." Helen rose to her feet. "I won't regret bringing you here. Will I?"

He knew what she had truly asked: *Are you dangerous?* "No, ma'am."

"Good." Before she could continue, a faint grumbling noise buzzed in the distance, somewhere not far past their property line.

Both of them turned to the window, looking out across the cornfield, toward the edge of the surrounding forest. A faded glow brightened a small cluster of trees. The drone grew increasingly louder.

Helen gasped. "Dear God, is it them?"

Judging the way her body quaked, Howie suspected she already knew the answer. "Yes. Turn out the lights." A tremble invaded his voice. "And, for God's sakes, hide me well."

☆ ☆ ☆

The knock on the front door came fifteen minutes later. Helen ambled across the foyer in her evening robe, reached the door, and flipped on the porch lights. Through the peephole, she saw three shadows staged in triangle formation. Behind them, idled a mud-speckled utility truck with a twelve-foot bed. The large, heavy object the white Ford had hauled around the county chilled her blood, projecting her worst memories. The wooden cross had been strapped to the bed so they wouldn't lose it during their journey. It had been constructed recently; she could tell by the fresh coat of paint and the absent blood stains. It wasn't worn and weathered like the one she had seen on the day her husband died.

"Miss Beckett?" inquired the man at the head of the triangle. "Miss Beckett, I believe you know why we're here. Would you let us in?"

She had no choice. She'd let them in or they'd come in. And, if they *came* in, that meant a broken front door and God knows how many other repairs.

She toggled the deadbolt and opened the door. A single grinning face greeted her. The two visitors behind the pack leader kept straighter faces, though she could see traces of recent smiles near the end of their lips.

"Hello!" the head of the triangle said jubilantly, as if presenting her with some game-show grand-prize. "I'm Officer Bankhold," he said, pointing to the name tag above his left breast. Above the right breast was a patch depicting a golden cross with golden squiggly lines around it, childishly signifying the symbol's radiance. The emblem had been stitched on and it stood out against the black fabric of the men's attire. "But you may call me Banky, and these are my two associates, Wilson and Hartley. May we come in?"

Helen Beckett stepped aside. "Please."

"Thank you kindly." Banky crossed the threshold and waved on his two associates. As he entered the foyer, he glanced around, noticing the peeling wallpaper and the clusters of brown stains on the ceiling. "My, my. Looks like you could use a handyman 'round these parts."

"Yes. I'm not very skilled when it comes to housework and since—well, since last year, I haven't gotten around to learning."

Banky winked at her. "I know a handy guy in Lansdale that will work for a bucket of peanuts. Have this place tip-top in no time at all."

"I wish I could afford a bucket of peanuts."

Banky laughed. "Well, then. Let's get on with it, shall we? Where's best to chat?"

"The kitchen," she replied, nodding toward the end of the hall.

She walked and they followed. Helen couldn't shake the feeling of their eyes on her neck, sensation lingering like the gentle touch of old cobwebs.

They reached the kitchen and Banky sat down at the lone table without waiting for an invitation. His company stood behind him like statues.

"Coffee?"

"For me, yes," he replied. "These two schmucks can do without. They're working." He clapped his hands together and the men fanned out. They disappeared into separate rooms. "Not that I need your permission, but you don't mind if they get started without me?"

Nervously, she shook her head. "No, of course not. What do you think they'll find?"

"I think you know what." There was nothing pleasant about his tone now. "I'd prefer to do without the games, but I understand your position, and, honestly—I respect it. However, I have a job to do and I'm going to do it. I hope you will supply me with the same respect."

She stood there, continuing to prepare the man his cup of coffee. "Cream? Sugar? We have goat's milk. Fresh."

"Goat's milk it is. And a drop of sugar, darling."

She mixed the ingredients, then waltzed over to the kitchen table. Placing the mug in the center, she sat down.

"Poison?" he asked.

She shook her head.

"I'll take your word for it." He picked up the mug and dangled his nose over it. Closing his eyes, he breathed in the bold aroma. "Dark roast. Mm-mm. My favorite."

Footfalls sounded on the floor upstairs. Her eyes migrated up the walls.

"My son is in bed. Sleeping."

Banky smiled, squinting one eye. "I assume you told him about the situation? Instructed him accordingly?"

She nodded.

"Good. As long as he cooperates, we should have no further infractions."

"He's only seven."

"Hm," Banky uttered while sipping. Needing a break, he set the half-empty mug down, propped his elbows on the table, and rested his head on his interlocked fingers. "This is damn fine coffee. They don't make coffee like this in the metropolis. Not as flavorful. There's something homey about country coffee."

"I'm glad you like it," she said through her teeth.

"We're gonna find him, Miss Beckett, I assure you. No matter how good you think you are about stashing things, I'm that much better at finding them. So, we can save a lot of time and trouble if you just tell me where my runaway contestant is. Please and thank you."

"I don't know what you're—"

"Now, Miss Beckett—"

"Mrs. Beckett."

His eyes narrowed wryly, which followed a long, knowing stare. "Used to be, but not anymore. I did my homework, young lady." He sighed. "I understand how you must feel about us and our work."

"You call what you do 'work?'"

His head knocked from side to side as if bouncing the answer between his ears, screwing up his eyes. "Yes, ma'am, I do. We all have to make a living in this world. You milk cows and tend crops, and I *Sacrifice*. Mine is a dirty, thankless job. But it's still a job, one I do well and take pride in. People don't appreciate what we do. The non-believers, such as yourself."

She glared at him. Her upper lip twitched with contempt.

"I'd think after your husband's *experience,* you'd be a little more grateful. After all, you're having a successful harvest. Aren't you?"

She shrugged. "Subpar."

"Hm. Too bad. Well, the gods can't always provide, can they? Maybe we should up our ante for next quarter's offering."

She kept still. Above, footsteps pounded on the floor. In one motion, she rose to her feet.

"Nelson!"

Banky stood up. "Your son is fine, Miss Beckett. We mean him no harm."

"Stop calling me that!" she snapped.

"Very well." The man nodded, then cocked his head back and faced the ceiling. The pounding grew louder. The walls rattled, the small worthless knick-knacks on the shelves clacking together. Helen bolted for the doorway but Banky's arm reached out and caught her around her midsection. He pulled her in. "No, no, no. See, I told you we'd find him."

Less than a minute later, the noise moved down the hallway, to the top of the stairs. She heard the grunting of three men amidst a violent struggle.

"Mommy!" Nelson yelled.

"My baby!" she screamed, trying to break free. Banky tightened his grip. "Let go!"

"I'm sorry, Miss Beckett. Please cooperate."

Feet stamped the wooden stairs. Creaks and hollow knocks sounded off in rapid succession like the finale of seasonal fireworks. Within seconds, the three men appeared at the bottom of the stairs. The two men Banky had introduced held Howie on his knees in a position he couldn't break free from. They had his arms locked between their legs. Howie struggled, but his efforts were useless.

From the top of the stairs, Nelson called his mother. "Mommy! The bad men got him!"

"Go back to sleep, sweetie!" she called back. "Go back to bed. Please…"

"They're gonna take him just like Daddy!"

Tears began to roll down her cheeks. Sadness bit the back of her throat. Her lips trembled violently.

"I really wish you people wouldn't teach your children to think of us as 'bad men,'" Banky said. "I mean, I get it. But come on now. We're only doing what we need to so the rest of us can survive."

"For the greater good," she said, almost in a growl. "Fuck you."

"Potty mouth." Banky forced his arm around her throat and pulled her head back, brushing his lips against her ear. "I hate potty-mouthed non-believers."

He pushed her forward, toward the front door. Banky's associates dragged Howie out the door, toward the truck.

"Tell your son to go to bed or you'll punish him." Banky squeezed tighter, nearly cutting off her oxygen supply. *"Now."*

"Go… to… bed, honey," she said, nearly breathless.

She watched her son turn slowly and pad back down the hall, toward his room.

Banky dragged her through the front door, across the porch, down the stairs, and onto the front lawn. His associates had already placed Howie on the cross, stretched his arms across the crossbar and bound his wrists with rope.

Next came the hammer and spikes.

Howie roared with revolt, pleading with the men, begging for his release. Wilson and Hartley continued without delay, without changing their expression, without any regard for the sanctity of life, the very meaning of the emblem stitched above the breast of their all-black uniforms. Wilson held Howie's fingers out while Hartley lined up the strike. With one blow, the nine-inch nail went through Howie's palm and sank four inches into the wood beneath. A second whack drove the spike home so the head settled flush against his skin.

Howie screamed until his vocal cords cracked. He didn't have anything left by the time they finished the other hand, and, by the time they went to work on his feet, he fell unconscious.

Banky forced Helen to watch the entire thing. When they raised the cross onto its stand, Banky lifted her on her feet.

"You will stand here," Banky said, "and watch this man die."

"No," she whispered, sniffling.

"I'll take your eyelids if I have to." He put her earlobe between his teeth and bit hard, but not enough to pierce her flesh. "Are extreme measures required, *Miss* Beckett?"

She hesitated and thought of Nelson. "No... I'll watch."

"Smart girl."

Howie opened his eyes an hour later, although lucidity avoided him. His head, tilted toward the ground, lolled as he struggled to keep conscious.

Helen prayed that he'd pass out again. She prayed, but, like all her prayers, the invocation fell on the ears of deaf Gods.

27 Years Later

The pickup careened onto the long, dusty driveway flanked by rows of Spanish moss. At the end of the stretch stood an old, southern-gothic house, complete with the full wrap-around porch the driver's mother had always desired. The driver found a vacant spot close to the steps, hopped out of the cab, glanced around the immediate area while fighting off the glare of the setting sun, and then headed for the house's front door.

He took the steps two at a time, strolled across the porch, and didn't think twice about ringing the doorbell. As he waited, he wondered what condition the old man would be in, if he'd be mentally aware enough to comprehend the current situation.

A woman wearing a traditional French maid's outfit answered on the second ring. "Hello?" she asked, cracking the door wide enough for one eyeball. "May I help you, sir?"

"I'm looking for a man named Wilbur Bankhold," the man said. "I'm told he lives here."

"I'm sorry," she said. "But who are you?"

"I'm from the metropolis. My name is Everett. My father used to be an old colleague of Wilbur's, and I was hoping I could have a moment of his time." He cleared his throat. "To reminisce. See, my father passed away when I was young and, well, I don't have a lot of memories of him."

The eye looked him up and down.

"Please. I went to great lengths trying to find Mr. Bankhold. I won't stay long."

The eye studied his face, particularly his eyes. A moment later, the door swung open and the maid revealed herself. She was a pleasant-looking woman, perhaps a decade older than Everett, but in much better shape. Oddly, the woman reminded him of his mother.

"Come in, Everett," she said in a tone that suggested she hadn't dropped her suspicions.

"Thank you." Everett entered the foyer.

She gave him another once over. "Mr. Bankhold is in his study. I'll walk you."

"I know the way."

The comment obviously stirred her suspicion because the woman's brow arched, nearly becoming one with her hairline. "I'll walk you anyway."

The second she turned, he dug through his pocket.

"Wow," he said. "I didn't think it'd be this easy."

She halted and spun on her heels, but it was too late. Everett had already equipped himself with the syringe and the needle darted into her neck. He plunged the contents into her system, and she fell to the floor before the last drop was administered.

Without caution, he scampered toward the study.

☆ ☆ ☆

"Do I know you?" the wheelchair-bound man asked. "Look vaguely familiar."

"I don't think so, Mr. Bankhold." Everett paced back and forth.

"Hm. You from the metropolis?"

"That's right."

"And I worked with your daddy?"

"More or less."

"Son, pardon me, but you ain't making a lick of sense."

"I was hoping you could take a ride with me."

Bankhold's expression fell flat. He gripped the wheels of his apparatus as if he meant to race off. "How exactly did you find me?" he asked suspiciously. "When I retired—" A series of hacking coughs followed. As he hacked, he pounded the armrest with his fists. Next, he scrambled for his oxygen mask. He sucked on the stale air for a minute straight, then placed the mask back on its resting hook. "When I retired, my accounts were deleted from the database. Permanently. That was protocol for those who... *Sacrificed.*"

"Yes, true." Everett toured the room once more, surveying the framed family pictures on the wall next to the bookcase. "It was extremely difficult to track you down. Computers and technology just aren't what they used to be. My mother told me stories when I was little. Said when she was young, you'd be able to research anything you wanted on something called the Internet in two seconds or less."

"Those were the days."

Everett nodded. "So I've heard."

"What do you want from me?" the old man inquired. "I can smell a pile of dog droppings a long way coming, and I smelled yours the second you rang my doorbell."

Everett smirked. "I want you to take a ride with me, old man. I have something important to show you."

"What the hell are you talking about?"

"It's about your kids." He pointed to the family photos. "All four of them."

Bankhold's face twisted with bewilderment. "My kids?"

Everett nodded. "Tommy. Patricia. Corben. Tanya."

The old man's eyes widened with alarm. "My kids."

"They're in a bit of trouble."

"Trouble?"

Everett tried to hide his smile. "It's probably better if I show you," he said, feeling around his pocket for the second syringe.

☆ ☆ ☆

Banky awoke to the nose-twitching smell of the truck's exhaust and the faint cow-shit aroma that was synonymous with driving through the country. The window was down, and the wind roared in his face. He felt the extra flab in his cheeks ripple with the forceful gusts of air. He moved his head to the side but found the rest of his body paralyzed.

"What did you do to me?" the old man croaked.

Everett focused on the road, not overly concerned with his passenger's lucid state. Effective drugs were hard to find nowadays, but Everett had hit the motherlode. These had worked to perfection and since he had timed everything just right, the man would remain numb from the waist down until they arrived at their destination.

"Do you know how many people the New Church of Old Gods *sacrificed* during those early years of operation, back when they believed they served a greater good and helped the people they governed? An estimated sixty-five-thousand. Not much compared to the three-hundred-and-twenty-million people residing in the U.S. around that time. Less than a percent actually. But still. Those sixty-five-thousand people had lives. Families. Parents. They were people and you killed them." Everett shook his head with disgust. "How many you kill, Bankhold?"

Banky glared at him, keeping his lips sealed.

"I bet you killed a bunch. Over a dozen. Hell, maybe two."

"I never killed anyone," Banky said, almost whispering. "Never killed a single one."

"No?"

"No. I only supervised."

Everett cut the wheel to the right and parked the pickup roadside. The tires howled as the rubber and dirt met with friction. The man erupted with crazed laughter, pounding the steering wheel with both fists. He threw his head back and guffawed until his ribs suffered.

"What's so funny?" Banky grumbled.

"You supervised?" Everett's jaw hung agape, seemingly astonished by the old man's memory. "You supervised? Man, if that's how you live with yourself, so be it. But you 'supervising' makes you just as guilty as if you fastened those people yourself." Hysterical laughter bellowed once again. "'Supervised.' Nice one, old man. I'll have to remember that one when the authorities come after me."

Banky felt a rock in his throat. He swallowed, but the knot refused to unkink and remained stationary at the base of his esophagus. "Why would the authorities be after you?"

The driver sat in silence, a sly grin stretching his cheeks.

It's about your kids...

"Why?" the old man asked, barely able to get the word out.

They're in a bit of trouble.

Everett swerved back onto the dirt road, punched the gas pedal and sped toward their destination.

"I asked you a question, you demon-serving maniac," Banky said hoarsely. He felt another coughing fit gathering in his chest and didn't see his oxygen tank readily available. He doubted his abductor brought it and figured it had been left behind on purpose. "Hey!"

Everett glared at his passenger, that sick smile tarnishing what Banky perceived to be his last shred of decency. "You'll see. Soon enough, you will."

It was worse than he feared; they were already dead.

Or if they weren't dead, they were well on their way and there was nothing a crippled old man could do about it.

In front of an abandoned farmhouse in desperate need of demolition, four crosses stood in a row. However, the derelict domicile wasn't the focal point; the crosses and their occupants snared his attention.

"No..." Banky hissed, his voice betrayed by a sudden rush of emotion. He didn't notice Everett had gotten out, walked around, opened the passenger's side door, and was now dragging him out by his collar. Banky began to cough and bark, fluid from his lungs filling his mouth. He spat the meaty wad of phlegm on the dirt below. "No, it can't be."

Tommy, Patricia, Corben, and Tanya.; each had their own cross. They had shared the same hammer, but each had received their own nails. Their own death. *Their own sacrifice.*

"You monster," Banky said, his voice wet with leftover lung gunk. "You goddamn monster."

"Oh please," Everett said dismissively. "You've killed dozens. I've only done four."

"My babies."

"Funny, it's different when it happens to you. Bet that was part of the arrangement with the N.C.O.G. Wasn't it? Employees and their family members were left off the ballot? Their names withdrawn from the lottery? Bet you never knew a single person drafted as a contestant. I'd bet my life on it."

Banky began to sob. His shoulders heaved as he screamed into his hands.

"Bet they were all strangers to you," Everett said, bending down next to him. "Well, my father was no stranger to me, and I watched his sacrifice when I was six-years-old. Then, a year later, you forced my mother to watch another man die on our front lawn."

Banky looked up from his hands. He surveyed his surroundings, the house beyond the standing crosses and the cornfield at his back. The dilapidated house suddenly became familiar, like a puzzling piece of a distant dream. Twenty-seven years ago, he had raided this place. He remembered the woman Everett spoke of. She had betrayed her country, her state, and, most importantly—the Old Gods. She had harbored a fugitive, an elected contestant worthy of the highest sacrament—*sacrifice*. And Banky had found him, like he had always done. That was his job—find the lost ones and return them to their rightful owners, delivering them to the Gods in exchange for crops, desires, and prosperity.

All bullshit, as Wilbur Bankhold had eventually found out, along with the rest of the country. Over time, statistics defeated superstition and the quarterly lotteries were abolished.

"Your name isn't Everett," Banky said, almost dreamily. "It's Nelson. Your mother was Helen. And the man she hid from us was Howie." He nodded. "I remember all right."

"Two out of three, bub." Everett clapped him on the back. "Not bad, but my name *is* Everett. Everett Longo. Legally anyway. It was changed from Nelson Beckett after my mother killed herself two years after you crucified Howard Jensen on our front lawn. See, my father's sacrifice didn't produce the necessary crops to keep us financially afloat. She went bankrupt. So, in order to save our family from a life of poverty and certain misfortune, she offed herself. I was sent into the system and, fortunately, a lovely couple who lived in the metropolis adopted me. Rich folk. Gods bless 'em, right? Guess, in a roundabout way, my father's sacrifice worked out after all. Only, I believe my mother's sealed the deal. And the state's lottery didn't choose her destiny—the offering was *her* choice. Maybe a sacrifice only works when the choice comes from within, without forceful interference from outlying entities. Something your precious organization seemed to overlook."

Banky scanned the crucifixes. "My kids."

"I doubt their sacrifices will be worth a damn. Just senseless killing. Something you're pretty familiar with, I gather."

Banky dropped to his knees and pressed his forehead against the dead, yellowed grass. A breeze ripped across the lawn, carrying the fetid odor of expired flesh.

Everett patted him on the shoulder. "So long, old man. I'll leave you here to wallow with the dead. Death will come for you soon, you being without your oxygen tank and all. Would have built you your own cross but I ran out of lumber. Which is fine. I think you'll die slower this way. Better that. More time to reflect on your life and the poor decisions you made. Time to look every person you murdered in the eyes and tell them why you did it. Why you sacrificed them for Gods that do not exist. I think that's fair, if you ask me."

"Sorry," Banky said with a heavy, throat-gurgling breath. "Sorry for it all."

"Too late for sorry." Everett stood, swaying in the wind, breathing in the stench nature carried. *"Reap what you sow.* Isn't that what you people preached once upon a time ago? Reap what you sow, Bankhold. Reap what you fuckin' sowed."

Banky listened to the man's footsteps as they drifted farther away. A second later, the driver's side door clicked open and slammed shut. The engine growled to life, reminding him of the white monster he and his cohorts had driven all over the county, tracking down runaways. He turned as the exhaust belched plumes of brown fog. The tires spun on the dead lawn, kicking up grass and earth, and the truck propelled ahead, down the long dusty path. It disappeared behind the abandoned, lifeless rows of corn stalks, sparse from decades of neglect.

Banky returned his focus to his hands, refusing to glance up at his dead kin. Soon after, that long eternal shadow slithered over him, lacing his bones with an icy chill and pulling him under, beneath the soil, holding him in the darkness, forever.

A RIDE ON THE RAINBOW

(THE BLACK HILL #4)

1986

"CAN I RIDE the rainbow?" asked Woody, a short, rotund gentleman who only had half—maybe a third—of the brains he was born with. He was wearing his Bernie Kosar jersey and a Cleveland Browns cap tilted slightly sideways and not on purpose. Food stains, old ketchup and mustard mishaps, showed up on the jersey's white numbers, the nineteen Woody worshipped on Sundays come autumn-time. He walked alongside his older brother, Austin, up the hill.

The Black Hill.

The spooky hill was made spookier by the late-October aura that had spread across Ludlow, Ohio. That, and everything else was spookier in Woody Turner's life. His daily fears were heightened by the incident, the car accident that had nearly killed him but had somehow—miraculously— spared his life, that had left him permanently disabled. There was a fancy *doctor* term for it, but Austin Turner called his brother's condition what it was—brain damage. The good physicians and so-called experts told their parents to expect Woody's brain to perform at the ability of a four-year-old, and that was the best-case-scenario. They were right, however, and Woody—who was once a promising young man, student athlete who might have been recruited as a D-2 offensive lineman—had been reduced to a bumbling, stumbling, occasionally stuttering, oaf. But a lovable oaf. A harmless human being that always meant well, even though he couldn't express certain things or get across certain points. Woody Turner's innocence matched his mental capacity, and he wouldn't harm so much as an ant.

All that aside, his brother knew there were things about Woody that made him different. Qualities that made him *interesting.*

The fear. Woody was frightened about a lot of things, scared of monsters under the bed and ghosts that patrolled the hallways of his parents' house. At first, Austin didn't think much of his brother's claims. Ghosts weren't real and couldn't possibly manifest in the hallways of the house he'd grown up in. But he thought differently when his parents had corroborated some of his brother's stories. They would go to bed with the furniture arranged one way, wake up with their couch flipped over, an end table on the other side of the room, their entertainment center reversed so the television faced the wall. Too much work for one mentally-deficient thirtysomething to do in the middle of the night without making too much noise, that was for sure.

The way Austin saw it, Woody could see ghosts. Not just *ghosts*; but he could see *things*. He'd say things that made absolutely no sense, but then, a few days later, Austin would connect the dots. Sometimes it would start off as simple as Woody mentioning ice cream. Ice cream. Just a comment. Like, *Hey, Austin, that ice cream is on fire.* Perfect nonsense to most, but to Woody, he spoke as if a blazing bowl of ice cream was the sanest thing in the world. And two days later, Austin would scan the local newspaper and discover that a neighborhood ice cream man had gotten so depressed by his personal life and impending divorce that he had driven his truck to the end of a dead-end lane and lit himself on fire, truck and all. *Ice cream* and all. *Austin, that ice cream is on fire.*

So it had been.

Things like this happened all the time around Woody, and quite a lot lately. More than ever. Used to happen maybe once, twice a year. Now it was almost every week. Gradually, he'd tell Austin more stories, see more ghosts, and sometimes—just sometimes—the television would tell him secrets that actually came true, such as six months ago when he had overheard the black screen talking about a "basement girl." It turned out that, down the block, one of the Turners' neighbors had kidnapped a seven-year-old girl and was keeping her chained up in his basement. The things he'd done to her were unspeakable, but the television told Woody every word, and he'd been able to recite the puke-worthy acts with such detail that Mrs. Turner fainted when she'd read about the depraved aspects in the paper some time later.

The whole situation freaked out Austin, made his skin crawl with invisible bugs, but he had decided it was a gift, a blessing and a terrible, terrible curse. The accident had undoubtedly played a part, damaged the boy in more ways than one, and Austin thought that maybe he could use his brother's newfound skill for good. Like, solving mysteries in the greater Central Ohio area. And there was no local mystery more famous than the *Black Hill.*

"Can I ride the rainbow?" Woody asked again.

"Bud, just calm down," Austin told him, taking the Polaroid and putting it to his eye, taking a picture of the lone tree that capped the Black Hill.

"Browns. Football. Kosar. One o'clock?"

Austin snatched the photograph out of the automatic feeder. He turned to his brother as he flapped the picture in the air. "It's only eleven, bud. We'll be home in plenty of time to watch the Browns."

"Can I ride the Rainbow?" Woody smiled like he always smiled. Woody smiled even when he was afraid, which made it hard to judge if something supernatural *was* happening. When he was really scared, he covered his eyes with his massive hands. Still smiled, though. Always smiled.

"What rainbow? Do you *see* a rainbow?"

"Rainbow. Rainbows everywhere." His gaze lifted toward the bright autumn sky. Dead, curled leaves fluttered through the air like drunken butterflies. Wind swept over the hill, the rustling of branches scratching the boys' eardrums. Fall in Ohio was in full-swing, and Austin loved every minute of it. October was his favorite, around Halloween. Something about the holiday excited him more than any other, even Christmas. Something about the mood, the *aura*. "Rainbows. Everywhere."

Austin looked up. He didn't see a rainbow. Instead, he saw a cobalt sky and clouds that moved as if they had left late for something. Just an ordinary day near the end of October.

"What else do you see, bud?" Austin asked. Still holding onto the photograph that was taking its sweet time to develop, he snapped another one. This one was of Woody looking up.

"Rainbows. Let me ride them, Austin, oh boy, please?"

Austin chuckled. "Bud, even if there were rainbows all around us, you wouldn't be able to ride them. They're invisible."

"In-divid-ible."

"No. *Invisible*."

He tried again but couldn't get the word out without botching it. Austin patted his brother on the back, a reassuring love tap that told him, *don't worry about it, bud.*

"Means they're not real. It's a trick of the light."

"Trick of the light," Woody repeated, his eyes rolling upward. He was trying to understand, wrap his brain around it. "Trick of the light. Trick. Trick? Trick or Treat?"

"Something like that, yes." He patted his brother on the back again. "Here," he said, handing him the undeveloped photograph. "Shake it. When it develops, it'll be a picture of you."

Woody did as his brother asked. Shaking the photo in the air delighted him, and he spent the next two minutes prancing around the crest of the Black Hill, giggling hysterically, shaking the photograph as if he were trying to rid his hand of something that was superglued.

When he was finished, and the picture was fully developed, Woody seemed charmed by the image. Though, when Austin saw it, he was not.

A rainbow.

A kaleidoscope of primary colors. That was what he'd taken a picture of, though, that was impossible. He'd snapped a photo of his kid brother. There were no rainbows to speak of.

Yet, there it was. The evidence rested in his left hand.

"A rainbow!" Woody shouted while bouncing in place. "It's a rainbow! Oh, let me ride it. Will ya, Austy?"

"This doesn't make sense," Austin said. He checked the first photograph, the one of the tree, and saw exactly that—a tree with no rainbows, no colorful smears of any kind. It was a normal photograph, one unmarked by things that weren't possible.

He snapped another picture of his brother. This time, Woody made a funny face, sticking his tongue out and wrinkling his nose. He found it hilarious. Austin did not.

"Lemme see the picture, Austy! Lemme see the raiiiiiiiiiiiiiinbow."

Austin let the photograph develop in front of his eyes, as if that would prevent the trick from happening again.

It didn't. For the second time, a rainbow covered Woody's face, masking his entire body.

Well, Austin thought, *this is what you came for, isn't it? To discover something?* Yes, it was, but Austin was thinking more along the lines of spotting a ghost or witnessing one of those black stars that Blake Weber had mentioned in the letter he had written to his wife minutes before he had split her head open with an ax. He did not come here expecting to capture photographic evidence of a *fucking* rainbow.

Woody danced around the Black Hill, galloping in place.

"Woody," Austin said. "Tell me. Do you still see the rainbow?"

Woody nodded. "Yep. Rainbow. Everywhere."

"Do you see anything else?"

Woody ended his gyration, remained still for a moment, and pointed to the top of the hill. Near the tree. "Just them."

A cold sensation traveled Austin's body. Shock tied his vocal cords in a knot, squashing any chance of speaking the thoughts that came to him. Above all else, he was paralyzed by his brother's action, and the unseen things near the tree atop the Black Hill.

After a moment, Austin found his voice. "What are they?"

Woody's voice was deep and serious, lacking the usual playfulness that accompanied every word. "Shadows."

Even though he felt like running, screaming for help, Austin snapped a photograph. When the machine cranked out the picture, he snatched it and began furiously shaking it in the air.

Once developed, Austin glued his eyes to what his Polaroid had captured.

Shadows was correct. Partially. Shadowy *figures* was more on target. Three of them, standing near the tree, looking down at the man taking their picture. They had long arms—impossibly long—looking more like apes than men. Definitely human-ish. But not human, not all the way.

"What the hell are they?"

Woody's finger shook. "RIGHT THERE! RIGHT THERE!" Panic commanded his voice, sheer fear. There was no denying that whatever Woody had seen, it had freaked him out.

Austin backed away, his neck hairs rising. His entire body went cold, a wintery chill striking his bones in the middle of autumn.

He took another picture.

In twenty seconds, he knew why Woody had been so alarmed.

They were in front of him. The shadows. They were crowding the shot. They were so close that the tree and the hill were hardly seen. It was mostly all shadows. In them, he could make out the stars. Not their universe's stars, but someone else's. He was a big fan of astronomy and had committed the map of their solar system to his memory, could name most of the stars without any help. But the pattern was all off. No constellations. No Big Dipper, no Little Dipper. Lyra and Scorpius, all absent. These were new constellations, a new planetary arrangement. And there were...

Black stars.

Constellations.

Black Star Constellations.

They formed images, sure, but Woody didn't know what. Constellations are just stars until someone shows you what they are. This collection was made up entirely of black stars against an equally dark backdrop, the stars highlighted by an orangish glow.

He closed his eyes, and that was when he saw the images.

First he saw Blake Weber crack his old lady's head open, and the splash of blood that followed and soaked into the bedsheets. Then he saw a group of kids ride their bikes up the hill; their bodies went missing in the summer of '62 and were never found. No one ever discovered what had happened to them, but the image showed the four of them floating down the Ohio River, their eyes torn from their sockets, replaced by shiny black stars. They were smiling as they floated on, toward a dark ruined city that couldn't have existed in the real world. Then he saw a couple in their car; Austin recognized them as Shady O'Quinn and Margaret Eastern. Shady, as far as Austin knew, was still serving time for the murder of his girlfriend. When he'd been questioned, Shady admitted to not being conscious during the murder, claiming the deed had been done by someone else, some unnamed killer. The bruises on her neck matched his fingertips and he was hauled off to the slammer with a life sentence. He saw a highlight reel of the other lives the Black Hill had claimed over the years.

Then he saw Woody. With a knife. Thrusting the blade into his brother's back.

A rush of pain spiked down Austin's spine, and he crumbled to the grassy surface. Woody stood over him, smiling that smile.

"I'm riding the rainbow, Austy! Riding the raiiiiiiiiiinbow!"

Austin pleaded for help, or at least he thought he did. He opened his mouth, but no words came out. Woody sunk the blade into him six more times, the last one catching him in that soft spot at the base of his throat.

Behind Woody, shapes formed. Shadows. Beyond those, the black stars moved in, forming constellations of their own. In them, he found death.

THE CITY OF BONES

THE CHARCOAL-GRAY TANK rolled over the city of bones.

In the distance, the ruined metropolis sat on the horizon, war-torn and smoking. Ashen skies blanketed the heavens, an endless canvas of bleak despair. The tank slowed to a contemplative stop and remained there for about three minutes. Inside, the soldiers argued about whether to advance, to head back to camp, or to abandon the promise of imminent defeat. The group was relatively split on the decision, but, when it came down to it, Skunk was in charge and whatever the cigar-puffing, neck-tatted sergeant said would have to fly, no *buts* about it.

"What do you say, Sarge?" asked Wolf, a young man whose nickname hardly matched his persona or his appearance. If a wolf had been starving, gone weeks with only eating scraps and no real meals, then maybe the moniker would fit. The scrawny twenty-something glanced at his superior with hopeful eyes, pleading for the Sarge to take them home, away from the madness afoot.

Skunk inhaled a lungful of brownish smoke. He held it deep, allowing the fog to fill his chest, and then released it throughout the tank's interior. The men didn't seem bothered by the rolling plumes, save for Wolf. The kid turned his head and closed his eyes, as if breathing in one short breath would inflict permanent damage.

"We stay," Skunk said gruffly. "We stay and we fight. We kill the bastards or die trying."

The other two soldiers, Bear and Peacock, nodded, and while both men would have preferred a different outcome, who were they to protest? Bear, broad-shouldered and hulking, a fine example of the human race, strutted over to his station—the turret hull. Peacock, a man who'd always worn bright, tropical-looking feathers on his helmet for dramatic effect to distract the enemy, faced his own duty, the map which hung on the back wall of the tank.

"We could head straight through the city," Peacock said, tracing his finger along the route. "Or we could go around it. No telling what we'll find doing either."

Skunk considered this a moment. "City looks lost."

"Aren't they all?" Peacock said, and the way he lowered his head suggested he hadn't meant to say *anything*.

The Sarge gave the options a few seconds to percolate. After he was done letting his thoughts stew, he breathed, and with his breath came more fog. "We head straight through the city. The fastest way from one point to another is in a straight line, no? Yes, I believe it is. We head straight through. Permission to fire on anything that moves."

Wolf cleared his throat. Timidly, he asked, "What if there're survivors?"

Skunk swung his head slowly, his eyes gliding across the room, settling on his young officer. He repeated, "Permission to fire on anything that moves."

Wolf knew what that meant. It meant that there were no survivors, and if there were, if there were people left alive inside the fallen city, then they were better off dead than the alternative. Living amongst *them*. Those monsters.

Those wretched goblins.

Wolf climbed back into the driver's hatch and put *Beast* in gear. *Beast* was Skunk's tank, had been since the war began. He'd named it after his first dog. Though he didn't care much for the Sarge and his decisions, Wolf liked that story, the story about his dog. It almost made the Sarge sound human. Skunk had once admitted to his crew— once a group of eight, now four—that he'd been a loner during his adolescence, and Beast was his only true friend. Coming from a military family, he'd moved around a lot. People changed, but Beast didn't. And that was why Skunk gave the German Shepherd's name to the tank. A lot had changed in the four years since the Goblin War started, but not *Beast*.

Beast had stayed the same.

Beast rolled on toward the city, crunching along the path of bones scattered before it. Bones of fallen soldiers. Bones of innocent people caught in the center of madness. Bones of fallen enemies, the goblins, those little mystical merchants of death.

Once they crossed over into the city, Wolf could sense danger all around them. He pressed the accelerator pedal to the floor, cranking the engine. The tank roared and picked up speed. Crumbling buildings whizzed by on the monitor ahead.

Skunk popped in behind him, and Wolf jumped when the Sarge said, "Slow down, fucker. We're moving too fast."

"Isn't that the idea?" Wolf asked, trying not to sound defiant and failing. "I mean, the fastest way between two points..."

"Never mind that shit." Skunk sounded aggravated and clearly wasn't used to being told anything other than *yessir.* "Now slow this fucker down before you run us into a goddamn deathtrap. Something smells funky about this place."

"We're not stopping, are we?" Wolf couldn't hide the tremble in his voice.

"What if we are? Would you have a problem with that, soldier?"

Slower to a response than Wolf knew he should have been: "No, sir. Not at all."

"Goddamn right," Skunk said, and then punched Wolf in his shoulder. It was no love tap. The jab rocked him in his seat, almost causing him to jerk the steering, forcing the tank off its straight path. "Goddamn right," he repeated and then he was gone.

Wolf continued to guide the tank through the dead city, fighting off the burn in the corners of his eyes.

☆☆☆

They managed another two-hundred yards before Skunk yelled, "All right, stop us up there."

Wolf pulled up to where Skunk had instructed, next to a small mountain of debris. In the mess, Wolf clearly saw some dead bodies, not yet fully decayed. Fresh. He wondered if other units had come this way recently, if there were indeed any survivors.

He wanted to protest Skunk's decision to stop here, but he knew where that would get him—nowhere.

"All right," Skunk said, lighting another cigar. Tendrils of smoke rose up, toward the now open hatch. A breeze blew through the cabin, cool and refreshing. "Let's grab some firepower and head out."

Bear and Peacock gave them no lip, which Wolf found a bit surprising. There was no reason to disembark their ride, no reason to go running through a city that had been claimed by the goblins. What was he doing? To Wolf, it seemed like madness. Like he'd lost it. Like he wanted out of this war and the only way to leave was getting him and everyone around him killed in action.

Over the last four years, *Beast* had lost four riders. Each death had taken its toll on the remaining members, but Wolf knew Skunk had taken it the hardest. He'd smoked more, cussed more, and had become curter with each loss. It affected him, Wolf knew, despite the macho persona he put on display daily.

No, leaving *Beast* made no sense.

This was supposed to be a shortcut.

This was turning into a long-cut.

This was turning into a mission.

"Sir..." Wolf squeaked. He'd climbed out of the pit and was now facing his three squad members. They were turned to him, each of them smoking, each of them giving the youngest member of their quartet their undivided attention. "What... um... what are we exactly doing here?"

Skunk looked to Bear and Peacock first, as if awaiting their approval. When both men shrugged, he turned back to Wolf.

"Son," the Sarge said, lowering his head, "there are just some things you don't understand about this war."

Wolf swallowed the egg-sized lump in his throat. "Help me understand."

Still pinching the wet end of his cigar between his teeth, Skunk sighed. "Okay, so, let's just say we didn't come upon this city by accident."

"What do you mean?" Wolf felt his heart plummet. He already knew he'd been lied to, sensed that much as soon as he was asked to park the tank. "Why are we here?"

"Well, we received some intel about a month ago. Intel claims there's a Stone Scepter hidden somewhere in this city."

A Stone Scepter? Wolf *had* heard of such a thing, back when the war had first started. A myth. An untruth. Something no human had ever set eyes upon. A goddamn rumor, that was all it had been. Something to keep the humans hopeful while city after city fell to the goblin hordes.

"A Stone Scepter?" Wolf asked, feeling his throat constrict. "I've heard of them..."

"Yeah, we've all *heard* of them. Intel claims someone actually saw one. *Here.* Not too far from where we are now." Skunk licked his lips. "The President himself asked us to check it out. Could be our only hope. Our only chance in this war."

"Why didn't you tell me?"

Skunk rolled his eyes. "Because, if we told you we'd be heading into a goddamn goblin nest, you would have freaked the fuck out. You're the only one who can drive this thing as good as me, and that means something, even if you are a cowardly little shit."

Wolf flinched as if he'd been spat at.

"Yeah, I know that probably hurts, but we ain't here to coddle your ass." Skunk dabbed his cigar out on the metal wall next to him. The orange-glowing ash fell to the floor like heavy feathers. "Anyway, we cherish your skills and you're a part of this team, whether you like it or not, so we couldn't have you lose your shit over this top-secret mission. Anyway, you don't need to worry. You can stay here, where it's safe. The three of us will head into that building," he jerked his thumb over his shoulder, "get in, get out, hopefully with as minimal contact as possible."

If there truly was a goblin nest inside, Wolf didn't think "minimal contact" would be possible. He'd seen a goblin nest only once in his life and it had been a nasty sight. They had lost two members of their team that day. Wolf had been lucky to live through it. If he thought back hard enough, he could still feel the warmth of his own piss running down his legs as he narrowly escaped the flood of goblins that had chased after him.

He knew he didn't have much of a choice. He couldn't say *no*. They were already in the city, they were already here, they were already—if intel's story were to prove correct— close to the Stone Scepter, which could be a game-changer in this seemingly lost war.

"Okay," he managed to say, breathing heavily. "I'll stay here. Wait for you guys."

"Give us fifteen minutes," Skunk said. "We're not back, you have my permission to roll on out of here, and go wherever you choose."

Home, Wolf thought. *That's where I'll go.*

But he wasn't sure he knew where that was anymore, or if it'd still be standing once he got there.

It was the longest ten minutes of Wolf's twenty years of existence. A minute felt like an hour. The entire ten felt like a day. And he still had five minutes to go. *Another eternity.*

He kept a watchful eye on the road to his right, which wasn't much of a road. More like a graveyard. There were dead bodies intermingled with fallen debris from nearby buildings, rubble and undesirable loot. Nothing moved in the distance. The city was still, dead, like every other city they'd come across during their journey. Across this derelict country, that was once The United States of America.

Before the goblins came. Before the creeps took over everything.

Sometimes it felt like they were the only ones left. That the suits in Washington were hidden underground somewhere and Skunk's squad were the last soldiers of the lost war. The last humans remaining.

Wolf looked to his left and surveyed the decrepit building, the one Skunk had led Bear and Peacock inside. Near the top, the corners had buckled, collapsed inside itself. At the bottom, near the foundation, a small yard of rubble lay in heaps. The windows were busted, dangerous shards remaining fixed in the frames. Wolf feared that if a strong gust of wind suddenly blew through the city, the building and the others like it would come tumbling down like a demolition implosion.

Wolf climbed to the top of the hatch and looked out, first up at the silver sky, then to the rest of the world. A powdery mist hid much of the city, the destruction lingering in stationed clouds. He strained his eyes to see past it, but it was no use. Wolf faced the building once more, checking his watch.

Two minutes.

He felt antsy. There was no way they were returning. What would happen when the fifteen minutes were up? He wanted to stay, wait it out, but Skunk had given him explicit instructions. *Roll on out of here.* And what if they came back in sixteen minutes? Seventeen? Twenty? What if they were still alive and, because of his impatience, because of his *cowardice*, his squad—the men he'd journeyed with for four long, hard years—were destined to die slow, agonizing deaths. Wolf knew he was no hero. This war didn't allow for heroes. Heroes died long before they could be labeled as such. Still... a part of him knew he couldn't leave his squad behind. They were a team. Live as a team...

...*Die as a team,* he heard Skunk's voice intrude on his thoughts.

Fifteen minutes had gone by. Still no sign of them. The city was as dead as ever, and eerily silent. No movement in the distance. No life within the building. No gunfire, cries for help. Nothing. Just the silence of a lost city, of a lost world.

Wolf climbed down the hatch ladder and went straight for the small weapons cache. He grabbed his M-4. Several magazines. Then he hustled back up the ladder. Slid down the side of the tank.

Rushing into the building, Wolf wondered how much longer he had left to live.

☆ ☆ ☆

Wolf took the corner fast, raised his M-4 and aimed at the shadows. The corridor was dim, populated with dark purple tones and shallow streaks of sunlight as it filtered in through the cracked concrete walls; however, the narrow walk was void of life. Crouching, he made his way to the end and peered down the next hallway. Much of the same. No goblins. No one representing the human race either.

He hustled to the end but stopped when a small figure appeared near his destination.

A goblin, Wolf immediately thought. He'd seen them up close only a handful of times. This one was short, about half the size of a regular man, and his hood veiled the slimy features of his face. Even in the distance, Wolf could make out the creature's hooked nose, bent downward awkwardly, like a banana only green like the skin of a cucumber.

The goblin glanced up, revealing its iridescent eyes, which changed from shades of piss-yellow to a cloudy gray. Wolf roared with surprise, and then aimed his weapon at the still-standing creature.

The thing only smiled at him. It held its staff, the goblins' weapon of choice, like a walking stick, and didn't raise it as Wolf had his. The goblin grinned, baring his shark-like teeth. Wolf wanted to turn away, run back to the tank and roll out of there. If this truly was a nest, then his team was—most likely—already dead.

The goblin muttered something in its native tongue. It sounded like a question. In the four years since the war had started, Wolf hadn't bothered to learn their language, sounds, common expressions. There were men who could but none of them had boarded *Beast*. He wished he could have learned, though. He'd have gladly taken up goblin studies instead of combat training. But there had been no choice in the matter. He'd been selected for combat.

The goblin parted its lips once again, making a sound that reminded Wolf of a truck engine stuttering to life. Wolf didn't hesitate this time around; he aimed, concentrating on the goblin's head, and pulled the trigger. The M-4 sung a short song and Wolf watched the goblin's head snap back, a splash of dark minty green splattering the wall behind it. The goblin crumpled to the floor, dropping its magic stick next to him.

Wolf struggled to breathe. That was his first kill with his field weapon. Over the past few years, he'd run over a few of the little green monsters with the tank, flattening their heads beneath the road-wheel's tracks, leaving their bodies behind for the vultures to pick apart. But that was it. Nothing up close. That was usually handled by Skunk and the others. Now, he was one of them. He was a killer.

And Wolf felt... surprisingly good.

He moved toward the end of the hall. He took the corner at once, keeping the M-4 out and ready, his finger trembling on the finger, not with fear but a nervous excitement. Adrenaline had flooded his veins and he suddenly felt invincible, like nothing in the world could stop him, not even a fierce legion of goblins.

Wolf kicked open a set of double-doors. He sprinted down the next hallway, which had been flooded with sunlight due to a good part of the ceiling having broken apart, crumbled on the street below. The way Wolf could see up into the next floor made him wonder how structurally safe it was to be in here, and, after he'd given it some serious thought, he thought it was best not to linger. With each step he wondered if the whole damn building would soon collapse.

He sprinted ahead, into the next room.

Two goblins rushed toward him from the opposite end of the corridor. They were squealing like tortured piglets, raising their wands, aiming. Wolf dropped the leading attacker with a three-second pull of his trigger. The bullets tore through the creature's body, shredding up its robe and skin. Green blood arced into the air, disappearing in misty bursts. The impact knocked the goblin back, off its feet, forcing it to the ground. Wolf immediately turned his aim on the next threat. He was a little late getting there, and the goblin already had his wand pointed, ready to fire. A beam of milky white light exploded from the end of his staff, and Wolf dropped to the floor to avoid being hit.

Burns like a sonofabitch, he remembered Skunk telling him once. *Seen a man's head melt. His face just turned into a puddle at his feet.*

From the ground, Wolf fired. The bullets caught the goblin in the lower half of its body, and as Wolf continued the assault, his aim traveled up its legs, up its torso, and ended with catching the goblin in the throat. More green blood sprinkled the air. The goblin dropped its wand and clamped its claw-like hands around the hole in its throat. Dropping to its knees, the goblin gurgled, trying to speak. Perhaps it was begging for mercy, perhaps it was cursing at Wolf, but, either way, Wolf didn't care. He got to his feet, and, while changing the magazine on the M-4, he strolled over to the kneeling creature. Once reloaded, he pressed the end of the flash hinder to the goblin's temple and pulled the trigger. Then he moved to the other fallen goblin, having noticed it was still alive and attempting to crawl away. Wolf ended its escape with one trigger squeeze.

Then he was off. Running down the next corridor. As he went, he heard something in the distance. It sounded like babies crying. He stopped. Listened. It was coming close. Slowly, he continued, then stopped when he realized the sound was a lot closer than his ears had led him to believe.

It was coming from behind a door about twenty feet ahead and to his right. Cautiously, he approached the door, walking lightly on his toes as if the slightest pressure on the floor would cause the world to drop out from under him. Once there, he opened the door slowly, allowing the noises to escape the room.

He backed away when he saw a room full of infants. Not human infants, *goblin* infants, about thirty little ones huddled together in a long, narrow maintenance closet. In the center of the room, a female goblin sat cross-legged, nursing one of the newborns. She glanced up at Wolf, unfazed by his presence. She didn't stop feeding the infant, nor did she scramble for the closest weapon, which Wolf saw there was none. Not really. A few broomsticks and rolls of paper towels, none of which would defend her against the firepower of Wolf's M-4.

For a few seconds, Wolf could only stare at the goblin and the small crowd of children around her, each of them awaiting their turn at the teat. Wolf raised his gun, began aiming, not sure exactly where to start. In fact, he wondered if he should start at all.

The mother goblin spoke, an inarticulate noise that sounded like gargling mouthwash. There was a hint of venom in her voice and Wolf knew she wasn't inviting him to get in line behind the infants. She repeated the words—if you could call them that—over and over again. Each time, she became more animated, baring her teeth and snarling.

Wolf looked the room over, surveying each of the young—

their little cherubic faces, hooked noses and inhuman eyes that changed color depending on the angle.

Future killers. Future rulers of this world.

Wolf knew he had to eliminate them, wipe them clean from the earth. Still, he couldn't bring himself to do it. He couldn't bring himself to slaughter the innocent.

Slowly, he backed away, shutting the door, leaving the room and everything inside just as he had found it.

Then he sprinted down the hall, toward the center of the ruined building.

There, he'd find his crew.

What was left of them.

When he burst into the main room, a capacious area with arched vaulted ceilings that might once have been a banquet hall, he saw his three fellow soldiers hanging from the center like a human chandelier. They were tied together, each of the men cut and bleeding. Their lacerations leaked steadily, and, even from the ground Wolf could see how deep their wounds ran. Their blood fell in steady droplets and dripped into a large chalice, which sat in the center of a small altar.

Wolf looked up. Of the three men, only one of them was conscious. It was Skunk. His eyes were open but just barely, on the verge of finding the long sleep. On the path to unconsciousness. Wolf took one step forward and realized what had been gathered around the altar—a collection of goblins, each one of them fast asleep. There had to be about fifty of the little filthy monsters, each one snoozing, snoring, sleeping their way through the apocalypse.

Wolf knew exactly what this was the moment he set eyes on the hibernating goblins, the blood falling into the golden chalice, and the scepter resting on the altar. He'd walked right into a *summoning gathering*. He'd heard the tales before, the legend of the goblin *Kings*. *Goblin Kings* were goblins of a higher order on the scale of magic, powerful beings that were said to have enough magic coursing through their veins to demolish an entire country with a single wave of the wand. Wolf never exactly doubted the tales, but he did write them off on account he had never seen a Stone Scepter before. Now he had, and he saw the altar, and the hibernating nest, and—the city of bones. All those human remains. It suddenly made sense.

The last requirement of the Ceremony of Kings.

It was humans—flesh, blood, and bones.

Wolf suddenly felt weak in the knees, weak all over.

He raised his M-4, wondering how many he could take out before the gunfire would wake every nest within a five-mile radius. He figured he could waste most of them before they overpowered him, but that would still leave him with the problem at hand—the Ceremony of Kings, and his friends being used as tools of the sacrament.

When Skunk laid his eyes on him, they immediately shot open. The leader of their pack squirmed in the netting that confined him and the other soldiers. *"Wolf,"* he whispered. *"Don't do it."*

Wolf's trigger felt as heavy as a bag of sand. "Why?" he asked, his voice trembling.

A few of the goblins stirred in their sleep.

"The mission. Don't forget about the mission."

Skunk was right. The Stone Scepter was their mission. He needed to bring it back to the nearest human camp, give it to those in charge so they could pass it off on the first available scientific research team. So they could study it. Learn everything about it. And... use it for themselves. Turn it against their enemies.

"Can't... let them live."

"Wolf!"

More of the creatures were disturbed by the voices, but not enough to be ripped from their dreams.

"Don't do anything stupid."

Wolf knew the Sarge was right. He needed the scepter. Not to kill these monsters.

"Get the scepter and get the fuck out of here. Forget about

us."

A deep trench in Skunk's legs dripped into the Chalice. Wolf knew the rest of his group was done for, and even if he did manage to get them down safely, the movement alone would be enough to wake up the entire nest. Instead, Wolf tiptoed around the sleeping party, making sure to place his toes on the spaces between the bodies. A few times he accidentally kicked one of the goblins, but it wasn't hard enough to disturb their sleep.

He'd danced his way to the center of the room and climbed the altar. Bending down, he reached and grabbed the Stone Scepter, and, as it glowed a heavenly white, he felt its power run through him. He was filled with a divine sensation, as if the power within the long staff would lift him up off the altar and into the clouds above the building. Take him on a tour through the cosmos. It was a funny feeling, one he wasn't sure he felt completely comfortable with. There was an unnatural prickling of his nerves. And it wasn't... human.

A part of him wanted to drop the damn thing and return to Plan A—waste every single one of the goblins while they slept.

Looking up at Skunk and reading his expression, Wolf knew the Sarge didn't approve.

"Get out of here. Get it to Langley. Get it there safely. And then tell them I relieved you of your duties. Go home, Wolf. Wherever that is for you."

Wolf didn't know if home was still there, and right now, home was the farthest thing from his mind. He turned, facing the exit.

Lining the doorway, were four goblins, each one of them hunched and breathing heavily, each armed with their magical weapons.

They screamed, a high-pitched whine that caused Wolf to drop the scepter and clap his hands over his ears.

The entire nest awoke at once.

Wolf grabbed his M-4, ignoring the awful pitch coming from the gathering, and fired upward, at the long rope attached to the net holding the three men. His bullets were true, severing the rope in half. He jumped out of the way as the three men fell toward the altar, a good twenty-foot drop. Everyone seemed to land safely, except for Bear, who landed foot first. His ankle snapped on contact with the stone slab, and Wolf watched his bone punch through the skin. The man's scream rose above the goblin's whining.

Without thinking, Wolf handed his knife to Skunk, and turned back to the crowd of gathering goblins. He swore they had multiplied in the seconds it had taken to shoot down his squad. Without waiting for his crew to ready themselves, Wolf fired on the crowd, aiming at the armed goblins first. He cut down two of them before they could return fire. But the other two were already aiming, the ends of their rods glowing with a whiteness that brightened the entire room.

"Get down!" Wolf yelled out and jumped from the altar.

Skunk and Peacock were able to move off the altar, but Bear—in his reduced state—could not. The two streams of white hit him in the chest, knocking him off the altar with force, sending him airborne. Wolf watched his chest deteriorate, watched the magical energy from the goblin's weapon eat through flesh and muscle and bone, until there was nothing but a see-through hole the size of a bowling ball in Bear's chest. The man slid across the dust-covered floor, dying as he went.

"Where are your weapons?" Wolf asked, as he poked his head over the altar, watching the goblins arm themselves via the weapons cache in the rear of the room.

"I don't know what they did with them," Skunk replied.

"We're so fucked!" Peacock bellowed, pounding his fist on the concrete ground, hard enough to break his wrist, or so Wolf thought. "Fuck this shit. Let's just use what ammo we have left and take the easy way out."

Skunk grabbed his subordinate by the throat. "No one is killing themselves, you fucking coward."

Peacock scowled.

Skunk turned to Wolf. "Kill the ones with weapons. We'll pick up some of theirs as we move on. Peacock?"

Peacock's lips quivered with anger. "Yes, sir?"

"You're responsible for the scepter." He handed him the goblin's treasure.

"Yes, sir."

Peacock didn't sound like he cared much for Skunk's decision, but he listened anyway.

Wolf stood up, putting himself in the goblins' view. "Okay, let's do this." He fired on the crowd, hitting some targets. Clouds of green blood exploded in the air. He moved down the steps, continuing to fire, clearing a path toward the exit.

The goblins returned fire with their globes of white light. Wolf dodged them, and watched the energy source melt through the floor, where it landed. The balls of light that sailed over his head punched through the wall, eating their way through the studs and sheathing on the other side. He wondered how far it would travel. If its path would end or if it'd go on forever. He wondered if the floor and walls slowed it down or if it covered the proceeding distance at the same speed. There were a great many things Wolf wished he knew about the goblins—*so much to learn.*

He took out three more of them, shooting them in the face at close range, watching their tiny little brains bloom into flowers of green filth, and made for the exit.

"We're gonna make it!" Peacock yelled. "We're gonna fucking make it!"

As he spoke the words, a crawling goblin, one who'd been knocked to the floor by the hustle of its brethren, latched onto his leg and bit into his ankle.

Peacock screamed and looked down. First, he tried to stomp on the thing's head, but that didn't do much except allow the creature to really sink its teeth in. Then he began thrashing the thing with the scepter, bringing the staff down on its head. By the time he killed it, cracked its skull open and watched green, syrupy liquid pool out from underneath its fractured cranium, he had another attacker. Then another. The goblins had leapt onto his back, began biting his neck and ears, chewing on his flesh. He screamed when one of them tore off his ear with its teeth.

Ferociously, the little beasts continued to sink their teeth into him, ripping away pockets of skin and muscle with each nibble.

Skunk turned and held out his hands. "Give me the scepter!"

In his last moment alive, Peacock tossed the scepter to Skunk. The second it left his hands, the nest of goblins swarmed him, covering every square inch of him.

As Peacock screamed his last screams, Wolf and Skunk made their exit, and headed for the street.

☆ ☆ ☆

They almost reached the exit without further interference from the goblin horde. As they sprinted down the last hallway out of there, shadows formed at the end of their path. Small shadows. Tiny shadows. *Hungry* shadows.

And one tall shadow. A female. The female Wolf had seen no less than twenty minutes ago in a maintenance closet, giving nourishment to her young.

The small army of goblin children leered at them. Their contempt was almost palpable.

Wolf knew he should have executed them when he had had the chance. But had he done that, then he would have awoken the sleeping goblins, which would have meant they would have never gotten this far. Had he slaughtered the goblin children and infants, their chances of getting the scepter back to Langley would have been lost.

Wolf raised his gun. As the horde rushed them, Wolf fired. The dead fell like bowling pins.

Skunk got busy with his knife, running straight into the crowd. He slashed and hacked his way through the horde. When he reached the female, he faced her with three goblin children clinging to his legs. They had chewed away his calves. She released a high-pitched scream in his face, and he silenced her with one quick slash across her throat. The slit erupted with a powerful green spray, splashing him in the face, painting him in the goblin's blood. Then he went to work on the three little bodies near his feet. He executed them swiftly, being careful not to slip in the small green river the floor had become.

More latched onto Skunk's back. There were just too many of them. Wolf did the best he could with his M-4, but they were outnumbered. Skunk couldn't hold his own with just the knife. He cut and cut, but he also had gained about five goblin children as passengers, and they were gnawing through his neck awfully quick.

"Kid!" Skunk shouted. He tossed the scepter to Wolf. The kid caught it with one hand, the other continuing to spray the hallway with bullets. "Take it. Run. As fast as you can toward the exit."

The room had thinned considerably. If Wolf took a straight path, firing ahead as he ran, then he'd probably make it. Unless he slipped on the slick floor, which was possible.

So much blood, Wolf thought.

He did as his Sarge commanded. He ran straight for the exit, firing everything he had, bowling over the goblin children as he went. When he made it through the throng and when there were no more obstacles standing in his way, he only had one leech on his back, which he was able to fling off with ease. He turned and sprayed the crowd with more firepower, thinning the herd even more. But it wasn't enough to spring Skunk free.

Wolf watched as the goblin children brought Skunk to the floor and jumped all over him, hiding him beneath their wall of young, green flesh. There were so many of them, Wolf couldn't even provide his Sarge with a mercy kill.

Wolf hopped up onto the *Beast* and entered the hatch at once. Once he was down the stairs, he tossed the scepter aside and headed straight for the controls. He fired up the tank and rolled on out of there. In the rearview camera, he saw goblins flood out of the building like ants from their hill. For a few seconds, he thought they were going to catch him, climb the tank, and find a way inside. But as the Beast picked up speed, they fell farther and farther behind.

In less than a mile, he'd lost them completely.

In less than five minutes, the city of bones was shrouded in sandy clouds and gray light.

Five minutes later and the city of bones was just a memory, one that felt more like a dream than reality.

Wolf drove to Langley. He handed his superiors the scepter, the item which he was told would "win them the war."

After that, he shook some hands, received several accolades, and was then granted leave.

Then he went home. To what was left of it.

HOW TO KILL A BEAR WITH A BOW AND ARROW

MILO MEDLOCK SAT in a tree, the tallest oak in Red River, and waited for the bear.

He'd seen the report on TV last night; a black bear had been spotted sometime between six and nine, going through garbage cans on Southland Drive, near the bay. Three people reported the bear's presence, and one of them had stood on their porch and shouted at the beast, hoping the loud noises would spook off the bear. But it hadn't. According to the report, the bear had ignored all human requests and continued sifting through the garbage for edibles. Once it had finished, it hustled into the nearby woods, and no one had ever seen or heard from the beast since, though, the newscasters hadn't been shy about pointing out that the bear could reemerge any time it pleased.

Milo aimed his bow and arrow down at the ground. It'd been years since he'd shot the thing, and only dug it out for occasions like this. He wasn't ordinarily a hunter—he'd never killed an animal in his entire life, unless you counted flies and the occasional hornet. Never killed anything bigger than his thumb. But, when times called for it, when the neighborhood was under attack by bears or by criminals posing as post office workers, Milo Medlock grabbed his bow and arrow.

True story: About two years ago, Milo and his wife, Tilda, were watching the news one afternoon when a report came across the screen, informing the good people of Red River to be on the lookout for a dangerous criminal posing as a mailman. Apparently the scumbag was knocking on doors, pretending to deliver the mail, and then breaking into houses. Milo, not having a gun in the house to protect his family from the outside threat, had gone straight for the bow and arrow, the one his father had made him when he was just a small boy, almost forty years ago. Tilda thought the idea was ridiculous—she thought most of his ideas were—but she couldn't convince him to keep the doors locked and the windows shut instead of sitting on the roof and scoping out potential burglars dressed like mailmen.

"Just let the authorities handle it, you schmuck," she had told him. "Who do you think you are? Robin Hood?"

He'd told her that he obviously wasn't Robin Hood, but he was a pretty good shot. He'd practiced regularly in the garage with targets, beer cans and such. He'd never entered any archery competitions, but Roman—a friend from the office—always encouraged him to do so. But Milo wasn't the confident type and he never could bring himself to complete the online form for Red River's annual archery contest. He'd known how well he could shoot, but what if there was someone better? Someone more accurate? Someone who could split his own bullseye right down the center of his arrow, just like in the movies. He didn't think he could handle that kind of defeat. Even though he'd hit that mailman when he'd come strolling up the driveway with no car behind him, no sack of mail on his back, hit him right where he'd intended. Luckily, it *had* been the burglar, otherwise there might have been legal repercussions of his sure shot. He'd hit the thug right in the leg, through the calf, and made sure not to inflict a mortal wound. He could have if he'd wanted to.

If he'd wanted to.

If I'd wanted to, he thought, as he shifted in his makeshift tree stand. He was by no means a hunter, had never even given the sport any thought; something about killing innocent animals made him uneasy.

But what about the bear? Wasn't he innocent? After all, the bear hadn't done anything. Not really. It had invaded a suburban street and raided some garbage cans for food. It'd probably been hungry. It'd just needed some snacks. Something to get by on until something better came along. No harm in that. It wasn't a man-eater for Christ's sakes. It hadn't left the street a bloody mess of haphazardly strewn people parts. It had done nothing except to attempt to satisfy its most basic need—to eat. And it hadn't shed a drop of human blood to do so.

Not yet.

And that was where Milo Medlock drew the line. He wanted to remain proactive. Like the situation with the mailman imposter, he wanted to down the beast before it could inflict damage on the community. Sure, it'd started with a few overturned trash cans, but what came next? A few butchered people? Kids shredded like rag dolls on their way home from school? What if the animal wandered into that sixty-five and older community down the block? Granny might be watering her front lawn one minute, getting her fucking arm ripped off the next. Milo didn't need that. Not in his neighborhood. Not when he had the means to do *something* about it.

"You'll never kill that bear," Tilda had told him. "You don't have the sack." She'd continued to smoke her Marlboro Reds and watch Drew Carey on the television. She was only forty but she acted almost twice her age. Constantly nagging and crotchety. She'd been the reason Milo collected so much overtime, why he'd spent so much time in the garage with his bow and arrow and his almost-endless supply of Miller High Life.

"You said the same thing about the mailman who wasn't a mailman," Milo had told her. "Said I wouldn't get him."

"Not what I said, numb nuts." She'd scoffed then, between

drags of her smoke. "Said you'd get yourself killed and unfortunately I was goddamn wrong about that."

"You know, you're a miserable wench, you know that?"

She'd ignored his comment, acted as if he hadn't said anything at all.

He'd leaned his head against the wall, and breathed in a cloud of second-hand smoke. He'd coughed something fierce and his asthma instantly flared. "Would it kill you *not* to smoke in the house? You know I have trouble breathing."

She'd flipped him the bird.

Sitting in the tree was peaceful. Milo breathed in the fresh atmosphere, his lungs full of healthy, clean air. It made him happy being alone. Happy to breathe. Happy to be amongst the silence of nature, those intermittent sounds of birds twittering and branches swaying, the swoosh of the wind passing through the trees. He closed his eyes and thought he was in heaven. He had no desire to head back, back home where hell waited.

☆☆☆

Milo hadn't any idea where to start. He'd watched a few Youtube videos on bear hunting but it hadn't seemed like a big enough sport. All the hunting videos featured deer or duck, and even less of them featured the bow and arrow. Everything was shotguns or rifles *(mostly rifles)* and those videos bored him. How hard was it to put down an animal using a gun? Seriously. At close enough range, a kill was almost automatic with a gun. Pull the trigger and the gun delivers instant death. No skill there. Now, to kill with a bow and arrow, one needed to be close. Real close. But not too close. Especially to a bear. Too close meant your head was coming off. Too close meant instant death, *for you.*

Milo had found one bear hunting video he liked and had watched it several times. One of the things the video preached was making sure to procure the proper license. Bear licenses were issued at certain times of the year depending on your State, and the instructor of the video told him not all states allowed bear hunting and to check the local gun shops for more details. Milo had done his research; New Jersey allowed black bear hunting and, sure enough, black bears were in season. He'd gone down to the local Waldo-Mart and gotten himself good and registered.

He was now licensed to kill... *bears.*

"Bet you're after that black bear everyone keeps talking about," the guy behind the gun counter had said to him.

Milo had nodded.

"Well, good luck, partner. Got any bait?"

"Bait?" The question had caught Milo by surprise. "What do you mean?"

"Need bait to catch a bear." The gun salesman had shrugged. "How else you gonna get that close?"

Milo hadn't thought about bait. He'd thought he'd peruse the forest that bordered Red River and hopefully pick up the garbage-sniffer's trail. That was what the Youtube video had taught him to do. Bait hadn't crossed his mind.

Now, in the tree, he looked down at his bait. It was a good choice, he thought, and he wondered if anyone else would agree. *Probably not,* he thought, smiling.

"Don't worry," he called down. "That bear'll be along soon and this will all be behind us."

His bait stifled a cry and called something back, words which were ignored. He'd heard something rustle amongst the leaves, and when he looked down in the direction of the sounds, he spotted a cluster of green foliage bouncing back and forth. Something had disturbed the shrubbery, something big.

Sure enough, a second later, a snout emerged from the forest. A massive, fur-covered cranium followed. Behind that, the bulk of the black bear came into view. It was bigger than Milo had expected, and, even from his vantage point, he could tell the beast was above average. In fact, he didn't think black bears grew to be that big. Its girth surprised him. No wonder the neighborhood had been shaken; if he'd seen that thing digging through his trash, he might have given this bear hunt idea a second thought. Suddenly the bow and arrow felt weightless in his hands.

The black bear moved out from the brush and into the clearing slowly, waddling back and forth, reminding Milo of the Youtube video. The bear in that video had been equally sluggish and in no rush to go anywhere. Milo thought that might change when the arrows began to fly, but he wasn't so sure. He didn't know how many it'd take to down the beast, but he'd brought two full quivers, twelve in each. He was hoping to only waste one arrow—hit the monster right between the eyes.

The monster.

The bear.

Were they the same thing?

Then the screaming started.

"OH MY GOD!"

Milo wished he'd put duct tape over her mouth. It would've been better that way, but he had needed something to grab the bear's attention. He couldn't risk it passing by without noticing the bait. He needed it close. He needed it practically on her so all he had to do was look down and fire. Shoot. Release the arrow, and watch it penetrate the skull right between its eyes.

The bear spotted Tilda and Tilda started screaming, really letting him have it.

"GET ME OUT OF HERE, MILO! GODDAMMIT! YOU SON OF A BITCH! I KNEW I SHOULD HAVE LEFT YOU! YOU WORTHLESS, LIMP-DICK FUC—"

The bear jumped back on its hind legs and roared. The bestial vocalization moved birds from their positions in the trees. It silenced Tilda at once. It gave Milo a rush of adrenaline and coated his skin in gooseflesh.

All of a sudden, things felt real.

There was no going back now. He aimed with his bow and arrow. He held his concentration on the bear's massive target of a head. The beast lowered itself down on all fours.

It jogged toward the potential meal tied to the tallest oak tree in all of Red River.

Milo waited.

"HELP ME!" Tilda cried.

The bear approached, closing the distance with more speed than Milo had anticipated. The gap between his wife and the black bear slimmed. He looked down the arrow, picturing what it'd look like buried in the beast's skull.

The beast.

The monster.

Which one?

When the bear was about five feet away from Tilda—Tilda who now screamed and cried and begged to continue on with her lethargic lifestyle—the bear roared again, pushing the hair back off the face of its next meal. The bear took the last five feet in a slow, calculated approach. It sniffed its food before attempting to eat it.

This is good, Milo thought. This hesitation on the bear's part would allow him to adjust slightly, allow him to ready his shot, steady his aim. He did so accordingly, making sure he wouldn't miss on the first attempt.

But when he was ready to release the arrow, let his fingers slip off the string, he found himself unable to do so.

The bear sniffed under Tilda's blouse. She whimpered and turned her head. Then she screamed when the bear opened its jaws and bit down on her thick thigh. It tore away a section of meat, a slab of raw muscle.

Tilda screamed until her vocal cords broke.

Milo continued to sit in the tree, keeping his aim on the bear, but as time slipped, so did his view on the current situation. He'd come here to kill a bear. A beast. A plight on society. Something that terrorized and killed; something that must not live for the safety and well-being of others.

But that wasn't the bear, was it?

The bear hadn't hurt a soul, not until it had met Tilda Medlock, the real beast, the real monster in Milo's life.

The bear ate a piece of the woman's thigh and decided it deserved seconds. It lunged forward, snout first, and tore away another piece of Tilda's leg, from her calf this time. She thrashed around and cried out, but she was no match for the all-powerful jaws of the woodland critter. It feasted on her muscle, wrestling with the blood and skin, digging its nose deeper into her, pulling away with more gore and muscle, more pieces of Tilda.

Milo thought he should look away. He thought he should do something, other than sit in the tree stand he'd made for himself, his front-row seat to his wife's evisceration.

He decided he should end the beast's life.

He readjusted his aim and let the arrow fly. It connected true with a wonderful *THWACK!*

He wouldn't need another arrow.

The beast was dead.

And the bear continued to eat.

SIREN'S END

CLENCHING FISTFULS OF wet sand, the man climbed his way up the beach. Behind him, the waves clapped against the shore, sounding like the duel of distant pistols. Rallying against the pain, he forced his head around and glared at the ocean, the rocky sheet of endless gray. In that moment, somewhere beyond his vision, he heard his men scream, deck boards crack, and disturbed waters growl.

Was it the waters that growled? he thought, looking up, spotting the sky and noticing it held the same colorless hue as the ocean—here, the world looked dead. *Was it really the waters?*

Or something else?

When he couldn't take any more of the dismal scenery, he returned to his long crawl. Up the beach, a stretch of dunes blocked his vision of the deserted coastal town, a place he'd been before, a place that ended up not being deserted at all. There was one place that had kept its lanterns lit—a small pub about two streets in from the dunes.

If I can make it, the proprietor will help me. He had to. It was the least he could do. *He'll nurse me back to health and then...*

And then what? The survivor had no ship; that had gone down in a glorious battle with the sea and...

Those things.

Whatever they were.

He had no outs. He was trapped here. On this godforsaken edge of the world. This little island off the coast of the mainland.

The survivor managed his way up the beach, writhing like a worm through the sand, kicking his legs in rhythm with his upper torso. Surprisingly, the dunes weren't hard to summit. He'd reached the top and scouted the first avenue he'd set his eyes on, located his bearings, and then decided which course to take.

He slid down the dunes on his bottom. When he reached the stony, uneven road below, he tested his feet. His knees wobbled with the slightest bit of pressure. He sat back down. Five minutes later he tried again. Better this time. Easier. Less wobble in his knees, less ache in his bones. Not perfect. He spent another quarter hour standing, allowing his muscles to acclimate. It felt like he hadn't stood in years.

How long had it been?

He didn't know how long he'd been drifting in the Atlantic, floating among the flotsam of his ruined ship. Days? Weeks? None of it mattered now. His life—the only precious thing he had left to worry about. What little of it remained.

He hobbled down the street, toward the small inn/pub combo. He took the cobblestone walkway two steps at a time, paused, and then took two more. This approach ensured his body would not become overtaxed. His muscles protested movement of any kind, and hot flares of pain streaked up and down his body. He longed for the comfort of a mattress and pillow, the warmth of a hot compress and kindling in a fireplace. Tea. Yes, lots of tea. The phantom aroma of a hot cup filled his nostrils and that alone was enough to keep him warm for the time being.

A half hour later, the survivor found himself before Siren's End, the last pub on the edge of the world. He glanced around the dead street, remembering the days when this seaside town hadn't been so derelict, when townsfolk of all kinds populated these streets, bustling about their day. Those days were long gone, and it had been years since the shops around Siren's End had seen business, save for the pub and their occasional visits from passing fishermen and semi-lost seafarers. The occasional crew of adventurous pirates.

Now, everything here was closed.

Everything here was dead.

Except for Siren's End.

And Garrett Means, last captain of the King's Folly, aimed to find out why.

The buildings he passed were covered in soot, the fires that caused their condition long since smoldered. Debris littered the streets; old newspaper pages blew across his path, wooden slots from ruined crates and rum barrels lay across the cobblestone walkways, and spoiled food lined the gutters, too rotten even for the rats to claim.

A town in utter ruin.

When he arrived at Siren's End, he marveled over the impeccable condition of the inn's exterior. Fresh paint coated the brick facade. Black smoke unfurled from the chimney, suggesting the fireplace was in peak working condition. Gulls circled the sky above, hoping to secure fresh scraps from the kitchen.

Captain Means heard nothing from his position. The place seemed quiet on the inside, along with the apocalyptic town it resided in.

This dead city on a dead island off the coast of—if what Means had witnessed was any inclination—a future dead country.

Means headed for the door and was surprised to find the entrance unlocked. He shouldered his way inside, stood in the open doorway for a moment and took in the sights of the interior décor. It was as nice as any other pub along the coast. A place nice as this should have packed in quite a crowd, but today the joint was empty. Not a single patron was cozied up at the bar or occupying the nearby tables and Means suspected the inn's check-in log would prove every available room vacant.

Behind the bar stood a shadow.

"You've returned," the barkeep said, drying a drinking glass with a dirt-smudged towel. "With far less company than when last we met."

Tempted to rush the man, Means controlled himself, harnessing his raw emotions. He was in no condition to fight. No condition to take another step but he did so anyway, fending off the dizzying lightheadedness that crawled throughout his skull, erasing his worldly perception as it circumnavigated his dome.

"You..." Means managed to say, continuing his little two-step toward the closest stool. "You..."

"Yes, me. I know. A bastard, ain't I?"

"Did you know? Did you know she was among them? My Isabella? My sweet?"

The elderly man scratched his thick mutton chops with his free hand. "Isabella? Isabella?" He squinted. "Yes, I seem to remember an Isabella. Your sweet, you say?"

"You know damn well. I told you we were searching for her during our first arrival at this godforsaken place."

"I recall, yes, I recall."

"Where is she now?" Means put out his arms, resting his palms on the edge of the bar. He didn't know how long he could support his weight like this—maybe a few seconds—and then lifted his leg so he could plant his rear on the cushioned stool. His other leg couldn't handle the shift in weight and gave out, causing him to fall to the floor.

The barkeep heehawed. Another gut-shaking outburst followed. "Sure are a persistent bastard, aren't ya?"

Harnessing a few shreds of strength, Means rolled over. He faced the barkeep, the reason his brain would manufacture nightmares for every sleep to come. His lips parted, revealing teeth as yellow as a ripe banana. More laughter came from the insidious proprietor; it echoed in the empty chamber that was Siren's End.

"You fed us to those things," Means said, his lips stinging with a numb sensation. He sat up, his spine feeling like it had separated in several places. "You... sent us to that island."

"Aye, I did." The barkeep was pleasantly okay with this fact, causing Means cheeks to burn with indignation. "If it's any consolation, I take no pleasure in feeding them. They mean nothing to me."

A lie. A bold lie. His smiling face told Means that he enjoyed the arrangement very much. *Too much.*

"You're a liar. A traitor to the Royal Navy."

The barkeep shrugged. "Perhaps. Perhaps, my boy. Perhaps."

Means felt a surge of energy flow through him, and he launched himself to his feet. The sudden movement caught the barkeep by surprise. The man's eyes flared, his lips naturally forming a tight oval. He backed away, seemingly expecting Means to clamber over the bar and begin his assault, a barrage of blows that would leave him bloody or worse. *Dead,* dead like the islands his little monsters ruled.

"Do I scare you, old man?" Means asked.

The barkeep didn't respond. He stared at Means, holding the dirty glass out in front of him like a pointy knife.

Means bared his teeth. "I should kill you."

The barkeep's rigid expression broke, and his twisted smile returned. "You won't hurt me. You won't dare. You've seen what the women are capable of."

"You are a devil."

"Of sorts."

Means couldn't believe what he was about to ask. "What sort of devil are you?"

The barkeep brayed with more laughter, a deafening outburst that threatened Means's eardrums.

"Man," the barkeep said, his voice barely above a whisper. "The worst devil of them all."

40 Hours Ago

A pillar of fire in front of him and Means realizes the foremast is burning. He turns and realizes the mainmast has been set aflame, too. His men are scurrying across the deck, searching for either means of escape or recovery. Judging from the chaos, it seems the latter isn't likely. Men are abandoning ship, jumping overboard head first into the rough waters below. The entire stock of rowboats has been deployed, already gone amidst the fog, the all-encompassing white glow that surrounds them all.

He quickly wonders how he ended up here. He remembers Siren's End, the barkeeper drawing them a map to the island located a little less than fifty nautical miles from where they had sat and drank ale, and ate until they slipped into mini comas.

An Island of Women, *he had said, which, to men who'd spent a great deal of time on the sea and limited hours amongst the company of women, sounded heavenly. They had set course at once and sailed west, toward the location of this great mystery.*

An Island of Women, Means remembers thinking. If Isabella is anywhere, she is there.

Without much effort, they found the island. They discovered the women. But what happened after was very far from what the crew had envisioned upon hearing the barkeep's tale.

What they had found there was death.

Means shakes away the haunted memory of their visit. If he wants to survive, he needs to focus on just that, not past tribulations. He pushes himself to his feet and scrambles toward the edge of the ship. He looks down into the turbulent waters, eyeing the majority of his cowardly crew. They're swimming in the water. No, not swimming. Thrashing.

They're not alone.

The women are with them.

Feeding on them.

Their screams echo across the sea. The encroaching fog envelops them. All that's left of them are their final cries for mercy.

Means turns back to the deck. The fire is out of control now, spreading down the masts, conquering most of the boom and the roof of the captain's quarters. His materials, most importantly the portrait of his Isabella and the diamond intended for her finger only, are most likely on their way to becoming char and ash. A tower of fire stands tall over the bow. There are minutes left before the flames will travel to the deck and burn away the last remaining lumber of the sinking ship.

There's no rescuing King's Folly. They say a captain should always go down with his ship, but that's not for him. He has a reason to live—he has Isabella. She's out there somewhere. Among the women. Among the chaos.

Maybe if I can convince her, he thinks. Maybe if I can show her how much I love her?

He hasn't yet, which is why she left in the first place, why she joined this secretive commune.

He thinks about hurling himself over the edge when he hears a voice call his name. It's soft and familiar, somewhat comforting despite the anxiety lacing his nerves.

"Garrett?" she says, and Means turns to her.

"Isabella?"

She's standing in the center of the deck, Her Majesty's torn sails ablaze above her.

"Isabella," he confirms. She doesn't look the same as she had seven months ago, before her disappearance. She still has her slender appearance, her gaunt face, the features prevalent in the poor and homeless, but there is something different. Maybe it's her gown, the stark white garment that covers every inch of her flesh, making her look more angel than woman. Maybe it's the blotches of blood around her mouth, the remnants of her last meal. Maybe it's the teeth, those sharpened twigs of calcium, those tools of carnage.

Maybe it's her nails, long and curled like hawk talons. It's the combination of these atrocities that contribute to her altered visage.

The woman he loves is no longer the woman he loves.

"What... what happened to you?"

She smiles, her bloody lips curling at the ends. "I've been reborn."

"You've become a devil."

"No, Garrett." Her face grows with concern as she steps toward him. "No, not at all. I've found a new way of life. That old life wasn't for me. You know that."

"We would have been happy together. You and I."

She shakes her head. "No, you would have been happy together." She nods her head to the side and bends her knee, a courteous gesture that comes off more like a warning. "I told you the married life wasn't meant for me."

"Your father... he promised you to me."

Her posture stiffens; her features constrict. "I am promised to nobody."

"We had an accord."

"I am not property!" she spits, flecks of blood sent airborne. "I am not his to pawn! Like some basic treasure!"

The venom in her voice nudges him backward. He feels the deck's rails against his back.

"Isabella, I'm sorry."

"You men," she continues, pointing at him as if he's every man that ever lived. "You men take and you take, and you don't consider us. Our feelings. Our wants and needs. You make us live like slaves."

"No, Isabella," he says. His mouth is dry and cottony, and the words almost don't come out correctly. "I love you. You know I do. You have to know that."

"You smother us with your love."

Three shapes form in his periphery. Three women, all of them clad in the same white material, all of their faces stained the same red.

"You smother us with your affection, your ideas of the perfect life." The closer she gets to him, the tighter his

throat becomes. *"But you don't know perfection like I know perfection. You've never tasted the flesh and blood of men, of God's so-called greatest creation."*

"Now hold on just a minute," he says, barely. Feels like someone is squeezing his vocal cords. *"You're sick. I can help you. I can nurse you back to—"*

"I don't need your help," she says, lunging for him.

Before he can react, her mouth is on his throat. A wave crashes against the ship, and a salty spray dots the back of his neck. The next thing he feels is his blood leaving his body via the gaping hole Isabella has created near his jugular. Squirts of hot blood run down his neck, underneath his attire, coating his chest and stomach.

"Good-bye, my love," she says with such disdain.

His heart breaks in two as he's flung overboard, and into the stormy waters below.

Means clasped his hands around his throat, feeling his way around every inch of flesh. His heart sank when his fingers danced over the open area where flesh and muscle should have been. The cavity was dry and deep. The crusty nature of the wound suggested his body had recovered from Isabella's bite and was on the mend. But the depth and size of the cavity concerned him. It was deeper than an ordinary bite, at least by an inch or two, and about the size of a clenched fist. It wasn't exactly the kind of trauma one recovers from, even with proper medical attention.

"Mirror," Means demanded hoarsely.

The barkeep had one handy behind the bar and brought it to him promptly.

Means discovered his reflection. His vision was immediately drawn to the missing flesh on his neck. His breath caught in his throat upon witnessing his disfigurement. Bruised flesh surrounded the crater in his throat, the same purple-black marking that covered most of his arms and legs. He gently patted the wound and found it numb, probably why he hadn't noticed it earlier.

The strength ran out of his fingers and he let the mirror fall on the bar top.

"Quite the wound, sailor," the barkeep said with certain admiration. "Injury like that could kill a man."

He'd thought about that. It was miraculous that he had survived.

"What were they?" Means asked, though he already knew the answer.

"They're sirens, sonny. 'Bout the meanest creatures on this side of the hemisphere."

"And you're their what?"

The barkeep squinted. "I'm their contact. I'm their caretaker of sorts."

The shadowy corners of Siren's End began to move.

The barkeep hung his head. "I'm their slave." He lifted his shirt to reveal a dozen of tiny bite marks, pockets of missing meat. "They're so damn hungry."

Means turned his attention to the moving parts of the room. Shadows closed in until the glow of the lantern reached their figures. They shrank back into the shadows.

"Light keeps them away most days," he said, covering his exposed belly fat with his shirt. "They won't kill me, though. Just feed off me when they want a little snack."

"Because you feed them much larger meals." Means gritted his teeth. "Men. Entire fleets of men."

"It keeps me alive." The barkeeper shook his finger at him. "You'd do the same in my position."

"This town? This island?"

"Ate their way through it in a few months." He sighed deeply. "Soon, there won't be any ships left in the Queen's Navy."

"What then?"

The barkeep shrugged. "The homeland. All of Europe."

"We have to stop them."

The shadows hissed.

The barkeep chuckled, an almost-silent vocalization. "There ain't no stopping them. They're determined." He continued to shake his finger at him like a parent dishing out a good scolding. "Men like you created things like that. Remember this. You fathered these beasts."

His memory recalled Isabella, not the beautiful creature she was but the wretched monster she'd become. "I couldn't have... I only wanted to love. *Her* love."

The barkeep scoffed. "Love... is a two-sided coin, my pathetic friend. Can't have unity without the other half present."

"You don't know me," Means told him, as it became increasingly difficult to breathe. Spotting the creatures in the darkened corners, his heart raced. They were waiting, biding their time.

"Enough of this meandering. You've made your choice, *captain.* You've doomed your ship, your men, all in the name of *love,* or your misguided views on the subject."

"Who are you to judge me?"

Leaning closer to the lantern on the bar, he shrugged. "No one. Just a man. Remember? Most dangerous devil there is." He smiled and then blew out the small flame that had kept the entire establishment aglow.

In the darkness appeared several pairs of eyes, too many to count. They were a radiant turquoise, bright like the Caribbean seas he'd explored when he was younger. The ovals were drawn to him. They sped forth at once, and quick, and when they arrived there was pain.

Means screamed the only thing that mattered, his lost love's name—"Isabella!"—as the creatures dug into him, drank his sanguine nectar, and separated his muscle from the bone with their hungry mouths.

BEYOND THE BLACK HILL

An Excerpt from the book, "Beyond The Black Hill" by
Joseph Allan Gecko

(THE BLACK HILL #5)

Copyright © 1997

*T*HOSE WHO LIVE in Ludlow, Ohio recognize the Black Hill for what it is—a place of evil where bad things happened and continue to happen, without end, until the last sand of time falls to the bottom of the universe's hourglass. Townspeople avoid the Black Hill at all costs, and the only people who make the climb are those from around the country, paranormal investigators and thrill seekers expecting to find the ghost of Blake Weber or Woody Turner's rainbow. Of course, no one who ever goes looking for the anomalies on the Black Hill ever find them. And that's part of its charm. It's been the highlight of one international and over twelve domestic documentaries, and has been featured on every ghost hunting reality television show known to man.

The legend of the Black Hill continues to interest those with a taste for the unusual. As previously mentioned, the Hill has a long history and has claimed many lives. Doubters will tell you there is a logical explanation for all of this. They'll say Blake Weber was just a sick old man and that the "black stars" he wrote of had nothing to do with taking an ax to his wife's head. They'll say Shady O'Quinn was equally nuts when he broke Margaret

Eastern's neck, twisted her head completely around. They'll also tell you that Woody Turner's mental state contributed to the stabbing of his brother, and that the unexplainable rainbow pictures had nothing to do with his actions, that rainbows can't talk and couldn't possibly have commanded Woody to execute Austin Turner. Naysayers will contribute the infamous disappearances, especially the 1962 neighborhood boys who vanished leaving only their bikes behind, to the fact that sometimes people go missing and are never found. They'll point to the statistics, state that a hundred thousand missing-persons cases are active in the United States at any given time. But the people of Ludlow, Ohio know different.

They know the Hill, and the Hill knows them, and there is a mutual understanding between the two, and the two never cross each other, never overstep the invisible border between them.

"Things are pleasant when people don't go messing around up there," said Patricia Martin, 63 years old, of 23 Terrance Street. "When out-of-towners explore the Black Hill, things just go wrong. Power outages happen. Water mains bust. Electrical fires burn down houses. I think if you look back at every single rotten thing that's happened over the last 40 years or so, you can attribute it to someone messing around up at the Hill."

It would seem the town agrees with Patricia Martin's stance. In fact, in 1992, the town petitioned to regulate traffic to the Black Hill. It became illegal to walk the Hill and lingering at the base would earn you a ticket. Climbers would not only earn a hefty fine, but a light jail sentence too. The city of Ludlow took the Black Hill very seriously, and for a good while, once they started catching violators and making their arrests public, the traffic to the site stopped almost completely. Of course, there were those who weren't going to let a town ordinance stop their once-in-a-lifetime pilgrimage.

Of course.

In 1994, John Davis Coolidge and his two college

buddies went up the Black Hill in hopes of documenting something for a documentary they were shooting for film school. The tapes of what they had recorded were completely blank (so we are told) and are currently locked up in the county sheriff department's evidence room. In any case, not one of the three boys came home alive. Evidence from the crime scene suggests that John Davis Coolidge went crazy while up on the Hill and attacked his two friends with some camera equipment. Jack Treadwell was beaten to death with the audio gear, the boom mic covered in his blood, which confirmed the murder weapon. Both of his eyes had been plucked out of his head and were found in John Davis Coolidge's intestinal tract during his autopsy. Eddie Ryan was also savagely murdered; his head had been smashed into the base of the tree that sits atop the Black Hill. According to the police report, it looked like a "rotten pumpkin that had been dropped on the blacktop." After killing both young men, John Davis Coolidge ripped a twelve-inch gash into his own abdomen and streamed his intestines across the Hill. After he was finished, he was still alive enough to unspool an audio cable and hang himself from a tree branch.

Just last year, a woman walking her dog—a little labradoodle named Curly—in broad daylight got the urge to walk the Black Hill. She was from town and knew the legends well. Close family members were very adamant that Jillian Marsh would never in a million years go anywhere near that place, so something must have "made her." Still, on June 6th, 1996, Jillian climbed the Black Hill and never came back down.

When police found her, she was face up, looking at the sky, an enormous smile stretched across her face, made wider by two thin slits that ran from the corners of her lips to her earlobes. Her eyes were not in their sockets, replaced by two black stones that had symbols carved into them. The symbols were later taken to the local university and studied by a team of professors, all of whom had determined the symbols were ancient hieroglyphics used in documenting sacrificial offerings to unearthly gods (a record of these symbols and their meanings can be found in the index). They found the woman's eyeballs several hours later, after Curly passed them onto a family member's front lawn. Weeks later, the labradoodle sold for $25,000 in a highly secret auction.

As of this writing, the town of Ludlow is in the midst of raising funds to erect a giant wall around the Black Hill, so that tragedies like John Davis Coolidge and Jillian Marsh never happen again. When asked why they don't just demo the whole area, blow it to Kingdom Come, a member of Ludlow's City Council (who would like to remain nameless) said, "Whatever is up there, we simply don't want to anger it."

APERTURE

PLACING THE FILM against the aperture plate, the old projectionist grumbled, to himself, words of indignation. He snapped the gate over the film, adjusted the framing, and then turned to face the control station positioned directly beneath the porthole. Looking out across the theater, over the Friday night crowd and toward the screen, he pushed the glowing green button in the center of the panel. The motor kicked on, drowning out the distant noise of anxious moviegoers and the collective hum of the other nine projectors. The platter system spun with life, all three in sync with one another, feeding the rollers seven reels worth of footage. The projectionist stepped away from his work, folded his arms across his doughy chest, and looked to his company, his new apprentice, the preppy-looking youngster whose face had been taken over by utter confusion.

"Um," the kid said, his eyes darting back and forth. "That was great and all, but I have no idea what you just did."

"Weren't you paying attention, numb nuts?" the hermit asked, wiping his dirty, oily hands off on a shop towel. Once he deemed them clean enough, he stroked his gray-streaked beard, combing loose the speckles of leftover

Doritos. Shooting the kid a steely gaze, the projectionist moved away from the machine, seemingly satisfied with the way the print was running. "I just threaded the fuckin' thing for ya. Pay attention next time."

Rob Garland wanted to take the timid approach. He thought about keeping hush, *really* thought about it, but he only had a week to learn everything the old hermit knew about being a projectionist. Instead of remaining quiet, he cleared his throat.

"I learn better when I *do.*" He kept still in fear that sudden movement would cause the hermit to start chucking empty reels at his head.

"You'll *do.* You'll *do* plenty. Patience is a virtue. Doesn't your generation know any-goddamn-thing?" He didn't allow a response, which was fine because Rob knew the question was rhetorical. "Goddamn millennials. We're talking about threading a projector here, not splitting atoms. Come here. I want to show you the building station."

Rob followed the man over to the secluded area of the booth that consisted of a work bench with two circular disks angled outward, jutting pegs in the center where the reels were commonly placed. Compiling five to six reels into one massive print looked complicated—Rob had seen it done before—and he wasn't sure if he'd "get it" in only five days. No, it wasn't splitting atoms, but it might as well have been.

The projectionist pointed to the splicer sitting on the bench. "See that? That's your best friend. That's what we use to splice the frames together. Get it?"

"Uhhhh... sure."

"Good. I'll show you how to build a print on Wednesday when the new movies come in. In the meantime, we can splice together some trailers for practice." He nodded in the direction of the cage on the far end of the booth. "Let me show you where we keep some supplies."

"Yes, sir."

Before he took his next step, the old man shifted his gaze back to Rob, his eyes barely visible between his lids. "You call me sir one more damn time and Imma splice your chode off, cock boy. Got it?"

Snickering, Rob nodded.

"Now call me Dan, my fuckin' name, or suffer the fuckin' consequences."

"Yes, Dan."

Rob followed Dan to the cage, a small corner of the booth sectioned off by raw wood framing and chicken wire. Dan popped open the gate and led Rob inside. The cage was trashed with what Rob considered junk. There were Christmas decorations and old projector parts, cardboard boxes filled with rolled-up movie posters dating back to the eighties and dozens of empty reels. Rob also noticed several unopened canisters tucked away in the corner. There was some crap, various marketing materials that never made their way downstairs, cardboard displays and paper handouts, covering the orange and silver canisters, but he spotted them anyway.

"Okay," Dan said, kicking a path to the far wall. "Here's where we keep the trailers. We got a ton of old ones we keep for training thumbsuckers such as yourself. Here's one for *Pulp Fiction*." He snatched the small hockey puck-looking disc off the shelf and held it to the light as if he'd discovered a blood diamond beneath the African soil. "You like Tarantino, kid?"

"He's all right," Rob replied, his eyes drawn to the corner and the canisters. "I mean, I like everything he's done, even though *Jackie Brown* was kinda boring."

Dan blew an irked breath between his lips and said, "Well, you're fuckin' boring" quietly, so Rob couldn't hear. But Rob did hear and only laughed at the crusty old bastard. "Nonsense," he barked, and continued to grumble on about kids and respect, and did so in near silence. "Anyway, have your pick. There are all types of trailers up here. Knock yourself out. I might take *Pulp Fiction* with me. Consider it my retirement gift from this piece-of-shit, no-one-gives-a-fuck-about-you place they call The Orchid 10."

"What are those?" Rob asked, pointing to the partially-hidden canisters.

Dan arched his brow. "Those?" He waddled over to the old dented cans and bent down on one knee. "Well, one of them is *Austin Powers and the Spy Who Shagged Me,* and the other..." He knocked over the marketing materials like the trash they were. They spilled across the floor, mixing with other throwaway items of little to no importance. The first thing Rob wanted to do when he took over Dan's job was to clean out the cage, make it look somewhat presentable. "The other is a rare print from my own personal collection."

"You collect prints?"

Dan rotated his entire body toward the kid. His lips carved out an almost sinister smile. "Yes. Yes, I do." A faint laugh lived and died in his throat. "Mostly foreign flicks. Rarities and B-sides. Stuff you've probably never heard of, stuff you might not even find on the Internet. Stuff that may or may not sell for a fortune if I live long enough."

"What kinds of movies?"

Dan's forehead bunched together, creating wrinkles and ripples across his pale stretch of skin. "Do you like horror movies, kid?"

Rob shrugged. "Sure. Rob Zombie's first couple were good. I'll see the new one."

The projectionist scoffed. "Rob Zombie? The man wishes he could make the types of films I'm talking about. The types of films I collect are true masterpieces. They're true art. They're... how shall I put this?" He pressed the tip of his forefinger against his chin. His eyes expanded as the words came to him. "They are morbid perfections."

Rob stared at him, unblinking. "Oh-kay, then."

"Take this one for example." He popped the latch on the orange canister and pulled back the lid. Inside sat three reels. "It's a short flick. Only about an hour. French title. *Ouverture.* English translation: *Aperture.*"

"Like an aperture plate?"

Dan winked at him the way one might near the end of a flirty date. "Exactly. Guess you were paying attention after all. An aperture is an opening. In our biz, it's the space that allows light to pass through the projector, allowing the image captured on film to project onto the screen. In this film's case..." He stroked the reels as if they were the spine of his favorite cat. "...it's... well." He laughed incredulously. "Never mind, kid. You wouldn't believe me. Not a thing like this."

Rob folded his arms across his chest. He'd just turned eighteen and had learned a long time ago the difference between when someone was sincere and when someone was putting him on. But in this moment, he couldn't decipher if Dan was serious or yanking his cord. At the very least, the old, nearly-retired projectionist *believed* in what he was talking about. He'd known Dan for about a year, since he'd started working at The Orchid 10 last summer. He'd only spoken to the man a handful of times since, and he hadn't seemed *too* loony. A man of few words, sure, but not the bat-shit bonkers turd everyone made him out to be. The man was a hermit, a real recluse, and Rob didn't know him any better than he knew the guy at Wawa who brewed his coffee every morning.

"Try me," Rob said, his curiosity piqued.

Dan flashed him an excited, grinning look. "You want to see it?"

"Sure." He didn't know if he did or not, but the answer came forth anyway, as if there were no possible way he could stop it. "What's it about, though?"

Dan rubbed his hands together in delight. "Oh boy. You're in for a real treat. A *reel* treat," he said, snatching a reel out of the canister and holding it up to illustrate his pun. "It's a story about love and death. Life and what lies on the other side of death's door. Some say," he said, that sick grin still pasted across his face, "that one viewing will open up a portal in your mind, allow you to see what's on the other side. A temporal gateway of sorts."

"An aperture," Rob mumbled.

"Yes, kid." Grinning still, the hermit revealed gums that had blackened over the last sixty years. Teeth that were long overdue for repair, maybe past the point of restoration. "An aperture into another world."

"So you've watched it?"

He looked down at the reel in his hand. "Well... no."

"No?"

"No," he said confidently. "Why would I? That sounds scary as shit."

"You've never watched it?" Rob asked, almost angrily.

"No. Nope. Started to once. Got about five minutes in and had to shut it down. Gave me a headache something fierce."

"What happened? What was on it?" Rob felt his obsession with Dan's story grow, as if it were some living, palpable thing inside him. Feeding on him. Gnawing from within.

A crown of sweat dripped from Rob's forehead. He felt lightheaded.

"You okay?" Dan asked.

"Fine. Tell me about the print. What happened?"

Dan shrugged. "It was just too... bizarre."

"Isn't that *why* you'd watch it?"

"Listen, kid. When did this turn into an interrogation?" Dan put the reel back in the canister and shut the case. "I just collect the shit, hoping it sells when I retire. Which is next week, by the way. Which means you're going to be the new lead projectionist. Which means we need to learn your ass."

"We should watch it."

Dan's smile danced off his face. His color paled. "You... really... want to?"

"Yes." He'd called the old hermit's bluff. "Yes, let's watch it."

"Oh... oh, okay. Tonight then. Midnight. I'll thread theater one."

"Perfect."

He didn't know why, but midnight couldn't come fast enough.

The lobby of Orchid 10 was unsurprisingly vacant for a Monday night after the last show had gone in. Rob drifted toward the popcorn stand where the cute new girl stood behind the counter, prepping the popcorn popper for closing. She had already emptied it and was beginning to wipe down the greasy interior.

"Jumping on that a little prematurely, huh, new girl?" Rob asked, leaning on the candy counter.

She twisted her neck, continuing to spray down the stainless steel kettle. Flashing him a superficial smile, she said, "Dude, no one else is coming in."

The second the words left her mouth, a couple stumbled through the front door, holding hands and giggling. They asked Rob if they were too late, if they had missed any part of the movie. While staring at the new girl, he simply said, "No," and then proceeded over to the ticket booth.

"And be sure to try our number one combo," he said loud enough so the new girl could hear, his lips pressed into a devious smile.

The new girl scowled, but when the couple came over to order a number one, she greeted them like the training videos instructed. "Anything else?" she bubbled and they shook their heads "no" and headed for the theater.

"There's always one," Rob said, winking at her.

She wriggled her lips and returned to her closing tasks, starting the process from the beginning.

Rob leaned on the counter again, the lower half of his face barely able to contain his grin. "Always one—"

"Cram it, Garland," she said sharply. She turned to him and pretended to squirt cleaner at him, mimicking the squishy sounds it made when it shot from the nozzle. (pshoo-pshoo). She returned his goofy grin.

The two of them had been playing this little flirty game the last week, basically since Brianne Welker's orientation. On her first day, she had told Rob that she had broken it off with her boyfriend and was looking forward to spending the summer before senior year single. He thought that info was a little too much to reveal on her first day, but he didn't mind; they had shared a strong connection from the second he had laid eyes on her, the second he had opened his mouth. Their first conversation felt like it would never end, be consumed by awkward silences or grow dull. They shared likes and dislikes and discovered they loved the same movies. They spent the rest of the afternoon cleaning theaters, discussing their favorite films, albums they'd require if stranded on a desert island, and which books they'd read over and over again. She was a little too much of a Harry Potter nerd for his tastes, but that was okay; he liked the books too and told her Universal was supposedly opening up a Harry Potter theme park, which she already knew about and claimed she'd be first in line when it opened next fall.

They talked for hours even though their exchange only seemed like minutes. And when the day was over, they continued their conversation via text message.

They next day they were making out in the ice room. Rob had her back pressed against the ice machine. She jumped up on his hips and wrapped her legs around his waist. It was a scene out of every romantic comedy he'd ever seen. They'd spent the next ten minutes swapping saliva until one of the other ushers had barged in. The usher's face had twisted with alarm and embarrassment, and he'd immediately thrown his arm over his eyes and backed out of the room.

Since then, they had made sure to carve out at least ten minutes of every shift to make kissy-face in the maintenance closet.

"What are you thinking about?" Brianne asked him.

"Nothing?"

Her eyes slimmed. Cocking her head, she said, "You're thinking about the broom closet again, aren't you?"

"No..." Rob winked and held the pose. "Okay, I was. Sue me. Wanna go?"

"I have to finish cleaning the popper. Then sweep and mop the stand. You know the routine."

"Yeah, I sure do."

"Plus, I was thinking we could do something else. You know, *besides* making out."

"Oh?" Rob perked up. His pants suddenly felt a little tighter. Sweat crawled down his inner leg. "Like what, pray tell, did you have in mind?"

Buffing the counter with a clean rag, she shrugged. "I dunno. Dinner? The diner on 37? IHOP? I'll even let you pay the bill."

"How gracious of you." Rob folded his arms. "Got a better idea. Dan just invited me to a movie tonight. A sneak peek."

Brianne's brow spiked with interest. "Oh? The new Nolan?"

He shook his head. "No, something a little more obscure."

She seemed almost disappointed.

"Some foreign film," Rob said, filling up the napkin dispenser. "It's French. *Aperture*, or something. Says it's supposed to be scary as fuck."

"Really?"

"Really."

"I do like French films. Ever see *Chocolat?*"

"No. God, no. And I don't plan on it either."

"It's so good. Plus, you know—Johnny Depp and stuff."

"Terrible." He slammed the top down on the napkin dispenser and tugged the first one through. "So... you in?"

"I don't know. Sounds weird. And creepy. And that guy Dan gives me the willies. He should invest in some deodorant."

"Come on. He's not so bad."

"He never comes down from up there. I met him once, my first day. I said 'hello' and he grunted something back that wasn't even English."

Rob squeaked with laughter. "Yeah, that's Dan. Man's a bit of a recluse. He's harmless. And a good guy once you get to know him. This theater will suffer without him."

Brianne finished the counter, and then bent over to put the lid back on the candy case. "Fine. We'll watch your French flick. But can we get food? Fuck, I'm starving."

Two minutes to midnight and Dan Galloway had finished threading *Ouverture*. The sensation in his fingers while placing the film on the rollers had been too strong to ignore. They'd gone rigid a few times, especially while he'd fed the film through the brain, the piece stationed in the center of the print that controlled the speed of the platter. Numbness ruled his hands, down to the bone, every nerve shredded. When the tingling sensation abated, a shooting pain took its place and shot up his arm, needling his elbow. Nerves swam like a school of sharks in a feeding frenzy. His brain felt cloudy and empty, like a veil draped over his thoughts, preventing any original content from forming. He got the sense that, if he tried to speak, his words would come out as inarticulate syllables.

When finished, he took a seat next to the projector. He inhaled slowly, heard himself wheeze with each breath. A funny tingle fingered his heart, and he wondered if this was it, if this was the big heart attack that had ended many other Galloways before him.

He rested, but, as the seconds ticked on, he felt no better.

Eventually, he pulled himself up. Looking through the porthole, he spotted his protégé, the kid who'd replace him in a week's time, and the kid's new squeeze, the saucy new girl who served up one hell of a number two combo.

His lips spread into a smile, but the emotion behind the action quickly faltered. The realization of his successor's dim future hit him hard. His mood suddenly soured and he felt awful for Rob. In a few years, this job would be gone. What was once a pretty decent-paying job complete with benefits and union perks, would give way to part-time minimum wage work only. True projectionists were a dying breed and he was the last of his kind. Dan predicted digital hardware would replace film in two year's time, maybe less depending on the market. Soon, any two-bit numbskull with the brave ability to press a button could start a projector. Projectionists were trending toward obsolete, like the clockmakers and switchboard operators before them, and that bent Dan's smile, crushed his high spirits.

APERTURE

Dan pressed the green button. The motor buzzed to life. The rollers fed the film along. The lamphouse glowed bright, projecting images on the screen. Dan raised his vision and focused on the front of the theater. Some French words were written in white against a black background.

Dan felt a presence behind him. A figure. Standing tall in the booth, looming over him, stretching like some indefinable shape, free from the constraints of gravity and other earthly restrictions.

He turned and saw nothing. No floating shape. No dim, jellylike figure reaching for his neck. Nothing but shadows and the small cone of light looking down at his workstation.

Silly, he thought, *you're being silly.*

He returned to the film. The black and white images appeared before him, changing within a few seconds of showing themselves. They were of random things. Grotesque things. Things he'd seen before, once, when he first acquired the film from some junkie ex-actor who'd stolen it from some big-wig Hollywood executive twenty years prior. He'd made it about five minutes in before having to shut the damned thing off; he wondered how long he'd last the second time around.

The feeling returned. Something behind him. Some unspeakable horror, some gangrenous creature dripping with black, vile fluids, reeking of death and disease, a limitless mouth filled with tiny white shards of teeth, motivated to destroy and defile all that made the human world good and perfect, all that made it *human.*

Dan turned and expected to see nothing again, much of the same; the dim light and shifty shadows the projection booth usually harbored.

But what stood before him wasn't a trick the shadows provided. It actually resembled the horrors his brain conceived.

Only worse.

The thing was real.

221

After the first few minutes of random gross-out frames and still credits, the meat of the film began. Rob threw his arm around Brianne and pulled her close. The top of her head fit perfectly in the space between his cheek and shoulder, snugly, like there was no other head in the universe meant for that special place. They locked together and fixed their eyes on the screen, waiting for the story to unfold and sink its claws into them.

(The woman on screen was folding laundry. She sat on her bed, piling the squared articles on top of one another. She was crying but trying not to. Sniffling.)

The scene changed: a dead bird spattered against the dotted line on the asphalt surface, a feathery blob of bones and blood. A hammer coming down on a human hand, smashing the fingers into twisted extensions of flesh and exposed white. A woman hurling herself off the balcony of a sky-high tower and a few frames of the black, soupy puddle she'd become.

"What the hell are we watching?" Brianne whispered.

"I don't know," Rob said, feeling slightly disgusted, slightly amused. A cold wave crashed against his arms and legs, causing a layer of gooseflesh to sprawl over him. "Whatever it is, it's cool as fuck, though."

"Cool?" She pushed away from him, breaking contact. "This is sick."

Rob turned to her. "We can go if you want."

On screen, an army of spiders crawled over a woman's mostly-deteriorated corpse. There was no denying the corpse was real and not a prop. Rob felt its authenticity in his bones.

Brianne seemed to weigh her options in silence, as more unspeakable acts of violence were projected before her. Scenes depicting real-life mutilation flashed between brief moments of what might have been a cohesive, coherent story had the filmmakers stuck with it.

"No," she finally said. "But I need to pee."

"Okay." Rob looked around the empty theater. "If you see Dan, tell him to come join us."

She nodded, and then took off down the aisle.

He cupped his hands over his mouth. "And bring me snacks!"

She gave him two thumbs up.

Rob reclined in his seat and focused on the picture.

(The woman moved to the window, looking out across the street. Below, townspeople bustled. As she watched, the woman said something in French and there were no subtitles to accompany her voice.)

"What the hell are you making me watch, Dan?" Rob whispered to himself.

More quick scenes: a man getting hit by a car, a tire rolling over his head, flattening his cranium, coagulated lumps of brains and blood spurting through the cracked skull and split flesh. A pack of lions tearing into a zebra, ripping huge chunks of skin and muscle away, still alive as the predators quarter the defenseless, struggling animal. An entire hallway of flyblown bodies, the surrounding walls dripping with dark fluids. A homeless clown sitting on the street corner of some busy intersection, munching on a severed hand, while several pedestrians pass by seemingly unaware of the menace's existence.

(With her back to the camera, the woman faced the open window. The bustle of Paris faded into the background, reduced to faint white noise. She turned to the camera. The woman's face had changed, suddenly different. She had morphed into a different woman altogether. It was...)

"What the hell?" Rob asked the empty theater, pitching himself forward.

The woman on screen was no longer the Frenchwoman.

"Help me, Robbie," the woman said in a voice that no longer carried a French accent. It was American. It belonged to Brianne. "Help me, Robbie," the new girl repeated. "Help me." There were tears in her eyes, streaming down her face, running off her cheeks. But she didn't appear sad like he thought she ought to, rather, indifferent about the situation. Maybe not even that. Maybe... *happy?* He swore the ends of her mouth curled, traces of a smile beginning to take shape.

"They're coming for you, Robbie. They're coming for all of us. They can't be stopped."

Rob launched himself out of his seat. He stood there, eyes glued to the black and white screen.

Brianne's body heaved as she began to sob. "They're coming." Her voice changed just then. Deeper. Several octaves lower. Eerily demonic. "They're coming. We let it out, Robbie. *We let it out.*" The last sentence sounded like a record played backwards, low and warbled. *"We let it out! We let it out! We let it out!"* Her screams sounded like the howling gale of a bad storm. Her fists beat against the camera, shaking the frame. No, not the frame. *Him.* She was beating him. He felt the impact of her blows on his chest and shoulders.

Rob turned to run but there was only darkness behind him, an endless, lightless void. He thought about jumping into the inky lake before him, but there was a sense of threat there, a notion that this was darkness not to be trespassed, that there was no return from this place. This was a place that kept *things*, his intuition told him. There was no coming back.

No coming back.

No coming back!

He turned back to the screen and faced Brianne, who was now standing in the row before him dressed in the Frenchwoman's attire, that silky satin robe.

"NO COMING BACK!" Brianne shouted in a voice that wasn't her own, and possibly belonged to some foul soul residing in the deepest depths of Hell.

Rob backed away as Brianne's mouth remained open, displaying rotted teeth, a tongue comprised of writhing maggots, which spilled over her lower lip as she continued to shout. *"NO COMING BACK! NO COMING BACK!"*

Rob jumped backwards expecting to clear the seat, but there was nothing left of the theater behind him except the dark abyss. Icy hands grabbed him and pulled him under, taking him to—

Rob flailed and cried out. Gasping for fresh air, he lunged forward. Brianne screamed and jerked the wheel, causing the tires to wail beneath them.

"What the fuck, dude?" she asked, flipping off the horn-honking driver to her left.

"I'm sorry," Rob said instinctively. "What-where? Where am I?"

"Um, you're in my car. On the way to IHOP. Like we said. Like two minutes ago. Before you passed out and went all *Jacob's Ladder* on me."

Rob wiped a layer of cold sweat from his brow. "I thought... the movie."

"What movie? *Jacob's Ladder?*"

He shook his head and suffered a sudden wave of dizziness. He fought off the urge to puke all over the glove box. "The one we were watching." He swallowed and tasted acid, the bile in the back of his throat. "The French flick."

"What the hell are you talking about?" She took turns between eyeing him warily and concentrating on the road. "We left work and decided to go to IHOP. There was never any movie."

"No," he said, shivering. A fever worked over him, and he could feel a sickness crawling through his veins, infecting each organ as it traveled deeper and deeper into his body. The sudden notion to rip his hair out became strong, and he found himself fingering around his scalp. "No, we were watching..."

"Are you feeling all right?" She felt his forehead. "Jesus, you're burning up. Maybe I should just take you home."

"No. Home." The highway lights became a shifting kaleidoscope of bright colors. He took another spin on the fever carousel.

"Fuck that," she said.

"No." But he had no choice in the matter. She had already pulled off the main drag and was heading down Green

Street, toward Rob's parent's house.

The next morning he felt much better, at least physically. He went to work with his head in a cloud, his brain polluted with weird thoughts, but his body felt all right. He wasn't hot or sweating pellets of ice; he was good. But his head, on the other hand, felt like someone had set off a fog machine in there, pumping ghostly images of things that should not exist directly into his mind's projector. He tried to remember the previous night in its entirety; the film, what happened during the viewing, the bizarre events that had followed. But he couldn't do it. It wasn't there, not all of it. There were fragments, just pieces. Broken images and shattered visions. Tidbits of a good bad dream, there somewhere beyond the veil of reality. Enough to verify what he'd seen was real, but enough to doubt its authenticity.

When he arrived at work, he decided what had happened last night was real. The film was real. The viewing was real. Everything that had happened was real right up until he'd awoken in Brianne's car, screaming like a newborn baby thirsting for the teat.

But what was real?

The movie he hardly remembered?

The reels in his mind began to spin, projecting the Frenchwoman while she pleaded for help. But it hadn't been her, right? No, it had been Brianne.

He remembered the sick, nasty scenes spliced between those involving the Frenchwoman. Yes, it was all coming back to him. Slowly. Fragments. Dirty, twisted concepts weaving together like fine threads until they had come together and become one complete garment. The closer he got to the projection booth, the more he remembered. By the time he passed theater six, he had recalled everything.

He found Dan sitting behind his desk, awkwardly slumped. He lifted his head from the blank wooden space before him, and smiled. His teeth had seemingly rotted completely black overnight. His eyes and the tone of his skin had yellowed with jaundice. Most of his hair had fallen out, leaving behind noticeable patches of scalp. A dozen or so clumps of silver strands remained.

Dan coughed. "You like the movie, kid?"

Rob had approached with no apprehension, but once he set eyes on the old projectionist, he found himself backing away. "What happened to you?"

"I watched it," he said with a bright smile. "I finally watched it."

"Jesus, your face."

"My face is beautiful." He touched a spot on his face where a boil had formed. The tumor-like growth had filled to the point where Rob thought it might break and discharge pink, toxic juices. "I'm transforming. Becoming one with the other side."

"What other side?" Rob trembled. "What are you talking about?"

Leaning forward, Dan squinted. "You didn't see it? You didn't stare into the abyss?"

"I saw..." What had he seen? He remembered gazing into the black and seeing nothing but the endless void. "I saw nothing."

Dan shook his head violently. "Oh no. You saw what I saw. You saw into the aperture. Into the dark world. And you know what?"

Rob was too terrified to respond.

"The dark world saw *you*."

He wanted to turn and run, but fear rooted him to the floor.

"You can't run," Dan said as if he'd read the kid's mind. "You can't outrun what is everywhere. The dark world is everywhere now, hidden behind the veil of our own precious domain. There. Hidden. Waiting. Gaining traction. The film," he nodded to the three reels sitting on the desk, "will be shown to the masses."

Rob found enough courage to speak but he was still trembling. "N-no. It can't."

"Yes, it can. And it will."

"W-we can stop it."

"Too late. Darkness is like wildfire; it spreads quickly. And this film is pure darkness."

"P-please."

"Go now," Dan suggested, sweeping the three reels closer to him so he could rest his head on them. "Go and live your life. What's left of it. Live until the darkness catches up with you. It's not far behind. In the meantime, I will protect the film, as I always have." He perked up. "Funny, how I've never watched it before. After all the years I've had it in my possession, I picked now to view it. Curious."

Rob thought it was curious too, but kept quiet. Too many of his thoughts were bumping into each other, fumbling.

"I never watched it until I met you," he added, before putting his head back down, where it would remain for a good long while.

Rob went downstairs, handed in his immediate resignation, and walked out the doors of Orchid 10 for the last time.

He thought he felt a cold darkness saunter after him and follow him into the parking lot.

☆☆☆

Rob grabbed the door handle and pulled.

"Where do you think you're going, hot stuff?" Brianne asked from behind him.

Rob turned, and the sudden movement brought a sickly sensation to his stomach. Brianne strolled toward him casually, twisting her body with each step. Overhead, roiling gray clouds closed off the sky. The atmosphere reeked of damp air. Rain was on the way. Lots of it.

"Didn't think you could quit and not say goodbye to me," she said with a friendly, welcoming smile that almost erased his uneasiness. "Did you?"

"I was gonna text you."

"Sure you were." She stopped a few feet away from him.

"You okay? You've been acting weird. First last night, now, you quit your job? It's not me, is it?"

"No, definitely not you."

"What then?"

Rob knew what it was—*that goddamn movie.* He couldn't bring himself to speak the words aloud. "Nothing. Just going through some stuff."

She clicked her tongue. "Got it. Say, wanna take a ride with me?"

He glanced around the half-vacant lot thinking he shouldn't, how he should go home instead and wait for Dan's darkness to slither over him like a bucket of poisonous snakes.

"Sure, why not."

"Follow me," she said, almost seductively.

He did.

When he plopped himself down on her front seat and shut the door, he felt better. Not perfect, but better than he had only minutes ago. Like he'd shut out Dan's darkness. Brianne's car acted as a safe place, a haven from the unnamable things released by the foreign film.

"Where are we going?" he asked.

She pulled out of the parking lot, onto the main drag. "I dunno. For a drive. We never got that IHOP dinner you promised me."

"I'm not hungry."

"No, I wouldn't imagine you would be." A horde of invisible spiders crawled down his arms. "With everything you've witnessed."

He snapped his head in her direction. "What?"

She smiled. Grinned. Much like Dan's jaundiced face had.

"Did you like my movie?" she asked. "I made it for you, you know."

"Wha-what?"

"Well, not *you* specifically. The children like you. My little puppets. There have been so many of you over the years." She giggled, a high-pitched noise that sliced open his nerves. "My little agents of darkness."

Rob went for the door handle but the child locks were already on. He tried to push the button, but it didn't move. He elbowed the window but the glass held, held through each violent effort.

"There's no escape, little one," she said, the lower half of her face complete with a crescent smile. "Did you know the Frenchwoman was my birth mother? Bet you didn't. That's a fun piece of trivia for you. One you won't find on IMDB. Though, you won't find *Ouverture* on there, either. Will you?"

No, he didn't think he would.

"What are you?" he asked, squeaking the words out.

"Oh, a little of this. A little of that." She let her head fall sideways and set her eyes on him. He stared back, looking into the shimmering black orbs that filled in her irises. "My kind are the creators of the void. And I'm its keeper. Its protector. Its mother. Like my mother before me and hers before her. And, like all good mothers, we need to feed our babies."

Her eyes were normal again, bright as two blueberries.

Rob could barely speak, his windpipe feeling about as wide as a drinking straw. He croaked. "W-what d-did you make us watch?"

"Just a film. One of my favorites."

"That wasn't *just a film*." Rob felt weak, barely able to move. His thoughts began to bleed away. "What... was it?"

She shrugged. "The void needs to feed, and there is nothing more nutritious than the human noggin. Not the outside, of course. The shell is too bony and tasteless. But what's on the inside, what exists within the brain, where thoughts and imaginative cognitive skills are brewed—now that's the ticket. One human imagination can sustain the void for a thousand years, which is a long time for your kind, but, in the grand scheme of the megaverse, it only equates to about a day or two in Earth time."

"Why... me?" Rob felt all strength abandon his limbs. As he wasted away, he looked into the sideview mirror and saw his features had yellowed, grown overripe with jaundice.

"Why..."

Brianne, or the thing she truly was, shrugged. "Because you were easy. And the film was here. Dan had his copy stashed away, the one he'd stolen once upon a time ago, just waiting for the right opportunity to come along. I thought I could nudge you in the right direction. You wanted to impress me with the film, didn't you? That was your plan? Scare your way into my pants? Hm, how shallow you are, Robert."

"Didn't..."

"Save your last words as they mean nothing to me." A sleek grin spilled across her features. "The only thing I require is what's inside here." She tapped his forehead.

Everything suddenly ached. His arms, legs. Bones. Head. His muscles swelled with pain.

"Now, come on," she said, leaning over him. "Give me a kiss."

She opened her mouth and instead of seeing a tongue, teeth, the hanging pink orb in the back of her throat, he saw nothing but a glowing, white light. A heavenly flash of nothingness. Like staring into a xenon bulb, completely blinding.

She pressed her lips against his and he tasted chaos. Scented ash floating above burning buildings. Sniffed salt in the air over eroding shores. Inhaled smoke over cities on fire.

She tasted like the apocalypse.

And then he experienced the void, that floating black ocean of perpetual nothingness.

YE SINNERS, COME DANCE WITH ME

THE GIRL ON the dance floor shuffled her feet along with the beat, a slow tune intended for lovers, yet Kate was doing just fine by her lonesome. The violins and angelic keys played on while the female artist moaned through the speakers on topics of romance and betrayal, sacrifice and lust. A sea of bodies floated around her, swaying back and forth like hammocks in the wind. The glitter ball spinning above her bounced prisms of ambient light off the walls and the collection of slow-dancers, flecking the entire gymnasium with muted rainbow colors.

Still rocking on the tips of her toes, she glanced over at the chaperone's table. Mr. Andrews and Principal Stewart were engaged in conversation and it wasn't long the before the two were concealing their laughter behind their hands, hilarity of the shoulder-shaking kind. Even from her position on the dance floor, she could hear their whispers. Their hushed exchange played in her head as if spoken directly in her ear. The topic of discussion was Kate's Calculus teacher Miss Roberts, and the risqué photos which she had accidentally uploaded to her public Facebook page. Within minutes, the private glamour shots had been downloaded and shared around town a hundred times over, a fact that had become quite funny to the principal and his physical education teacher.

Monsters.

Little did they know that, following her suspension, Miss Roberts would attempt suicide. She'd survive but the damage to her wrists would be so severe that she'd have to wear sweatbands in public for the rest of her life. A part of Kate wished Andrews and Stewart would ask her to dance. They'd be perfect. She wouldn't even feel bad for what came next.

She averted her attention elsewhere, hoping to lock eyes on another loner, someone who was also brave enough to dance alone. But every wavering body had a partner. Logan Thomas and Emily Jones were closest to her. Over the next three years, Logan would become a drug-addicted sociopath and Emily would become infamous for leaving her crying six-month-old son in a hot car for thirty-five minutes while she "just ran inside to pick up a few things." *Perfect candidates.* But they were clinging to each other as if looking down over the edge of some steep cliff. Nothing short of prying them apart would grant her an opportunity, and interference was against the rules.

She needed to be *approached.*

Father and his rules, Kate thought, as the ocean of high school students suddenly parted. Through the opening walked Benson Hall, the kid who sat behind her in Chemistry II. They had shared a lab once, and she was sure she'd caught him cheating off her exam more than once. He was cute, much too cute to be locking eyes with her in the center of the dance floor. She wasn't on the ballot for prom queen or a member of the cheerleading squad—she'd been modeled after an average high school student with fair looks. The popular kids had no problem reminding her of this several times since her transfer a few months back.

Benson had dark features, brown eyes and matching shaggy hair that curled just short of his shoulders. He wore a navy-blue suit and a scarlet tie which played well with his appearance. Pinned above his breast was his boutonniere, the bud as red as a fresh droplet of blood. He looked trendy and oh-so handsome.

She felt her hands grease with sweat.

"Hey there, Kate," he said, looking back over his shoulder. In the distance, Kate spotted Benson's two immature lackeys. They flashed their teeth and vibrated with a severe case of the giggles. He turned back and faced her, bringing with him a smile of his own. "I was hoping we could dance."

She felt her eyelids close. "Why?"

He shrugged. "I don't know. You look... pleasant. And lonely."

She wasn't sure about the "pleasant" part, but lonely—absolutely. She needed to choose someone and fast. Time was running out and she didn't want to keep *Father* waiting.

"I'd love to," she replied, offering her left hand.

Benson grabbed her, forced her close.

As their flesh mingled, Kate saw everything; twenty years later; Benson holding a shovel; sinking the spade beneath the dirt; digging through six feet of earth; kicking a body rolled in painter's plastic into the void; removing the flashy ring from her finger before piling the soil back on, a ring he'd later hawk to the local pawn shop; then the lies he'd tell the police, a story about his wife absconding to Canada with no clear intent to return.

Kate smiled. *A prime choice, indeed. Father will be proud.*

Benson's grin faded, and Kate wondered if she had somehow shared her vision. His lips formed a straight line. He cleared his throat.

"Something wrong?" she asked.

"No. Suddenly don't feel well."

"Shush. Come dance with me."

She touched his face and

[pillars of fire; a bed of thorns surrounded by flames; his hands and legs bound to bedposts comprised of human bones; blood pouring from his wounds, running like water; his chest ripped open, the white of his ribs exposed; looking down at the crimson cavity where a skeletal wall tied together with cartilage used to be; his heart on display for

all the demons in Hell to see]

brought him close to her face. She puckered and kissed his soft, still lips.

[a shadow approaching the bed, dark and towering; the skinless man looking down at him; his raw muscle glistening red; breathing heavily; shadows all around him; the pain from where the thorns had entered his soft skin; spotting Kate in the corner, only it wasn't Kate, but a skinless version of the girl who had sat in front of him in Chemistry II; Kate laughing, pointing, blood dripping steadily from the tip of her finger; pulsing incarnadine flesh; the shadows closing in; their teeth filling up his view]

"Are you okay?" Kate asked, her grin wide and unwavering.

Benson shook his head. "What... what is... *what are you?"*

She stood on her toes, brushing her lips against his ear, and whispered, "I'm here to bring you home, Benson. *Father* and his friends are waiting for us."

Before he could protest, she pressed her lips to his forehead, showing him the rest of his future, where the raw bleeding figures ripped him apart, limb from limb, and dined on his flesh and blood.

She laughed at his expression when she revealed the segment where they spat him back out, molded and stitched him together, and repeated the process. Again and again. Forever and ever.

Sinners, she thought. *They all look the same when they're screaming.*

THROUGHWAYS

<u>Now</u>

"**We found it,**" the priest said hoarsely.

The truck driver's muscles tensed, his jaw quivered, his hands so weakened by fear he could barely grip the steering wheel. The priest stepped off the truck and hopped onto the pavement. The Throughway stood before them, tall and majestic, an aperture between discordant worlds.

The driver swung his feet, allowing them to hover a few feet above the ground. After careful consideration, he shoved himself off the seat. His knees surprised him; landing on the pavement, he managed to keep his balance. He followed the priest toward the Throughway, almost losing him in the kaleidoscope of bright, shimmering colors.

He knew what he needed to do, just lacked the confidence to see it through. The knife in his pocket felt like a bowling ball, weighing him down.

He walked. Followed.

The Throughway called to him, sang to him, offered him everything and nothing.

He walked.

EARLIER

After stopping for fuel and a turkey sandwich on rye, Nelson Park pulled his eighteen-wheeler out onto route 79 south, headed toward Arkansas. He'd get the load to the Costbusters in Little Rock sometime in the early morning and, without any delays, he'd be back in his trailer park home in South Carolina by the late afternoon, asleep before nightfall.

Only to get up and do it all over again.

It wasn't the greatest way to earn a living, but Nelson didn't mind the long hours and hundred-mile journeys. With no wife, no kids, parents he barely spoke to and siblings he spoke to less than that, the job was ideal. Nelson was a loner, had been most of his life. During his growing years, he had never considered any one person a "best friend", the phrase meaningless to him. In high school, he had hung around the same small group of friends, most of them now either dead, jailed, or had left Planet Earth without notice. He had no Facebook friends because he didn't have Facebook and shunned social media of any kind. Computers gave him anxiety, which no prescription could combat. He kept a cell phone only because his work required it and even that made him feel uneasy from time to time.

At forty-five, Nelson had no one.

And he kind of liked it.

Honestly, it wasn't that he didn't like people. He did. Loved them in fact, but for some reason he never connected with them. Though, when he thought about it, he did nothing to promote his social life. Never reached out to anyone, never made an attempt to connect with people, never really tried at all. His social existence consisted of a series of acquaintances. One would think, in a world built on communication and instant interaction, it would be damn near impossible to go forty-five years and not hold onto one past relationship, but that was Nelson. It seemed odd to others but had never struck him as so. He used to joke he was born an interplanetary being, that his parents found him in a barn, abandoned by his extraterrestrial birth-givers. After a while, he had started putting stock in his own jest.

Deep down, he wanted to fit in. Wanted friends. Wanted social acceptance on some level, any level.

Therefore, he had the very bad, very dangerous habit of scooping up hitchhikers.

As Nelson sped down the empty highway, endless stretching forests flanking the road, he sipped from his Big Gulp and tore open the plastic packaging of his Little Debbie brownie with his teeth. Biting into the soft chocolate goodness, he heard his CB crackle with static. A peculiar sound, one he didn't expect considering he thought he had shut off the thing permanently some time ago. Nowadays the CB was rarely used and the only voices that came across were racist loudmouths spewing hateful garbage and lonely, desperate people looking to elicit sexual gatherings.

Lo and behold, the CB had been switched on and someone's voice broke through the intermittent white noise.

"Hel..." a voice crackled. *"..lp me."*

Nelson was hesitant to pick up the receiver, but did so anyway, curiosity driving him. "Hello?" he asked. "Someone there?"

Strange numbness danced across his neck. A shiver coiled around his spine, corkscrewing the bones of his lower extremities.

"Hello?" he repeated.

"Help me." The voice came through clear. *"My name is Father Matthew Kohler. I'm currently at the Star Sky Diner near Tunica."*

A priest?

Although odd, Nelson punched the diner into his GPS anyway and saw it was only twenty minutes from his current location, and not entirely off-route. He'd never encountered someone asking for help over the radio before. This was a first. Usually, his hitchhikers were already roadside, begging for a lift by raising their thumbs in the air.

This was new. And exciting. An opportunity he couldn't

exactly pass up.

"Father Kohler, this is Nelson Park, codename Godzilla, over?"

A pause. Then: *"I hear you, Mr. Park."*

"10-4." He opened his mouth, the rational side of his mind taking over. "Father, are you hurt? Can I call you medical assistance?"

"No." He said this as if Nelson's offer insulted him. *"I mean, no. I'm fine."* The holy man drew a deep breath, interrupting the silence with static. *"I just need a lift."*

"10-4, sir. Hold tight. Be there shortly."

A crackle and the priest was gone.

About two minutes later, his cell phone buzzed and sang inside his breast pocket. A country ditty, one about cowgirls and rodeos and locking lips underneath the glow of a full moon, filled the silence. Nelson glanced down at the number, foreign and unknown. Not only that but there were far too many digits, fifteen in all, five over the standard United States format. Normally, he'd ignore such a call, but between the enticing string of numbers and the peculiar conversation with the hitchhiking priest, he figured *why the hell not*; this was a night full of firsts and thirsty curiosities.

"Hello?"

The voice on the other end did not even introduce himself. "Do not do it," the man said, his tone direct and edgy.

"Excuse me, partner?"

"Do not pick up the priest." He paused and sucked in a series of deep breaths. The man sounded like he was on the run, the phone bouncing in his hand. "I implore you."

"Who are you? How did you get this number?" Nelson had no idea what was happening, but he played along anyway. A part of him felt frightened. The mystery of it all vitalized the other half of him, filling him with panicky intrigue. "And how did you know—"

"Listen to me, Park." What felt like a tornado raged

inside Nelson's chest. "Do not—under any circumstances—pick up the priest. He is dangerous. He will try to kill you. Understand me?"

"No, I don't understand you." He pressed harder on the pedal, accelerating toward his new destination. "Explain yourself."

"No time. Do yourself a favor—do the *world* a favor—and keep on driving. We'll get him. We'll take care of that bastard, once and for all."

A click in his ear and the man was gone.

What the hell was that? For a good minute, Nelson harped on the man's words. *'Do the world a favor?' What does that mean? And 'we'll get him.' Who's we?*

He could have driven on. Could have put this nonsense behind him and finished up his route, journeyed home, cracked open a fresh Pabst Blue Ribbon before hitting the pillow and forgotten all about this cryptic weirdness.

But he couldn't. He knew that. The curious part of him won out, and he navigated his eighteen-wheeler whichever way the GPS commanded.

It was raining near Tunica. The priest was exactly where he said he'd be—standing outside the small diner, a turquoise and pink throwback from the olden days. He had his trench coat draped over his head, a makeshift umbrella. Water poured over him. Dark skies showed no sign of letup. Flashes of light brightened the horizon and claps of thundered followed their lead.

Nelson leaned over the passenger's seat and popped open the door. Hurriedly, as if the rain contained acid that was melting his skin, the priest clambered inside. Once positioned, he sat back, bumping his head against the rest, and removed his cowl. His hair was black, salted with patches of gray, his thin goatee much of the same. If Nelson had to guess, he'd say the man was close to the same age as he was, maybe closer to fifty. Father Kohler sighed, his eyes shifting toward his rescuer. "Thank you," he said in a grateful breath. Gently, he laid his fingers on the truck driver's forearm. "Thank you, Nelson."

Nelson wanted to tell him about the strange phone call, wanted to know exactly what the hell it was all about, but he refrained. Something in his gut warned him not to. Instead, he smiled at the priest, put his rig in gear, and listened to the sound of the engine drown out the deluge.

Five miles down the road, after brief introductions between moments of semi-awkward silence, the priest rotated in his seat and faced Nelson. "I need to request a favor."

Nelson closed his eyes. *Oh, here we go.* He'd been waiting for this. His parents had raised him Catholic and if all those Sunday mornings had taught him one good thing it was that the grabby palms of the church were never full.

The priest put on his best sad-hound-dog face. "Just a small favor. One I think you can fulfill." He sounded desperately hopeful, like a teenager asking her overbearing father permission to date a boy three grades older.

He sounded tragic, hitting Nelson in all the right places. Though a loner, when it came down to it, he was a great big softy.

"What is it?" Nelson asked.

"I need a lift to a specific location. Somewhere not far from here. Hopefully not far from your destination."

"Where?"

Kohler bit his lip. "Outside of Pine Bluff. It's off the highway. There's a... a *Throughway* there. I must see it."

He added up the miles and determined Pine Bluff would make him two hours late for his appointment. Not exactly a big deal, but, depending on the receiving manager, it could ruffle a few feathers. Worst-case-scenario, the manager could submit a low-level IR, which would be the first scratch on his clean record. It wasn't really worth granting a hitchhiker's request, but, then again, this was no ordinary hitchhiker. This was a priest, a Man of God. Not that the receiving manager would give any shits if Nelson had told him Christ Himself had been riding shotgun, but it made *him* feel better about shirking on the agreed time.

He nodded, told Kohler he'd be happy to take him. "But why did you say that word weird?"

With a snakelike gaze, Kohler curled his lips. "What word?"

Nelson rolled down his window, spat a bad taste into the rain-misty atmosphere, and cranked the window back up. "You know what word. The only one you said weird. Now, I'm a lot of things, Father, but a dummy ain't one of them, hear?"

Kohler smiled. "Yeah. I hear you loud and clear, Nelson. Loud *and* clear." He grinned. "So, you want to hear about the Throughway."

"I want to know why you said it weird."

"Okay then. Just remember when I'm done that it was you who asked me." The father folded his hands together, interlocked his fingers, and set them on his lap. Story time was about to begin. The father opened his mouth and said, "There are a lot of *Throughways* out there, thin places most human beings will never see..."

When the story ended, Kohler expected Nelson to call him crazy, pull over his truck, and insist that he get the hell out, none of which happened. Instead, Nelson kept driving down the two-lane back road, staring past the rain-battered windshield, listening to the patter and the constant roar of the diesel engine as he shifted gears.

"Well?" Kohler asked.

"Well what?"

"What do you think?"

Nelson shrugged. "Sounds fun."

Kohler fixed his eyebrows up. His mouth twitched as if something spicy-hot had touched his tastebuds and he wanted to hide his reaction. "Fun? Not sure I follow you, partner. I don't think I mentioned anything about fun."

"No, but you mentioned that there are portals to other worlds—*Throughways* you called them?"

"That's right."

"Yeah, you said *that*, and how you plan on shutting down the one near Pine Bluff, stopping whatever's on the other side from coming through." Nelson shrugged again, same as before. "Hell, sounds like fun to me."

"It's not fun. It's a job. It's work. Dangerous work at that." Kohler rapped the dashboard with his knuckles. "You like driving? You think that's fun?"

Nelson grinned. He got a bit of a rise out of Kohler's flustered attitude. "Suits me."

"Well, that may be. But this isn't fun. I surely don't like it."

It was then Nelson decided the priest was harmless. A little crazy if he believed in things like portals leading into other dimensions, but harmless, nonetheless. He had no weapons on him, Nelson had been certain. The drenched trench coat lay on the floor at his feet, and, even if there were a knife or a gun or some other concealment intended for violence, Nelson could have the six-inch blade tucked under his visor imbedded in Kohler's throat before the priest could even think about reaching for it. Nelson felt safe. Secure. Kohler was no more dangerous than any other hitcher he'd provided transportation for throughout the years.

One of these days, he had always told himself. *One of these days you're gonna be wrong.*

But today was not that day, he was sure of it.

"Some man called me," Nelson said, the grin sticking to his face. "Told me not to trust you. That you'd kill me."

"What?" Kohler asked. Nelson watched his complexion pale. "What man? What was his name?"

"No name. But I think he's after you."

Kohler pressed his face against the window and peered into the sideview mirror, his mouth open, puffing frosty fog on the glass. Nelson knew no one was following them—he'd been checking the whole time—but watching Kohler panic was too satisfying to tell him otherwise.

"Relax, Kohler," he said with a chuckle. "You're fine."

Although the downpour prevented them from reading the sign, they made out enough to tell they had passed over the Arkansas-Mississippi border. They'd arrive in Pine Bluff in less than two hours.

"Hurry," Kohler said. "I have a bad feeling about this."

Nelson didn't, not at first, but the closer they got to Kohler's alleged "Throughway" the more his stomach began to knot, twisting violently like a speared snake. As the counter on the GPS dropped below fifteen minutes, he was convinced—nothing good waited at the end of the road. Nothing good at all.

And that was when the text message came through from the same odd number the stranger had called him from. KILL HIM, the message said. FOR THE LOVE OF GOD, KILL HIM.

Now

Kohler stood before the portal, arms stretched wide, spinning in circles like he had just hit the Mega-Millions jackpot. He was about ten feet away, too close for comfort, so Nelson thought. Nelson gripped the six-inch blade he'd retrieved from the sun visor the second Kohler had scuttled from the truck. He knew he wouldn't obey the message from the stranger, but the knife made him feel safe, safer than if he approached the Throughway with absolutely nothing. Kohler had said he needed to shut down the thing, prevent something from coming through, and though he didn't say exactly what that something was, Nelson had every right in the world to be prepared.

The fact remained: Kohler had been right. He let that sink in, permeate his thoughts. The priest had told him about the Throughways and the portals and the gateways to other dimensions, and it turned out the holy man was right, which got Nelson thinking about what kind of "holy man" Kohler was in the first place, if one at all.

The Throughway extended the length of the two-lane road. It wasn't transparent—not exactly—rather translucent. It sparkled with various bright colors—red, pink, blue, purple, shades of teal which danced and disappeared, then reappeared as more vibrant versions of their former selves, a wall of chromatic prisms. Nelson thought he heard a mechanical drone, a low, vibrating drum beneath the patter of rainfall. The storm continued to rage on, the deluge carrying through with its assault. Lightning came in brief, bright flashes, slow-rolling thunder following closely behind. Pine trees stood like drunken giants on each side of the road, swaying back and forth, waving their leafy arms over them, casting their oscillating shadows on the steamy asphalt.

Nelson drifted forward on numb feet, barely feeling anything, much less the downpour. He listened to the priest revel in his discovery, dance in the street like a courtyard jester, drunk on humor and full of raw energy. The closer Nelson got to the Throughway, the *less* energy he had. It was as if the damned thing was draining him, bleeding him dry. Nelson disliked everything about it. He clutched the hunting blade his daddy had given him once upon a time ago, held it closely at his side. Knowing he was well-equipped battled the effects of the Throughway and gave him strength to carry on.

"Isn't it beautiful!" Kohler cried. If Nelson had been closer, he would have seen tears streaming from the corners of the priest's eyes.

Nelson nodded, staring at the Throughway, getting lost in the exotic assortment of color popping like miniature supernovas. So entranced by the portal's odd radiance, he didn't catch Kohler reaching behind himself, extracting the .45 ACP that had been secretly tucked into his pants. When Nelson finally broke free from the Throughway's hypnotic facade, Kohler had the gun aimed at him, motioning toward the otherworldly exit.

"Get in," Kohler said, no amusement in his voice.

Nelson slipped the blade in his pocket, undetected. Then, he raised his hands in the air and stood his ground. He wasn't going anywhere near that thing unless Kohler dragged him there, the personal escort he hoped for. Wished for. Counted on.

"No," Nelson said nonchalantly. He was frightened on the inside, but, on the surface, he remained calm, collected, and managed to stay perfectly still.

Kohler paced back and forth. "Don't make this hard on me, Nelson. Okay? I've traveled long and far to reach this Throughway, and it won't be denied a worthy sacrifice."

"A sacrifice?"

Kohler beamed. "Yes, a sacrifice. How do you think we shut them down, prevent them from crossing through? Ask politely? No, they demand an offering. Sustenance. They're like small children that need attention, constant playthings."

Nelson didn't understand anything except that Kohler wanted to feed him to some portal, or rather, whatever was on the other side of it. He wanted to ask who "they" were but opted to tell him "No" instead.

"Not asking you." As Kohler began his approach, Nelson lowered his hands, slipping them into his pockets. He curled his fingers around the grip of the blade. The turmoil in his chest fluttered with the rage of a thousand pissed-off butterflies. He picked the softest spot out on Kohler's neck, the best place to sink the blade. He'd never killed anything before, not even an ant. Thoughts of murder had never once crossed his mind in his entire life. There wasn't an ounce of evil in Nelson Park's body, but this wasn't about good or evil, right or wrong, this was about survival, about doing what needed to be done.

As Kohler got within striking distance, Nelson withdrew the knife from his pocket and lunged at the false priest, taking him completely by surprise. Kohler, who had let down his guard and had allowed the .45 fall to his waist, couldn't get the gun up fast enough. The blade was halfway in his throat before he'd lifted his arm an inch, the result Nelson had hoped for. A shot popped off, but the bullet hit the pavement, sparked, and died there. Kohler's body instantly went numb from the pain and shock, and his fingers betrayed him, letting the gun slip, fall to the road. Nelson kicked it away immediately, letting the darkness of the forest's shadows swallow it up. Knife embedded in Kohler's throat, blood funneling off his hand, Nelson walked him over to the Throughway.

The closer he got, the weirder he felt. He could sense the Throughway calling him in, drawing his body closer like a strong magnetic pull. He thought it was best not to linger. No time to waste. No time to let the Throughway absorb him, the way it had when Kohler was arming himself. About five feet away from the swirling, sparkling starbursts, Nelson heard voices, chittering communication that sounded somewhat human and somewhat animal all at once. His brain couldn't decipher what was being said, but his intuition told him the Throughway—or whatever was on the other side—wanted the offering Kohler had spoken of.

Nelson thought it was best not to keep it waiting.

He retracted the knife from Kohler's throat and dodged the bloody, spurting stream that followed its exit. Still alive, Kohler kept to his feet, his balance that of a toddler attempting first steps. Nelson didn't hesitate; he rushed forward, throwing his hands out, pushing Kohler off his feet. He watched the Throughway collect the man, screams and body and all. The bestial noises on the other side became louder, a cacophony of snarls and growls and insect-like buzzing. For a brief second, the length of a flash of lightning, Nelson thought he could see past the Throughway, catching a glimpse of the other side. The temporary transparency showed him images of blob-like beasts with long tentacles towering over dark cities of ruin, parading across barren lands of apocalyptic waste. Their stretching arms shared Kohler, pulling him in several directions at once, lengthening his limbs until they reached their maximum resiliency and tore free.

Then it was gone.

All of it.

No more Kohler, no more alien worlds...

No more Throughway.

Nelson was alone, just like always.

The way he liked it.

GOOD JOB, the message read.

He'd driven two hours since the incident near Pine Bluff. The sun was rising above the trees, basking the road in lavender shadows. Nelson sipped his pumpkin-flavored coffee and did his best to ignore the message, removing it from his thoughts. His curiosity bested him within a few minutes.

OK, he replied.

WE HAVE WORK FOR YOU...

...IF YOU WANT IT.

Nelson concentrated on the road. Work? He had a job, one he liked. He enjoyed the long drives, appreciated the solitude, welcomed the silence. The occasional hitchhikers.

THERE'S A LOT OF MILES INVOLVED.

The stranger sure knew how to play him.

THERE ARE A LOT OF THROUGHWAYS.

Ignoring his curious side was not one of Nelson's better characteristics.

WHEN DO I START? he replied.

NOW. YOU START TODAY.

THE PUMPKIN PEOPLE COME AT MIDNIGHT

WHEN THE CLOCK strikes midnight, a child from Sandpoint is given to the Pumpkin People. That's the way it was, that's the way it is and forever will be.

Most idyllic small towns have their fair share of superstitions and quirky traditions, and most of them go unspoken, as is the case of Halloween in Sandpoint. Because of their rich, bloody history, the beloved holiday goes mostly uncelebrated in Sandpoint, and the surrounding towns hardly make it a big deal. While Sandpoint schools don't exactly forbid children from dressing up, wearing masks and donning the costumes of their favorite cinematic heroes, they don't do much in the way of promotion either. Parents don't buy candy unless their kids force them to. Decorations aren't put up unless the kids force them to. No one answers the door on October 31st...

...unless forced to.

No one really knows when the anti-Halloween tradition started, when the legend of the Pumpkin People had first been told, the story of how a foursome of orange-headed creatures came knocking on Sandpoint's doors, requiring the annual sacrifice of a single child. The legends vary. Some say it began when the town first settled. Pilgrims, deeply rooted *in their religious beliefs, sacrificed one child on All Hallow's Eve in order to prevent the town from adopting cultures that seemed... well, for the lack of a better term—Satanic. If that had been their intent, I would say it had worked. Other popular theories include a cult from the 1920s that sacrificed children to Samhain and continued to do so throughout the years—a story I find too dumb and oh-so 70s paperback horror—and some say it's a group of lunatics running around in masks, abducting one child and slaughtering them in the name of their favorite holiday—much too Hollywood for my tastes and been done to death, no pun intended.*

Some say it's always been this way.

At midnight, a child goes missing.

At midnight, the Pumpkin People come for what's theirs.

"That's bullshit, Trudy," Cameron Fenton called out over the spooky Halloween music his babysitter had cued up before turning off the lights and grabbing the emergency flashlight his mother kept in the junk drawer. "That's such bullshit and you know it."

"Hey!" Trudy Marlowe said, sitting up from the couch. "Language, mister. You're only eleven. You can't be cursing yet." Trudy glanced over at Cameron's younger brother, who hadn't said a word during her story. "What about you, Langdon? Think the tale of the Pumpkin People is all poppycock?"

Langdon didn't know what poppycock was, but he was quick to swing his head back and forth.

"No, you don't or *yes, you do?*

Langdon squirmed in place. "Yes, I do. All poppycock."

The babysitter stuck out her lower lip. "Hm. Interesting. Then let me ask you two gremlins a question—how come your parents never take you Trick-or-Treating?"

Langdon and Cameron looked at each other, their eyes lingering, waiting for one another to respond. Together, as if by some telepathic arrangement, they turned and faced Trudy.

Her wide forehead crinkled.

"Well?" she asked, throwing herself back against the couch cushions, placing her hands on the back of her head. She even kicked her legs up on the coffee table, something Langdon knew his mother and father would *hate* had they been there to see it. "How's about it? How come they never take you?"

Langdon glanced around the living room and noticed the lack of décor around this time of the season. Most of what he'd seen on television, during the Halloween specials of his favorite programs, the months following summer seemed like the perfect time to dress up the house in the style of autumn. However, the Fentons didn't seem to embrace the season, never had now that Langdon had given it some thought. It was October 30th, just hours before Halloween, and there wasn't a single black or orange decoration stationed throughout the house.

But Trudy had been wrong. Not every house was as weird as theirs. He'd walked to school and passed pumpkins on porches, witches riding broomsticks on front lawns, graveyards of cardboard ghouls. Sandpoint celebrated Halloween, all right. They didn't go crazy for it like some towns; there was no big parade or center-of-town celebration, but people surely got into the spirit, erecting macabre statues on their front lawns and carving wicked jack-o-lanterns that wilted with rot well before the big day. These cases were few and far between, sure, but definitely not the dull, dreary ghost-town Trudy had painted during her fable.

After considering this, Langdon thought his brother had put it best: *Trudy's story was bullshit.*

"Well, no," Cameron said timidly.

"And why do you think that is, champ?" Trudy asked.

She was just trying to scare them, that was all. Trudy was usually a good babysitter and kept mostly to herself, texting her boyfriend and only paying attention to the boys when it had come time to microwave leftovers or to make sure they went to bed, were actually *in* bed, or sleeping.

This was the most the brothers had interacted with her since they had met last year.

"I..." Cameron said, his eyes falling. "I don't know."

"It's because of the Pumpkin People, you guys."

"Who *are* the Pumpkin People?" Langdon heard himself ask. He hadn't meant to—honest—but had found himself swept up in the babysitter's story. "Who are they really?"

Cameron whipped him in the arm with the back of his hand. "Idiot! There is no Pumpkin People, dumbass!"

Trudy clicked her tongue three times. "Cameron Fenton! Firstly, it's 'there *are* no Pumpkin People.' Who the heck taught you English? And secondly, don't call your brother a dumbass. I have a feeling he's much smarter than you."

"Hey!" Cameron rose to his feet. "I'm older *and* smarter than him."

"Yeah, okay, well, the latter is debatable and I'm not going there. It's getting late, almost *midnight,* and I haven't finished telling you the rest of the story." With an unsettling grin, she slowly rotated toward Langdon. "You really want to know who or what the Pumpkin People are? Do ya, sport?"

Langdon nodded and he suddenly felt very nauseous.

Every town has their haunts. Coastal communities see ghost ships. Towns surrounded by woods have Sasquatch sightings or regale visitors with tales of the Wendigo. Swamp towns have their voodoo magic. Farmers discover crop circles and can't seem to explain why their scarecrows go missing overnight, the only plausible explanation being "those darn kids again."

Every town has their secrets.

Sandpoint has theirs and no one is telling. The origin of the Pumpkin People has gotten murkier over time. Their story changed, their history altered depending on whose mouth the legend came from. I have my own story, my own opinion on the subject. I'll tell you what I believe and maybe you'll believe me too.

I believe the Pumpkin People legend indeed comes from

way back when, when settlers first discovered Sandpoint. They say Indians used to occupy these lands, especially around the marshy areas near the county line, not far beyond ol' Marv Parker's place. You know the one: the old cape with the white clapboard siding and faded pink shutters. Yeah, you've been there. Every kid has. Parker's place has always been said to be haunted, rife with ghosts of dead Indians, natives who were lined up and slaughtered like cows by the town's founding fathers. The tale of how Sandpoint came to be is a bloody one (for another night, perhaps) but the tale of the Pumpkin People is far more macabre and, considering the calendar and the clock on your parents' wall, timely.

They say on the day four Native Americans were butchered, their heads severed by their own hatchets, the settlers of Sandpoint were to throw a Halloween feast. The villagers had already dressed the table with pies and smoked turkey legs, squashes and pumpkins. Allegedly, the four Omahas showed, just before the founding fathers could recite Grace, from the woods with their hatchets in hand. The tallest tales say the Native Americans were soaked in blood, that they had savaged a nearby village on their way to Sandpoint, but I tend to believe they were innocent in all this. But maybe not. Maybe the Indians were angry that Sandpoint and the surrounding marshes no longer belonged to them, cast out of their homelands on grounds of eminent domain.

Whatever the case, the Native Americans were overtaken by the settlers' leaders and put to death, their heads forcibly removed from their shoulders. The founding fathers wanted to make sure no other tribe visited Sandpoint, especially with the intentions of ransacking the village and attempting to take back what was—in actuality—theirs to begin with. So, before the town sat down to indulge in their festive autumn feast, the villagers marched the headless bodies out to the center of Hammon's field—where ol' Marv Parker's place sits now—and fixed the dead to large wooden crosses, crucifixion-style, nails through their hands and feet, and replaced their heads with hollowed pumpkins. They carved haunted faces into their orange masks, what has become a modern-day tradition for the rest of the world—toothy grins, ferocious snarls, seedy eyes, sinister scowls—the works. They left them there to rot. A week later, after the neighborhood vultures had finished a feast of their own and the maggots had reveled in their death orgies, the dead Omahas were taken down from their crosses and buried in the empty field.

A year later, as soon as the clock struck midnight on All Hallow's Eve, the dead came back.

And they sought revenge.

Some say the Omaha ghosts snatched a small girl from her bed while her parents slept. Others swear the founding fathers willingly sacrificed one of their own to the cause, and did so annually, to appease the pumpkin-headed spirits. Others will tell you a lottery was drawn every October 30th. It's impossible to tell what actually happened but whatever it was, the Pumpkin People were born, and they were here to stay, and they demanded their annual bag of blood.

They demanded the life of a youth.

"Still call bullshit on that," Cameron said, rolling his eyes.

She scowled at him. "I'm telling your mother that you've taken up cursing."

He shrugged. "Fuck it."

Trudy's mouth dropped open and hung there, half with surprise, half with amusement. "You little shit."

Cameron folded his arms over his chest. "Even now?"

"Not hardly."

Clearing his throat, Langdon turned off the television, effectively killing the spooky background music. "I want to hear the rest."

"What rest?" his brother asked. "Her story is over. These pumpkin douches are some dead Indians or something stupid like that. Story over, bro." He yawned. "It's getting late. We should probably go to bed. Mom and Dad will be home soon, and they'll be pissed if we're still up on a school night."

"Oh, there's more," Trudy said with a wink and a terrible smile. "There's plenty more."

Cameron rolled his eyes. "Oh jeez. What now?"

"Don't you want to hear about the missing children over the years?"

Langdon felt his heart skid. He glanced over at Cameron; the kid was smiling, looking like he was about ready to burst into a fit of laughter. He wasn't buying any of his babysitter's story. Not a shred of belief on his part.

Langdon didn't particularly believe her either. At eight years old, his tolerance for believing in boogeymen and closet monsters was still fairly high, but, every time he thought he saw shadows moving about his room in the dead of night, he closed his eyes and counted to ten. That usually worked and the shadows—*whatever they were*—ended their midnight parade.

But this seemed different. There was history here. Missing children. Hadn't he heard about a missing child last October? He thought he had. There were whispers amongst his schoolteachers in the hallways. He vaguely remembered seeing a "Missing Child" poster stapled to a telephone pole, and again tacked to the classified board in the foyer of Super Shop. Those were actual memories, he was sure of it, and not something his brain had paired with his babysitter's history lesson.

The Pumpkin People were real. And tonight, they'd come again.

"I'm going to bed," Cameron said, waving his hands in the air. "I've had enough."

"I want to hear more," Langdon said, hopeful.

Trudy checked her cell phone. "Shit, kids. It's getting late. Y'all should probably climb into bed before the 'rents get home. Okay?"

Langdon sighed dramatically, clearly not happy with his babysitter's decision.

She walked with them upstairs, which Langdon now noticed had not a single black and orange decoration, just like the rest of the house. The only thing the Fentons had done for Halloween was place an un-carved pumpkin on the front porch, which had grown wrinkly and warped weeks ago. They'd already tossed it in the trash after the squirrels began to eat it and never replaced it.

He had never understood why it wasn't a big holiday around these parts. They'd lived in Sandpoint all their lives and the yearly tradition of grabbing candy from strangers and watching spooky movies on the couch had never been their thing. A select few in town celebrated—that he knew of—and the more he thought about, the stranger it all felt. It was weird now that Trudy had mentioned it. Halloween had come every year and few people noticed or cared.

Trudy tucked them in and turned out the lights. Before she left, she stood in the doorway, appearing as nothing more than a darkened shape formed by the dim hallway lighting.

"Pleasant dreams, my little pumpkins," she whispered to them. "Pleasant dreams."

"I think I scared them shitless," Trudy said into her phone as she walked down the unlit sidewalk, toward her house, which was only a few blocks away. She popped the last bite of her Kit Kat in her mouth and chewed. "They won't sleep a wink tonight. No way."

"You're such a bee-yotch, Trudy," her boyfriend buzzed in her ear. Ted was two years older and away at college, about an hour from Sandpoint. He'd meant to come down and spend the night with her, watching the Fenton brothers together, but he claimed he'd gotten behind on some schoolwork and needed to stay in and catch up.

"Yeah, well. What can I say? I like scaring people. Halloween is such a fun holiday. I hate this town."

"Yeah, it sucks. Up at school, the Halloween parties are sick. I mean, the frat houses throw some real bangers."

"Man, I can't wait to get to college. Totally done with this town."

"Yeah, Sandpoint is the sweaty ball sack of the United States."

"Just walking home makes me *so* depressed." She passed about sixty houses on her way home and counted the number of pumpkins on one hand. None of them were carved. Not a single house had put up lawn art. Had it not been for the trees in the midst of shedding their green garments and the chilly gusts of wind bustling down the empty street, no passing soul would recognize late October in Sandpoint. "Like, I can't believe I've lived here for sixteen years and have only been Trick-or-Treating twice in my life. With my aunt. An hour away."

"Yeah, no, I get it. Terrible."

"Yeah, anyway, I'm walking up to my house. I'll call you later."

Just then, a shadow jumped in front of her. It roared in her face, a guttural boom that caused her to scream. Her outburst rose above her attacker's, filling the night with a shrill, piercing cry for help. She turned to run but the shadowy beast's hand grabbed her shoulder, twisting her back around.

"Trudy!" the masked voice yelled.

She stopped screaming and stayed absolutely still, recognizing the voice at once. She felt her face scrunch with confusion, traces of anger ruffling her brow. "Ted?"

Ted peeled back his ski mask, revealing that bony—almost skeletal—facial structure she'd fallen in love with two years ago. "Ta-da! Surprise. Knew I'd get you!"

"You're a dick," she said with little emotion. "I almost died. Literally almost had a heart attack."

"Come on. You said you wanted to experience Halloween. Lying to you about schoolwork was totally worth it."

She stormed past him.

"What?" he asked, holding out his hands. "You're mad?"

From the stoop, she turned back to him and with a curt wave of her hand, she invited him in. "Just get inside. Quick. Before my parents come home."

Ted surveyed the street as if he expected her parents

to pull into the driveway right that second. But there was no one. The street was dimly lit by streetlights that barely worked; some of them hadn't functioned properly in years. The bulbs needed to be replaced or the fixtures themselves needed revamping, both of which the town of Sandpoint had neglected to address. Like much of the town, Trudy's street pulsed with a dead and haunted vibe.

"Hey," he said, turning back to the house. "It's just after midnight."

"Oh?"

"Think we'll see some Pumpkin People?"

She smiled. "Silly ass. You know I don't believe in ghosts."

Trudy went to the fridge to grab a glass of milk. She noticed her father's beer—a six-pack of Coors Light—and asked Ted if he wanted one. Or all six.

"Light beer?" he called back from the bathroom. He was washing his hands. He was *constantly* washing his hands. Everywhere. At all times. He always carried around sanitary wipes wherever he went. It was his most annoying habit, but Trudy couldn't complain. It was better than being with someone who didn't wash their hands, didn't shower, didn't use deodorant. Yes, this was better. She knew she could do much worse than a germaphobe. Over the last two years, she had worked hard on letting the quirk be. "I guess that'll do."

"Okay, it's on the table."

She lugged herself across the kitchen and sat down, facing the dark forest that her parents' home backed against. Deep in the woods, a little more than a mile, sat ol' Marv Parker's place, the site in her story where those Omahas had been executed. *Her story.* The one she hadn't exactly made up but had embellished so the Fenton boys would likely soil their pajamas. She couldn't remember which parts had been based on actual history and which she had flat out fictionalized; she'd practiced reciting the tale so many times over that she'd forgotten what her father had told her growing up and what her imagination had added after the fact.

As she watched the dark, something moved in the distance. A shadow within the woods. It was a slight movement, and, at first, she wrote it off as a trick of the light, the way the recessed floods reflected off the patio door. But, as the seconds crawled by, she became less sure. In fact, she thought she was seeing a shape take form. A shadow. A body.

A person. With a rounded head, big like a...

Attempting to stand, her shoeless foot slipped on the tile floor and she fell. Scrambling backward, she crab-crawled her way to the far wall.

Still, the pumpkin-headed shadow stood there, just beyond the back deck, about six feet into the woods. It stood. It watched. And it waited.

No, it can't be.

She stood and felt the wall for the light switch. Knocking down the plastic lever with her whole hand, the kitchen went completely dark, allowing her a clearer look into the backyard and a few feet into the forest.

No pumpkin-headed shadow.

It was gone.

Relieved, she sighed, cursing the shadow, her mind, her father's silly old tales, the strange town of Sandpoint, and everything else responsible for her seeing things that weren't really there.

She moved back to the fridge, wondering exactly what was taking Ted so long. Surely, he had scrubbed every last germ from his flesh by now.

"Ted?"

No response.

Her heart fluttered, and not with the occasional butterflies Ted's full lips and charming personality sometimes gave her.

She moved closer to the fridge, now noticing a sticky note that she'd missed earlier. On it, someone had written her name and two simple words: *We're sorry.* Below the impersonal apology, her parents' names had been signed.

What the hell?

What a weird thing to post. And where were her parents anyway? They were supposed to be home by now, hours ago, well before her babysitting gig ended. And here she'd come home to an empty house, which she didn't mind at first considering Ted's surprise visit, but now, after the unsettling note on the fridge door, she wanted nothing more than to see her parents' faces. To see them, hug them, tell them she loved them and that she was sorry she hadn't turned out to be the ideal daughter, the only child of their dreams.

Where were they?

She started to panic, and she didn't know why, not exactly. *We're sorry.* Just what the hell did that mean?

She rushed down the hall, toward the half-bath where Ted had chosen to rid himself of all the germs he'd collected in the past hour or two. When she reached the door, she found it slightly ajar. "Ted?" she called, and threw her forearm into the door, pushing it wide open.

She shrieked.

She noticed the walls first, how they bled. What looked like strawberry syrup speckled the sheetrock, dripping in spots where the murderous decorator had laid it on thick.

She screamed again when she saw Ted on the floor, lifeless, also covered in a shiny coat of glistening red.

She backed her way to the front door, mouth open, nearly breathless.

Something solid stopped her. Spinning on her heels, another high-pitched noise escaped her mouth. When she turned completely around, she was face-to-face with a wall of flesh. Backing away, Trudy glanced up, slowly, taking in every inch of muscly skin. When she reached the summit of the intruder's body, she saw the pumpkin. Where there should have been a head, there was orange. The pumpkin had been carved—black, soulless sideways triangles for eyes, a right-side-up triangle for a nose, and a banana-shaped mouth with six sharp points that were supposed to be teeth. All filled in with black. All soulless, void of light. Trudy stared into that darkness and the darkness looked back; whatever unseen horrors lived inside sent shivers across her shoulders, erecting the tiny hairs on her arms and neck.

She tried to scream again but the tan figure, who wore nothing but a pumpkin for a headpiece, reached out and covered her mouth with his massive palm. Then he squeezed. She felt her bones break, her jaw collapsing from the intense pressure.

The dead Omaha took her by the hair and dragged her through the house, toward the patio door. Next, he hauled her outside, down the steps, into the woods.

For a mile, he towed her. She didn't struggle. Didn't fight. Didn't scream. Through a carpet of dead October leaves, the Pumpkin-headed figure dragged her out to ol' Marv Parker's place, where the Native American and his trio of innocents had been executed over three-hundred years prior. He brought her to the edge of a deep, seemingly endless grave and tossed her near-lifeless body inside, down, into the same void that existed beneath his pumpkin skin.

Trudy looked up at the clear October sky and surveyed the stars, the moon, the never-ending stretch of midnight. That was the last thing her brain took in before the earth fell over her eyes.

THIRTY YEARS LATER

It had started to drizzle about five minutes before Langdon Fenton reached his brother's grave. He knelt and rested a bouquet, alive with the colors of autumn, down before the ankle-high gravestone, as he did every year on October 30th an hour before midnight. He wept softly but not before checking the cemetery, making sure he was alone, that no other souls were wandering about, a nervous tic he caught himself doing in almost every public place. He couldn't help it. Ever since his brother went missing almost twenty-nine years ago, he had felt compelled to check everywhere and everything for monsters; closets, under beds, in the backseat of his car, even in the basement of the office building where he worked.

Monsters, Langdon Fenton had realized, were just about everywhere.

And there were *actual* monsters out there, not just the child predators, serial killers, and sex offenders of the worst variety—those were bad, sure, *horrible,* but they paled in comparison to the *real* monsters; the beasts that drank blood, stripped human flesh into ribbons with their claws, feasted on the souls of the living. *Those* monsters were what scared Langdon Fenton. All because of his babysitter and his brother, both of whom had gone missing in Sandpoint exactly one year apart. Just after midnight on October 31st. Just like the stories had warned.

The Pumpkin People come at midnight, he could almost hear Trudy saying as she sat on his parents' couch trying to scare the ever-living piss out of the Fenton brothers. Cameron hadn't been scared, or at least he hadn't shown it. If he had allowed himself to become a little more frightened, then maybe he'd still be alive. But maybe not. Langdon never figured out how the victims were selected. It almost seemed random, though, as he discovered through years of research, it seemed there had been a secret group, a hidden society of elected officials who oversaw the process—who picked which kids were sacrificed to the pumpkin-headed *monsters*, those slain Indian ghosts who were hellbent on revenge and retribution.

That never sat well with Langdon. Research suggested that the town's parents chose the victims, which possibly meant Langdon's own mother and father had handpicked Cameron to die. When confronted with the allegations, when presented with all the research, both his mother and father had denied everything. Not that he expected them to admit they were responsible for their son's death. But he thought they'd give up something, some tidbit of information that blew the whole thing wide open, that clued Langdon in on the truth.

But they gave up nothing. Langdon had zero to go on but his own findings. And tonight, after almost thirty years of waiting, researching, drilling his way into the truth, he was going to end it. Or at least die trying.

Tonight, he was going to kill himself a Pumpkin Person.

He was going to hunt the ghosts or the slaughtered Omahas. He was going to save Sandpoint, end the madness, cure the disease that had plagued this place since its conception. He'd start at ol' Marv Parker's and work his way through the woods. He had a shotgun, a book full of spells, and some garlic. He didn't know if the latter would be of much use, but he'd read ghosts hated garlic. Despised it. Like vampires, garlic was like acid to their weak, nonexistent flesh.

There were monsters out there in the dark and Langdon Fenton aimed to find them.

He kissed his brother's grave, then stood up as a strong gust of wind whipped through the cemetery, brushing his longish hair away from his face. He rested the shotgun full of salt pellets—another trick learned through endless hours of research—on his shoulder and turned toward the horizon. The woods to Marv Parker's place sat less than a fifteen-minute walk away. If he hurried, he'd reach the spiritual grounds by midnight.

If he hurried.

Something told him he would.

He was motivated.

He was ready to take on the world.

A world full of monsters. Evil things. Unspeakable horrors.

His first step toward the woods ended with a crunch of dead leaves, and to Langdon Fenton, the bones of autumn breaking beneath his feet sounded like progress.

FOR THE LOVE OF THE TREE

(THE BLACK HILL #6)

2019

*D*ALE GARDNER KNEW what he had to do—his life's calling, so to speak. The Black Hill in Ludlow, Ohio was a great source of inspiration, had a great influence on his interest in strange happenings and supernatural sightings. Growing up, he had a framed photograph of the Black Hill on his wall despite his parents' hesitance and half-assed protests to keep it hidden, away from the eyes of probable guests. "You know, in case someone sees it, a family member, grandma or grandpa, and think it's in poor taste." But the shot that had once been taken by Austin Turner's Polaroid and had continuously been circulated on the Internet over the last twenty years plus, a shot that had been immortalized by Black Hill enthusiasts alike, never did come off the wall in Dale Gardner's childhood bedroom. In fact, it was still in pristine condition and was currently hanging on the wall in his downtown apartment, located in the center of Ludlow.

That's right; Dale was such a big fan of the Black Hill lore that once he graduated college, he specifically targeted a job *in* Ludlow. Imagine that. Imagine what his parents thought. They didn't think much of it, and though they knew the legends of the Black Hill were mostly likely embellished truths, a terrible story that had snowballed into this great big conspiracy, a Creepypasta wannabe, they still feared for their only son's life. That he'd get caught up in the hoopla and do something incredibly... dangerous? Illegal? Morally corrupt? Maybe all three, and every time they spoke to their son on the phone—which was three times a week—they reiterated the fact that sometimes stories were just stories, but sometimes they weren't, and to, for the love of God, not go looking to become one of those stories.

Dale laughed them off. "Goodnight, Dad," he'd said on the night of his trip up the Black Hill. Even though a wall had been erected around the site, that wasn't going to stop Dale Gardner from pursuing his childhood dream—to touch the tree atop the Black Hill. To carve his name into the bark.

Nothing would stop him.

He arrived at the base of the hill around eleven forty-five, after a patrol car that had been—for the last hour—circling the territory left and disappeared down the connecting side street. Dale waited another two minutes just to make sure. He was certain the area was under constant surveillance; rumors of cameras and audio devices being mounted on the wall itself had been passed around for years. Dale didn't see any visual evidence of any such thing, but that didn't mean they weren't there.

"You ready for this?" Holden asked him. His oldest friend from his elementary school days, Holden Peters, had driven over six hours to accompany his friend on this enlightening journey. Holden held out his iPhone, keeping the camera aimed at Dale, waiting for him to answer the question.

"Of course," Dale said. "Remember," he said, holding up a walkie-talkie, "you see anyone coming or see anything unusual at all, radio me and I'll come running."

"How do you know the fence isn't electrified or something?"

Dale stared up at the twelve-foot chain-link fence, knowing it wasn't boobie-trapped, but that he could possibly trip some sort of silent alarm. That was why he needed a lookout. *Holden.* "Because of lawsuits. They know people are gonna try to get in. This just makes it more difficult. More worried about it sending an alert to the boys in blue."

Holden nodded. "Of course."

"All right. Document everything."

Holden agreed and continued to keep the camera aimed at his friend.

"Here goes nothing."

Dale rushed the fence, keeping the wire cutters out in front of him, ready to start snipping the moment he came in contact with the fence. As soon as he was close enough, Dale dropped to his knees and slid in the wet, dewy grass. He slipped the cutters over the chain-link and began to snip away. Once he had cut a four-foot slit into the barrier, he pushed back one side which allowed him to slip through without getting hung up on the sharp metal edges he'd created.

He ducked through unharmed, and the realization he was that much closer to his dreams filled him with a sudden rush of nervous excitement. He almost danced up the hill, toward the tree. He glanced back over his shoulder, saw the light from Holden's iPhone follow him up the incline. Holden threw him the thumbs up sign, letting him know that the coast was clear... so far. Dale continued to watch the neighboring streets for activity of any kind.

Once he had reached the top of the Black Hill, he no longer concerned himself with what was happening below.

Because of the tree.

His eyes were immediately drawn to it, like a kid seeing his favorite baseball player, in person, for the first time. Stumbling his way forward, Dale nearly cried at the sight of it. It was everything he'd thought it would be and more. He moved toward it, dreamlike, his outstretched arm reaching through the dark, wanting nothing more than to place his skin against the bark, to feel what so few others had felt and lived to tell about it. This was the Holy Grail. *His* Holy Grail. He would not be denied access.

Even if a patrol car had entered the scene, Dale Gardner was certain he couldn't be torn away. He'd come too far, waited too long for this moment—he was going to carve his name in the bark, even if it was the last thing he'd do.

In the background, he heard Holden shouting. Exactly what, he couldn't make out. Dale turned his head slightly, viewed his best friend of almost twenty years out of the corner of his eye. He jumped up and down in the middle of the street, shouting and pointing. His voice came out warbled, not a single word decipherable through the filter this place had bestowed upon the world. Dale ignored him, deciding it was best to do this thing quickly and not waste any precious time. In all the stories of the Black Hill, in all the lore, those who lingered usually ended up getting caught in the spider's web and were never heard from or—in some cases—seen again. Alive anyway. No, it was best not to linger.

Dale laid the snips on the ground and released the hunting knife from the case attached to his hip. He dropped to his knees, put the tip against the bark, and began to carve. He watched the bark flake and fall away under the sharpness of the blade. He had gotten through the straight vertical line of the "D" when he heard someone scream from behind him, a harrowing noise that hit his ears and caused every hair on his body to rise. When Dale turned his head around, he expected to see shadows closing in on Holden, his mouth open, screaming his last scream. But what he saw was almost worse.

Nothing.

A vacant street.

He blinked and the black top disappeared, hidden beneath a veil of shadows. The street vanished, along with the small patch of woods that stood on the other side. It was all gone, reduced to a hazy wall.

He swallowed hard. His tongue felt like it weighed a hundred pounds. He managed to squeak out the name, "Holden?" but it was hardly loud enough to reach the man's ears, if he *was* still out there, somewhere, beyond the rolling fog that had seemingly come from nowhere.

Dale faced the tree, his entire body shaking. Something

was happening here. To him. A part of him knew he'd eventually become part of the story, just another notch on the Black Hill's long, endless belt. That the Hill would take him, absorb him like it had so many others.

And, sadly, he didn't care all that much. Because he wanted the knowledge; the knowing was important to him, more important than life itself.

"I have to know," he told the tree. "Show me."

As he began to cut the arch of the "D", the earth trembled. The tree bark split, a zig-zag crack that ran up the length of the trunk. A rainbow light pulsed from within, projecting a myriad of colors on Dale's face. The rainbow lights were comforting to Dale, eased his nerves though he knew he shouldn't feel that way. He should have felt fear. Panic. A terrible notion should have come over him, the realization that the next moment would most likely be his last.

But those emotions never surfaced. Instead, something akin to pride washed over him. A sense of accomplishment.

A sense of *knowing*.

The tree split in half, obliterating the work he'd started. A flood of primary colors escaped the inside, illuminating the Black Hill, which no longer held a shred of darkness but bright, radiating colors instead.

Dale didn't know how to explain the feeling that came over him next, only that it overwhelmed him, took hold of his body. He thought he saw, standing many yards away, way beyond where the tree had once capped the hill, three shadows with longish arms, their limbs bent awkwardly at the joints. Misshapen beings that had come from somewhere else, perhaps squeezed through the spaces between dimensions and ended up here. Dale remembered hearing about these shadows but couldn't recall from which account. Maybe these creatures were mentioned in Blake Weber's letter to his wife, or maybe in Shady O'Quinn's testimony. Either way, it didn't matter who else had seen the shadow people; Dale was seeing them now in all their glory.

Their arms undulated, reaching up, as if they meant to

catch something falling from a sky that wasn't there. They moved like those inflatable dancing characters you'd find in a car dealership's parking lot on a holiday weekend, only they flowed in slow motion.

Dale blinked, but that did nothing to rid his eyes of the images before him. Not that he wanted them gone. But he knew if he had any chance of surviving, he'd have to abandon his pursuit of the truth. That was the thing about the Black Hill—it knew how to keep its secrets.

Dale couldn't look away though. The swirling rainbows and shadow figures were all he could concentrate on. He felt as if he were floating. Weightless. A prisoner to this place of no gravity. He drifted toward them, toward the figures and the center, where the rainbow originated. In the distance, he thought he heard police sirens screaming, coming to rescue him. But, as he got closer to the figures and their gangly arms, reaching everywhere and nowhere all at once, he knew it was too late, that he'd soon become the next victim of the Black Hill.

Dim hands reached for him, grabbed hold. He felt them inside and out. Feeling. Probing. Taking from him, thoughts and pieces of his soul—if there was such a thing. And right now, Dale believed it was true. Souls existed; he felt his being stolen from him, collected by the shadowy things. In the midst of the rainbow world, Dale watched his essence leave his body in the form of a bright white trail that ascended above, became absorbed by the rainbow sky. As the beings extracted every last bit of his intrinsic nucleus, Dale departed from his body and watched himself. His body—in fast-motion—lost its youthfulness. His skin grew loose and dangly, his face now infested with endless wrinkles. Bones became brittle, fragile, ready to crack at the slightest amount of pressure. His hair had grayed to white. The extreme curvature in his back forced him into a hunched position.

Next came the cold; it settled within him, latching onto his bones, filling his veins with streams of ice. He knew now that he was dying, and he prayed for the death to be quick. The shadowy things continued to draw from him, purge every essential fiber of his being. The rainbows had dispersed, giving way to an endless black expanse. Here, in this field of nothingness, floated thousands of souls, far as his eyes could see. They drifted in his place, this palace of empty darkness and dead dreams. Soon, Dale would become one of them, just another victim of the Black Hill.

He felt the dark vacuum absorb him; his body become one with this bottomless sanctuary. Here he'd remain for all eternity. He glanced around at the other black stars. They winked at the worlds below, an entire vast universe of perpetual life and death, and whatever lay beyond the veil of the one true cosmic blanket that covered everything and anything, especially those in-between places. The unseen margins between worlds. Access points and entryways into impassable places.

Even there, the black stars shone.

HOW STARS ARE BORN

(a few words on BLACK STAR CONSTELLATIONS)

For my previous collection, I went through each story and told a brief tale about where the idea for that story came from. I'm not going to do that for every story here. Instead, I'll select a handful. Hope you enjoyed this collection as much as I had putting it together. Huge thanks to the publications that originally put them out, and a shout-out to my editor, Jenny Adams, who went through them and cleaned them up. Lastly, thanks to Matt Hayward for using his formatting magic to make this book's interior shine. You're the best.

STORIES

LOST IMPORT – This is an easy one. I saw an open call for a weird fiction publication that wanted dinosaur/shark stories. It was aptly titled SHARKASAURUS. I couldn't resist. I think I wrote the story in two days because I was so enthralled with the concept. I'm glad they published it. It's a fun book and if you liked that story, I recommend picking up the collection.

THE CHORUS BOY – After writing this story and examining it from a close distance, I can see certain parallels to Jack Ketchum's "The Box." Two different tales, sure, but there's the similar "children in danger, and adults being powerless to stop it" theme happening. Of course, "The Chorus Boy" is nowhere near as masterful as that story. Also, the ending of "The Box" is probably one of the biggest ballkickers in the history of short stories. Anyway, the idea came to me when I was researching the Internet about different boogeymen from different cultures. I came across *El Cuco,* who seemed severely underused as a horror-story villain. So I decided to set him loose and "The Chorus Boy" was the result.

THE BUTCHER OF BROOKLYN – This story was inspired by Hunter S. Thompson's *HELL ANGELS: A STRANGE AND TERRIBLE SAGA OF THE OUTLAW MOTORCYCLE GANGS* and the music of Lana Del Ray. A weird combo for sure, but I love bringing together two things I adore, infusing them. Anyway, the result was this story.

HOW TO KILL A BEAR WITH A BOW AND ARROW – I originally put this story at the end of THE SWITCH HOUSE as a bonus short, mostly because it takes place in the same fictional town as that novella; Red River (also the same town in IN THE HOUSE OF MIRRORS). But it also has similar themes, the whole husband/wife relationship falling apart, crumbling to pieces. The main idea for this story came when, randomly, I wondered whether it was possible to kill a bear with a bow and arrow. I wasn't convinced it was possible, but the main character of this story proved me wrong (insert smiley-face emoji).

ON THE EARS OF DEAF GODS – One night, in the middle of the night, my wife and I woke up to the sound of a loud engine running. We peeked through the blinds, and, across the street, a rusty-white pickup truck was parked. In the truck's bed was a large, wooden cross. The driver stayed there for several minutes. Idling. What he was doing, I hadn't the foggiest. About five minutes later, he drove off. The next morning, I wrote this story.

APERTURE – I used to work as a movie theater projectionist and it's undoubtedly the best job I've ever had. Sadly, with advancements of technology and the emergence of digital media, that job is pretty much obsolete. Anyway, my adventure in movie theater projecting (sounds weird, but okay) was the grounds for this short story. I never did discover a lost film that drove people to madness, but gosh, I'd always hoped to.

TIM MEYER dwells in a dark cave near the Jersey Shore. He's an author, husband, father, podcast host, blogger, coffee connoisseur, beer enthusiast, and explorer of worlds. He writes horror, mysteries, science fiction, and thrillers, although he prefers to blur genres and let the stories fall where they may.

You can follow Tim at https://timmeyerwrites.com
OR like his Facebook page here:

www.facebook.com/authortimmeyer